TRUE MAGIC

COLIN SIMS

Prologue

A Quick Note Before I Begin

OKAY, HERE'S THE DEAL: I'm new to this whole "writing" thing, so forgive me if this sucks. Lucky for you, though, I've just thumbed through *Creative Writing For Dummies* and picked up some useful tips. One of them—which is apparently very important—is to show and not tell. So instead of writing a sentence like, "Bob is a jerk," you write one saying, "Bob is a forty-year-old man who enjoys throwing rocks at pigeons." See the difference?

Anyway, I only mention this because I'm about to break some writing rules and tell you a few things. First off, my name is François Lemieux and I am *not* from France. I'm from Palo Alto. My parents emigrated from France and gave me a French first name to go with their French last name because they weren't thinking about the future cruelty of third grade classmates. (Hey, it's the snail-eater! Let's get him!) Secondly, I'm a sophomore at UCLA and up until very recently, I was the most average guy you've ever met. Medium height, slender build, non-athlete, sandy hair, a 2.9 grade point average, a few friends but not too many, a puke-brown Prius (which the brochure called "Toasted Walnut Pearl"), and last but not least, I was hedging my Film Studies major with a second one in Finance. Technically, I hated Finance. I hated math. Yet deep in the heart of every pragmatist is the knowledge that destiny is a cubicle—not a director's chair.

The one thing in my life that wasn't average was my girlfriend, Meagan. To say that she was ridiculously smoking hot would be a massive understatement. The girl put Victoria's Secret models to shame. (Kind of.) She stood a few inches shorter than me, had long blonde hair, crystal blue eyes, high cheekbones, a smile that could melt your heart and—okay fine—a very, *very* nice body.

We met freshman year in the dorms. She lived on the same floor as me, and one day when I was studying in the courtyard, she marched over, gave me a brief, appraising look, stuck her hand out and announced, "Hi! I'm Meagan."

The next thing I knew, I had a girlfriend.

No one understood it. Especially not me. Why this girl—who could've gone out with anyone—chose me was an enigma on par with other great mysteries such as: Where did the universe come from? What happens when we die? How did Donald Trump win the presidency?

Still, I wasn't about to look a gift horse in the mouth. If Meagan wanted to sleep over on Friday nights, I wasn't going to argue with her. She smelled nice and liked to light lots of candles. It was heaven. Or at least, so I thought. Sometimes a girl's charms can blind you to other aspects of her character that are not so pleasant. But more on that later. I don't want to get ahead of myself. The point is Meagan and I were only a day away from our one and a half-year anniversary on the night my life changed forever.

What follows now is a true story. Every single thing, down to the smallest detail is one hundred percent the truth as it actually happened—including the part about the zombie skeleton cop who nearly killed me on Hollywood Boulevard.

Chapter One

The Vampettes of Mulholland

Sometimes the great urban sprawl of Los Angeles thinks as one. It says to itself, "Even though it's Thursday night … *screw it*. It's Friday."

Tonight was just such a night. It was early spring, the air was warm, and a certain electricity danced between the city's inhabitants. This was a night for partying and everyone knew it.

As for me, I was staying in. An open copy of Robert Schrader's *Nail the Interview: Get the Job and Change Your Life* sat in front of me as I forced myself to read the chapter on internships. The first sentence stated that they were the gateway to every professional's future, and as such, needed to be accorded the utmost attention and seriousness.

I didn't disagree. Tomorrow was a big deal. At eleven a.m., I had an interview for a summer internship with Goodman, Sachs & Morgenstern, a prestigious wealth management firm downtown. (See? I was putting my Finance classes to good use.) As such, my plan for the evening was this:

1.) Study *Nail the Interview* until ten.
2.) Lay out freshly dry-cleaned suit.
3.) Drink glass of milk. (Possibly chocolate.)
4.) Be in bed by eleven.
5.) Get long, peaceful night's sleep.

That was my plan.

Unfortunately, there's an old saying—which I believe guys in the military like to use—that goes, "no plan survives contact with the enemy."

In my case, the "enemy" was a house party in the Hollywood Hills. One of my roommates had just scored an invite from some friend of a friend, and now all three were in the kitchen doing sake bombs. I could hear each of their voices distinctly. First there was Nate Buckner—my best friend from the dorms last year. He was a tall, skinny aspiring actor who hailed from Texas and had the accent to prove it. He was also the only one of my friends who knew how to talk to girls. Next, there was Brian Kim, who was about five feet nothing and knew more about hip-hop than anyone on the planet. Lastly, there was Vikram Singh. I actually didn't know him that well. He went by Vick.

Anyway, it sounded like they were having a great time out there. The music was blaring and I'd counted three "KANPAI's" so far.

I, on the other hand, was quiet as a church mouse with my door securely locked and my overhead light switched off. My aim was to create the impression that I wasn't home. I'd already gotten three missed calls and eighteen text messages demanding to know where I was, so for the time being, my ruse seemed to be working. If I held out another twenty minutes, they'd leave for the party and I'd be home free. Glass of milk and an early bedtime—here I come.

Then I casually leaned back in my chair, and apparently a screw had come loose, so the back fell off and I flipped over, kicking my feet up and knocking the desk over sideways.

Nuclear explosions have made less noise.

The next thing I knew, I was peaking bleary-eyed through an open crack in my door, explaining myself.

"I was, uh, sleeping," I said, rubbing my head. There was already a nice-sized bump that was going to need some ice.

"Dude you were, uh, jerking off!" Brian laughed and shoved open the door. All three poured into the room and the rap music from the kitchen followed. Brian found the light switch. "Jesus Christ! You were really going for it, weren't you Lemieux?"

My room looked like the aftermath of a hurricane. My chair lay in three pieces, my desk was overturned, my reading lamp was shattered, and a sheaf of papers littered every surface like fallen snow.

"Don't hate me," I said, "but I was on Facebook and saw this picture of your mom. One thing led to another and—"

Brian was about to cut me off, but Buckner interrupted him first. "Be that as it may," he said. "You're coming out tonight, Lemieux. We ain't taking no for an answer."

"You guys go ahead," I said as casually as possible. "I've gotta do something tomorrow."

This was dangerous ground. Under no circumstance could I tell any of them about my interview. They would all strongly object to the idea—especially once they learned *where* I was interviewing.

"*Tomorrow?*" Brian asked. He looked flummoxed. "I'll tell you what's happening *tonight.* We're hitting the wrap party for a modeling shoot. A modeling party! Don't you understand?"

"Why would I want to go there?" I said. "I have a girlfriend. And secondly, why would *you?*"

"Dude, what are you talking about? They're *models.*"

"Every one of them is gonna be a foot and a half taller than you."

Vick laughed and put a hand on my shoulder. "Bro, that's why you gotta come! We gotta hoist the little guy on our shoulders."

"Look, Brian," I said. "You don't have to go on anyone's shoulders. That's embarrassing. Just wear roller skates. Like that girl in *Boogie Nights.*"

Like all guys under six feet, Brian's height was something of a sore spot. As such, he clearly wasn't appreciating the Heather Graham reference. "Dude you're not tall either! What are you like 5'8"?"

"5'9"," I said.

"Bullshit. And even if—"

"Hold up a second." Bucker held up a hand. "I see what's goin' on here. Lemieux's bein' cagey. This is a Meagan issue, ain't it?"

Crap.

"Who?" I said.

"*Who?* God almighty. Now I *know* it's about her." Buckner looked to Brian and Vick. "You two give us a sec. This is serious. I gotta talk to my boy here a minute."

They both left laughing at me. Brian said something about my "labia getting in the way," but I wasn't sure what he meant by that.

The door closed behind them and now it was just me and Buckner. He bent down to put my chair upright and pointed at it. "Alright," he said solemnly. "Take a seat."

I did. Not really because he told me to, but because the bump on my head was throbbing like crazy.

"Buck, you're wasting your time," I told him. "I can't go to the—"

"Shut up for a second," he said, and then stabbed a finger at me. "I'm gonna ask you a series of yes or no questions, and by God if you say something other than yes or no, you're gonna regret it. Understand?"

I raised my hand in a salute.

"Good. First question—and tell the truth. Is this a Meagan thing? Is she draggin' you to some kinda nonsense tomorrow?"

Technically, the answer to that question was "sort of," but I elected to lie and say, "Meagan? No."

"Then let me ask you this," he said. "Do you think you're a bitch?"

"What?"

"I ain't tryin' to be mean. I'm just tryin' to make a point. Remember that movie *Swingers* you made me watch? 'You're so money and you don't even know it?' That's you. And Meagan? Shoot. She just don't fit in that equation."

I still wasn't understanding, so I just stared back blankly. I mean, I already knew my friends hated Meagan—they told me every chance they got—but I wasn't making the connection. Why were we talking about my girlfriend all of a sudden? What did she have to do with any of this?

Buckner's eyes dropped and he suddenly looked a little bashful. "Look," he said. "I get it. She's a real looker. You think you're batting out of your league, and you're the luckiest guy on Earth, right? But you gotta trust me on this. That girl is a one-way ticket to Shitsville."

"Okay," I said. "So what happened to the yes or no questions?"

"We're past that now. The point is you gotta let loose. I can tell by the look on your face that whatever you got goin' tomorrow, that woman's playin' some kinda part in it."

"Dude, it's not like I'm marrying her. She's just my girlfriend. And tomorrow's got nothing to do with her."

"Then what's so dang important you can't have a little fun tonight?"

My face scrunched heavily and involuntarily. The same exact thing happened whenever I got dealt a bad hand in poker. It was a weakness. "I, uh, can't say …?" I offered.

"See?" he said. "This has Meagan written all over it. Now listen for a second. She's a beautiful girl, and when she wants to be, she's almost charming. But I'm telling you, girls like her are Future Monsters."

"They're what?"

"They've got it all mapped out, amigo—their future career, their future husband, their future kids. I hate to say it, but at this very moment your name is probably written in a little pink notebook somewhere with a checkmark next to it. Is that all you want to be? I've been your pal for two years and I promise you, you could do better. Don't get trapped in some girl's plans. Make your own—starting with right now and coming to this party tonight. Or at least, come have a beer—or two—and then see what you think about things."

I mulled this over a moment. On the one hand, Nate Buckner could've written a book on how to effectively peer pressure someone. He was definitely pressing all the right buttons. On the other, he was dead wrong about Meagan. She was cool. She'd never mentioned anything to *me* about future husbands and kids. And she *hated* the color pink. Maybe the guy was just jealous.

Nevertheless, the thing about "making my own plans" nagged at me. Technically speaking, the internship at Goodman, Sachs & Morgenstern *was* Meagan's idea. I mean, she told me it was just a suggestion and I didn't have to do it or anything, but still …

Did I want to spend the whole summer getting coffee for stockbrokers?

Twenty minutes later we were all packed into the Toasted Walnut Prius and heading up Sunset on our way to the Hills. Was it lame that we rolled the windows down to blast the dance party beats of Martin Solveig? Maybe. But I'd done two sake bombs and the world was making a lot more sense. The air was warm. Girls were out. Los Angeles was alive.

As for me, I was an S.T.A.R. because I was big in Japan.

• • •

If you've ever been to a party in the Hollywood Hills, then you're familiar with the optical illusion of its houses. When you pull up to any driveway, all you see is a simple one-story structure that looks incredibly unimpressive. However, once inside, you realize that the house is actually five stories tall, as the back of it cascades down the hillside into a ranch-sized backyard with an infinity pool, a helicopter landing pad and a Ferris wheel.

I'd parked the Prius a little ways up the street, finding a fortunate spot nearby. The house itself was a straight up Hollywood mansion—an angular, modernist labyrinth of hard edges, gleaming white walls, Andy Warhol paintings and floor-to-ceiling windows overlooking LA. Also, I noticed, the ceilings were accented with royal blue mood lighting, which reminded me of the Starship *Enterprise.* (The remake, not the old TV series.) Plus, the dizzying laser show and electronic DJ music added to the starship effect.

Buckner pointed out the kitchen and we pushed our way forward. A long countertop covered in half-full bottles of every liquor, liqueur and mixer known to man greeted us. Buckner immediately set to work splashing every bottle into a single cup to make what he called a "Texas Tea! Yeehaw!"

I poured myself a cranberry juice and Brian shouted into my ear that "those girls over there are so freaking hot they have to be models!" I looked where he was pointing.

"I bet they are," I said.

He shouted back, delighted. "What?"

"Nothing," I said.

"Yeah!"

"So go talk to them. I'm sure they'll find you adorable."

"What?"

"Go over there!"

"*What?*"

And now we come to the reason why I suck at parties. The music is always too loud to talk—which is fine if you're talking to Brian Kim because, you know, who cares? But if you want to talk with a *girl*, then you have to do it in the only other way available—*dancing.*

I don't dance. The very concept baffles me. I mean, I understand that some guys can look cool doing it, but I'm not one of them. The last time I tried to fast dance with a girl was at my eighth grade mixer with Jen Bettencourt. I snuck up behind her, bobbing my head like a turkey until she spun around, screeched, and ran away. In retrospect, it was all my fault. I probably looked like a serial killer.

So, dancing? No thanks. I'll take a night in with my girlfriend any day. Speaking of which ...

I checked my phone and found a pair of texts.

MEAGAN: Hey! Just wanted 2 wish u luck 2moro! Daddy's going to luv u I promise! So proud of u!

MEAGAN: P.S. If u get the internship I have a surprise for u

Yowzers.

A surprise, heh?

I suddenly pictured Meagan in a whipped cream bikini saying, "Oops! I think I need some help," and then I approach—wearing a tool belt and a hardhat—and say, "Looks like you've got a problem there, little lady," and then *she* says ...

Alright, never mind. I don't want to get carried away. Besides, I only got to indulge in the fantasy for a couple seconds. A large hand reached over and snatched the phone from my grip. It was Buckner. His eyes flicked over the screen and he asked, "What internship? And what's this about her daddy loving you?"

Shit.

"It's nothing," I said quickly. "She just meant that—"

He ignored me and looked to Brian and Vick. "Boys, am I piecing this together right? Is François tryin' to work for Meagan's *dad*? I'll be God damned, this is worse than I thought!"

Yeah okay. I left that part out. The "Goodman" of Goodman, Sachs & Morgenstern happened to be Robert Goodman III—Meagan's illustrious father. He was pretty much what you'd expect from a guy who put "the third" at the end of his name. He was a tall, WASPy rich guy with a shock of blonde hair, an orangy fake tan and a politician's smile. He also hated my guts, but only when Meagan wasn't around. He'd say things like, "You're a dead man, Lemieux. I'm not kidding," and then she'd re-enter the room and he was as friendly as the Easter Bunny. She assured me that was just his off-brand sense of humor.

"Alright look," I said, holding up my hands in surrender. "It's not a big deal. It's just for a couple months."

"Lemieux is *what* with Meagan's dad?" Brian shouted. He was still having a hard time hearing.

Buckner leaned forward and yelled, "He's working for him!"

Brian wheeled on me with a look of shock. "Dude! Why don't you jump into a vat of acid while you're at it?! What's wrong with you?"

"It's a great opportunity," I explained. "There's a lot of job security in accounts."

All three paused before recoiling in disgust. Brian spoke first. "I don't even know what that means!"

"Bro," Vick shouted in my ear. "You gotta get on top of that situation. Tell Meagan thanks but no thanks."

I was about to explain it was actually really nice of her to set everything up when my phone vibrated. I took it out and saw that she was calling. *Crap,* I thought. *I can't answer it here. I'm supposed to be in bed right now.*

"Wait, that's Meagan calling him!" Brian shouted.

"Ask her what she's wearing!" Vick jumped up and down.

I scowled at both of them and then pushed my way to the balcony. By the time I got there, Meagan had sent a couple texts.

MEAGAN: Why rn't u answering me??

MEAGAN: 2moro is important!

My thumb automatically went to type a response, but I caught myself. If I responded now then she'd call again and I'd have to answer. Then she'd hear the party and I'd be screwed. My only option was to pretend I was already fast asleep and blissfully unaware of my phone buzzing. Then tomorrow I'd say something like, "You called? Oh, wow. I slept right through it! Yeah, the interview went great!"

Minutes rolled by as I stared blankly at my phone. I felt guilty. Meagan was just being a good girlfriend. She wanted the best for me, she really did. Was there anything I could do? Should I go home? Should I text her when I got there? Yes. That was it. I'd come up with some sort of explanation on the drive back.

I was about to go inside and make my excuses when a voice suddenly chirped, "Hi!" and I looked up.

A cute, tipsy brunette in a short cocktail dress beamed at me and held out a drink. "Your friends said I should give you this," she giggled, thrusting the glass into my hand. Her eyebrows then curved in sympathy. "I'm so sorry about your girlfriend! You poor thing!"

"What?"

"They told me what happened," she said with a frown. "It sucks to get cheated on."

"Cheated on?"

She nodded. "I know the feeling." Her eyes then glanced over me and she smiled brightly. "It's her loss, anyway. What you need is to dance with me!"

And just like that I found myself getting dragged back inside.

Now, on a side note, most people believe that astrologers who claim to predict the future are full of it. However, in certain situations, predicting the future is actually quite real and very easy to do. For example, I could predict with total certainty that in five seconds when this girl spun around to start dancing with me, I was going to look like an idiot.

Five.

Four.

Three.

Two.

One.

She whirled around, smiled up at me and I ... well, remember that dance 'The Macarena?' That's what I started doing. I don't know why. It was an old dance. It didn't fit with the music. It looked ridiculous. And yet there I was: hands on my head, hands on my hips ...

I got about halfway through it before she stopped me. "I think you need more to drink!" she shouted.

I looked up and saw Buckner in the kitchen slowly shaking his head. The next thing I knew, the girl was pulling me to a crowded bar at the other end of the room. Before I could object, she shoved a new drink in my hand. It was a shot glass with a strange green liquid in it. I stared a moment, perplexed.

Absinth?

Oh dear.

A few minutes later she was gone, dancing somewhere with her friends, but I didn't care. I was on top of the bar, standing on my head with a beer tap in my mouth as the crowd counted to fifty. (They only made it to sixteen.) ((I think.))

Then I was bartending. I'm not sure how it started. Someone must have asked me to grab them a drink and the idea caught on. It was only natural. I was the best bartender on the planet. And oddly enough, the more I drank, the better and better and better I got. Before long, I was spinning bottles and tossing them in the air like Tom Cruise in *Cocktail*. Girls loved it.

I was in the middle of pouring a whiskey behind my back—absolutely none of it missed the glass—when I first saw them. They came in as a trio, and the crowd parted all around them. This was probably an illusion of some sort, but either way, these girls stood out. All three were dressed in a distinctly gothic fashion, with spiked collars, knee-high stomping boots and an assortment of corsets and torn up t-shirts that displayed dangerous amounts of cleavage.

I won't lie—they were actually kind of scary. Still, I'd never been more attracted to three women in my entire life. They were *stunning*—easily the hottest girls at this entire party, and that was saying something. And Meagan? Who's Meagan?

All three were heading toward the bar, and unless I was seeing things, they were looking right at me. I handed off the whiskey, and in a blink, the goth girls were there. Under ordinary circumstances, I would've gotten weak in the knees with these three pale beauties staring at me, but like Popeye with spinach, I'd already consumed copious amounts of a certain green wünder drink.

"What can I get you ladies?" I asked, twirling a bottle for effect.

The tallest one, who had several inches on me in those spiked heels, smiled. "Surprise us," she said.

I made them three Blue Hawaiians.

Honestly, I'm as surprised as you. I still don't know why I did that, but the ingredients were there and it just sort of happened. Still, if they were disappointed, they didn't show it. The tall one gave me a smoldering look over her cocktail umbrella as she took a long, slow sip through the straw.

"Hmm." She licked her lips. "I think you're in my film class."

There was no way she was in my film class. If she were, I would've noticed. There were only a dozen girls in that lecture hall every week, and she wasn't one of them. But that hardly mattered. She could've told me she was an astronaut and I would've gone along with it.

"Yeah, I thought you looked familiar," I said.

"Your name is François, right? François Lemieux?"

"The one and only."

She smirked and looked to her two friends. They both smiled at me in a somewhat … *weird* way. There was a better word to describe it than "weird," of course, but it wasn't coming to me. Besides, I didn't have much time to think. The shortest of the trio, whose steampunk corset made it very difficult to look above her neckline, traced her finger along the bar as she slunk around the side. Her chest pressed against my arm while she ran a hand through my hair. "You look delicious," she said. Her tone was breathless and awestruck, like she was in a trance. I found it oddly erotic.

"Uh, thanks," I said. "You, you're … very pretty."

Her hand slowly fell to the back of my neck. "I know," she said, and looked up at me with big, soot-stained eyes. "Have you ever slept with three girls at once before?"

I cleared my throat. There were certain questions in life I never expected to answer, such as, "Would you like to have magical powers?" or "Have you ever slept with three girls at once before?" I wasn't sure what to say. Obviously the answer—to the second one—was no. Heck, I wasn't even sure if I *wanted* to. I mean, I *wanted* to, but … *oh wait.*

I knew what was going on here.

Buckner, I thought. I scanned the party but didn't see him. He must have charmed these girls into coming over here to mess with me. He, Brian and Vick were probably hiding behind a pillar somewhere watching and having a good laugh.

Thus, I figured: *Well, my friends, two can play at that game …*

"No, but there's a first time for everything," I said and raised an eyebrow in what I hoped was a mean impersonation of James Bond.

Corset Girl smiled broadly, while Tall Girl finished her Blue Hawaiian. I noticed that their friend—the one with cherry red pigtails and a nose ring—hadn't touched her drink. She looked—I don't know—*angry?* It was hard to tell.

Tall Girl reached forward and grabbed my collar like she was about to punch me. "You're coming with us," she stated.

Once again, I wondered what old 007 would say in such a situation. What I eventually settled on was, "What I do now, I do for Queen and country," and then let her yank me around the bar. Corset Girl remained glued to my side while Pigtails followed.

A few twists and turns later, we were in a dark bedroom on the top floor. The sounds of the party still thumped through the walls, but it was quiet. I honestly couldn't believe these girls were taking the act so far. I kept thinking that at any moment, they'd laugh and tell me it was all a joke. I mean, heck, I didn't even know their names.

Once the door was locked behind us, all three drifted into the darkness. I could barely see with only the moonlight trickling in through the large window to my right. Then there was a spark—and then another and another. They were lighting candles. Which wasn't *that* weird, except they were lighting them on the floor, which ... yeah was kinda weird. Once they were done, I recognized the shape. They'd drawn a large pentagram in the center of the room. I scratched my head. Weren't pentagrams some sort of devil worship thing? I mean, I guess these girls were into the goth thing and all, so ...

Corset Girl materialized in front of me and I flinched. "Come with me," she coxed, tugging lightly on my sleeve. She led me to the bed and stopped. "How about we take this off?"

Her hands found their way under my shirt and slid up my stomach.

Any second now, I thought. *The lights are gonna come on, a camera crew will burst from the closet, and Ashton Kutcher himself will tell me I'm punk'd.*

"Let me help you with that," I said, and lifted the shirt over my head.

Next she was at my belt buckle while I kicked off my shoes. She popped open the clasp with practiced hands and yanked the leather from the loops. Then Tall Girl was at my side. With a single finger, she turned my face to hers and lightly put her lips to mine.

That was surprising. I didn't expect her to go *that* far. Clearly, she was very committed to the role.

Her kiss grew in intensity as I felt my jeans sliding down. They were around my ankles when I pulled away. "Wait," I said. "I, uh, actually do have a girlfrie—"

"Shut. Up."

Those were the first words Pigtails had said so far. She now stood directly in front of me, looking as cross as ever. I was about to protest when she shoved my chest. I landed on the bed with a *pomf,* and she pounced on me. Her nose was inches from mine as she declared, "You're ours," and then kissed me ravenously. I felt the bed dip slightly as Tall Girl and Corset Girl crawled on either side. Were they pinning my arms? That's sure what it felt like …

Pigtails slithered down my body, moving from my neck, to my chest, to my stomach. Then she tugged my boxers down and her lips brushed against my … *whoa.*

It was at this juncture that I realized this might not be a prank.

"Um," I said. "I think we've all got the wrong idea here."

Her eyes flicked up to mine with a flash of annoyance.

"Just relax," Corset Girl cooed beside me.

She and Tall Girl then sat up to their full heights and removed their tops. Their knees still pinned my arms, but for a brief second, my immobility was the last thing on my mind. Flickering candlelight revealed that neither wore anything underneath. They both smirked before descending on me with their lips. Tall Girl went to my neck while Corset Girl bit at my chest.

So, when I was ten years old, my dad accidentally ran the family minivan off the road and it tumbled down a ravine. I was in the backseat, and I remember the car flipping end over end for what seemed an eternity. It kept going and I had this odd sensation during the middle of it—like a moment of supreme clarity. I realized, "This is really happening. This is what it's like to go rolling down a cliff in a car. I wonder how it will turn out?"

I only mention this because I had a very similar sensation when I looked up and noticed the ceiling had a mirror. (Whoever the owner of this house was, he/she knew how to live.) I saw the aerial view of all four of us—three gothic beauties writhing on top of a thoroughly confused college guy. And to be honest, I barely recognized myself. How in the world was I—François Lemieux, a.k.a. The-Guy-Who's-Never-Done-Anything-Remarkable—actually having a *foursome* in a Hollywood Hills mansion? It didn't make any sense. And unlike the car crash when I was ten, things like this DID NOT happen in real life. At least not to someone like me. And if that alone wasn't enough to raise an alarm bell, then *this* certainly was: a thin trickle of something black was running down my torso and pooling on the bed. I had to blink to make sure I wasn't seeing things. Once I did, however, my heart nearly bounced out of my chest.

Was that ...?

All three girls seemed to read my mind, and tightened their grip on my limbs. The message was clear: "You're not going anywhere." I felt a sudden pinprick on my upper thigh as Pigtails diverted her attention elsewhere. Then I heard it—a faint, wet gulping sound. I saw Tall Girl's throat working rhythmically. She was *drinking*.

At that, I closed my eyes, counted to three, and then proceeded to flip *the fuck out*.

And let me just tell you this: There are two types of flip outs. The first happens when you lose your wallet or discover your car got stolen. The second type occurs when you realize someone is trying to kill you. It's a whole different ballgame. The adrenaline pumps into your veins, long-forgotten instincts resurface and you discover firsthand where Stan Lee got the idea for The Incredible Hulk.

I wrenched my arms free and kicked my legs savagely, knocking Pigtails to the floor with a grunt. Corset Girl and Tall Girl turned on me with blood dripping down their chins. They both smiled gleefully, revealing long, reddened fangs.

At that moment—one I'm not particularly proud of—I gave an alarmingly high-pitched yelp and twisted to scramble away. Both girls leapt forward, grasping for my arms. I elbowed back at them, but they were strong.

My next move came from pure instinct. I saw a fancy, metallic lamp on the bedside table and grabbed it. When Tall Girl flipped me over to dive back into my neck, I cracked her across the face. It was a good blow, too. Solid. With a nice follow-through. So when she slowly turned back to me, revealing her skin to be little more than a thin mask concealing a gnarled goblin face underneath, I wasn't nearly as surprised as you might expect.

She quickly tore the rest of her face off, taking some of her left shoulder with it. By this time, Pigtails had jumped back on the bed and let out a monstrous shriek. She too decided her skin was no longer necessary and ripped it off. Gooey, saliva-soaked wings sprouted from her back. Corset Girl stood to do the same.

Clearly, it was time to get crazy. I still had the lamp, so I swung it around like a madman while yanking my pants back up. I managed to scramble backward and put some distance between me and the three … *girls? Monsters?* I'd figure that out later.

All three were between me and the door, so my only escape was the window. It was closed, but I could fix that. Without thinking, I grabbed a Scandinavian-looking desk chair and hurled it through the glass, shattering it into a million pebbles like that breakaway stuff does in the movies.

The girls lunged for me, but I spun around and kept swinging the lamp. They backed off a few feet, hissing like cats. I then seized my chance.

You see, sometimes in life, you have to take a leap of faith. You don't know what's on the other side, you don't know if you're going to fall to your doom—but you jump anyway.

That being said, a smart person would at least jump feet first and be ready for a tough landing. I, on the other hand, dove out the window like an Olympic swimmer.

The most I can say is that I didn't fall to my doom. I fell about ten feet into a bush and somersaulted onto a patch of dirt. The impact and accompanying scratch-fest on my bare skin probably hurt, yet I was in no condition to notice. I did, however, thank the gods for the illusionistic design of Hollywood Hills mansions. The "top floor"—where I'd just jumped from—was even with the driveway, putting my car only a short, barefooted sprint away.

Once back on the road, some stray party girls giggled when they saw me. I'm sure they thought I was doing a walk of shame, or perhaps I'd been caught in bed with the wrong woman. There was no time to set the record straight. I simply screamed for them to, "Run! Run! Run!" but that only made them laugh.

A moment later, I was fumbling for my keys outside the Toasted Walnut. Now as you might imagine, it usually takes about 0.5 seconds to get one's keys out of one's jeans pocket. Yet in circumstances like these, with three bloodthirsty gargoyles coming after you, it takes roughly six to seven times longer.

"François!" one of them called with a much deeper voice than before. "Get back here!"

I finally unlocked the door and got behind the wheel. (Don't judge me for still being wasted; these were desperate times.) I pressed the annoyingly unsatisfying "start" button on the dash, and the Prius came to life with a whisper.

Something banged against the windshield and I looked up. A long-clawed and gangly-limbed monster crouched on the hood. It was hard to tell which one was which anymore. My guess was this was Pigtails—but I could've been wrong. Either way, she informed me with a newly demonic voice that running was "futile" and that I was a "fool."

She probably had a point, but that didn't mean I was going to give up.

"Oh yeah?" I said, and stomped on the gas.

For a full second and a half, nothing happened. Nothing at all. Somewhere deep inside the hybrid's microprocessor was a design spec insisting, "But … I'm a *Prius!* You're not supposed to drive me like this!" It eventually got the hint, however, and gave the engine full battery power. The acceleration knocked Pigtails against the windshield and I swerved to shake her off. It worked. Her leathery wings caught the wind like a pair of sails and she was gone. Now it was just me and the dark, winding road of Mulholland. I kept my foot on the pedal, steadily picking up speed. It felt good. The Prius and I were one. I was a race car driver. A pro. I hugged the turns, I gunned the accelerator and I smashed into every mailbox and trashcan the roadside had to offer.

I twisted in my seat, searching for any sign of the monster girls. All I saw was another pair of distant headlights winding up the road behind me. I wanted to scream at whoever it was to turn around and flee. Yet it was possible the girls were gone. I hadn't seen them for a solid minute. Maybe they didn't want to be seen in public?

That hope was dashed when my roof caved in and an upside-down goblin face snarled at me through the windshield. She didn't have two fangs anymore; she had a whole mouth full of them.

I yelled for her to get off and yanked on the wheel, but it didn't work.

Her face *did* disappear, though, and for a split second, I actually thought she was gone. Then a bony, clawed hand crashed through my side window and tried to grab my face. Now before you judge me for the exceedingly girly screech that followed, just imagine how *you* would react in this situation. At least I had the presence of mind to grab its wrist and keep it from tearing my head off.

A frantic battle ensued until there was a sudden explosion of gore across my windshield. It was like an oil drum of red paint got tossed against the glass. I couldn't see a thing. I also noticed that I was no longer holding the clawed hand at bay—I was just *holding* the clawed hand. It now ended in a bloody mess somewhere along the mid-forearm. The girly screech returned.

I flipped on the windshield wipers and tossed the hand out the window. I could barely see the road through the streaky-red smudges. Then bright headlights shone aggressively into my rearview mirror. The car from earlier was nearly on top of me, honking its horn. Did it want me to stop? Did it want me to get out of the way? The message was unclear. For all I knew, one of the monster girls had found herself some wheels. Thus, I stomped on it.

Another of them landed on the roof and tore off the passenger-side door. It was actually pretty amazing. How strong does someone have to be to do something like that? I jerked the Prius to the right and scraped against a new Mercedes. It didn't stop her. The next thing I knew, I had my hand on her throat keeping her snapping jaws away from my face.

She hissed something unintelligible, and I shouted something even more unintelligible right back. To be honest, I was surprised I could keep her at bay at all. She had just ripped the door straight off its hinges. You'd think she could overpower a simple hand on her neck. Either way, I couldn't keep this up forever. I was driving with one hand and fighting a demon with the other.

I decided on a drastic move. Or perhaps, "decided," isn't the right word. I *reacted* with a drastic move. I took my hand off the wheel, opened my door and jumped out. It was just like the movies. I hit the pavement, rolled a bunch of times, and landed right side up in time to see the Prius launch itself off a cliff. I heard it crash, flip over a dozen times, and then—honest to God—explode.

Apparently that really does happen …

The car behind me screeched to a halt, doing a half spin at the cliff's edge. A girl jumped out carrying a tactical shotgun—I watch a lot of action movies—and started firing down the hill. Seven shots later she went back to her car, popped the trunk and casually took out a bazooka. I stared, dumb-faced, as she widened her stance, aimed upward, paused, and then fired. The resulting explosion looked exactly like a firework display. She nodded once and tossed the bazooka back in the trunk.

So …

Let's start with her car. It was a brand new, jet-black Mustang that had been tricked out to the point of resembling a poor man's Batmobile. The windows were tinted; the exhaust pipes were jet-like; the side paneling looked armored; and the engine—even at an idle—sounded like something from NASCAR.

Next, there was the girl herself. I noticed three things about her:

1.) She was tall.
2.) She had a ponytail.
3.) She was wearing pajamas.

Because why wouldn't she be wearing pajamas? I'd just been attacked by three skin-ripping, blood-drinking gargoyles—why should the girl who just showed up in a Ford Mustang wielding a shotgun be wearing normal clothes? She even rocked some *Hello Kitty* slippers, I noticed.

Then she was standing over me, looking confused. "You okay?" she asked.

I stared up at her blankly, and she frowned.

"You are François Lemieux, right?"

I continued to stare.

"*Parlez vous anglais?*" she asked. "*Êtes-vous François Lemieux?*"

Jesus Christ, was that *French?*

"I'm from Palo Alto," I said numbly.

I'm pretty sure that at this moment I was in what para-medics might refer to as, "a state of traumatic shock." I was shaking all over, the world was spinning and I couldn't think. When I tried to stand, I toppled over in a heap. I settled for remaining seated in the middle of the road.

After a pause, she plopped down beside me and cocked her head. "So ... you're not like a wizard or anything?" she asked.

My teeth chattered by way of response. It was possible that even if I weren't in shock I still wouldn't have known how to answer that.

"Wow." She looked baffled. "You're just a regular guy?"

I nodded slowly. My eyes were transfixed on the glow of the flames from my car just over the hillside.

"Well, you're doing great," she said. "Just breathe. But we have to get out of here soon. The police are coming."

"The police?" I said.

"Yeah. I mean, they're not a problem or anything. Just a hassle." She stood up and offered me her hand. "Come on. I'll take you home."

I looked up at her but didn't move.

She pulled a face and then took me by the arm. "Okay, upsy-daisy," she huffed with a surprised grunt. Once I was on my feet, she shot me another curious look. "Huh," she said. "You're *heavy*."

"Heavy?" I said.

"Yeah, it's just … you shouldn't be."

I had no idea what she meant by that—I barely weighed a buck-forty—yet I figured it was a question that could be answered another day.

She helped me into her car, and a minute later we were rumbling through the Hills on our way to Sunset.

"You live in Westwood, right?" she said.

"Uh huh."

"Palm Towers?"

"Uh huh."

"Second floor? Apartment 212?"

"Uh huh."

It wasn't freaky at all that she knew exactly where I lived. And of course, on a more average day, I would've had a lot of questions. However, in my current state, the only thought my brain was capable of producing was the smooth, tranquil thrumming of a massage chair.

When we arrived, she hopped out of the car and helped me up the stairs to my apartment. When we got to my room, she gave it a quick survey and asked what had happened to my chair.

"My chair?" I asked.

I had now slipped into a pattern where my only mode of response was to repeat the last word of whatever she just said.

She brushed some of the debris off my bed and then planted herself in front of me. "Okay." She put her hands on my shoulders. "I'm sorry about this, but it's for your own good."

"My own good?"

In a blink, her eyes turned a deep shade of florescent purple. "You will forget about tonight," she said in a slow, even tone. "You will remember going to a party and nothing else. When you left, you discovered your car was stolen. The scratches on your body are from drunkenly falling into a bush."

I squinted at her. "A bush?"

She squinted back. "What?"

"What?" I repeated.

She frowned. "Are you not hypnotized right now?"

"Hypnotized?"

She stared at me with her glowing eyes a moment in confusion. "Weird," she said with a light gasp. "This should work …" Her eyes went back to normal and she gave me a pitying look. "Well now I really *am* sorry."

Before I could respond, something amazing happened— something more unusual than anything that had happened so far. The girl spun around and a *Hello Kitty*-slippered foot collided with my head. She'd thrown a *roundhouse* kick. Nobody does those in real life. *Nobody.*

All the same, I was knocked out cold.

Chapter Two

Bigger Than You Thought

ONE OF THE THINGS BEER COMMERCIALS never show is the morning after. Sure, they show freshly filled pint glasses with frothy foam on top; they show friends clinking glasses; they even occasionally show Clydesdales pulling antique sleighs through the snow. What they *don't* show is the rotten, smelly next day with the sun seeping through the blinds as stale booze steams from your pores and you want to wretch. They leave that part out.

Now as a UCLA sophomore, I was all too familiar with the effects of a hangover. Yet as I woke up that morning, I learned that there are hangovers, and then there are *hangovers.* This was neither—because usually a night of drinking doesn't end with a car chase and getting knocked out by a mysterious girl who kicks you in the head.

Plus, the situation was made worse by my alarm clock beeping like a midnight freight train. The numerals 7:25 flashed across its face in a taunting reminder of my original plans. I groaned and rolled over, but the overwhelming need for water pried me from my mattress and sent me staggering into the kitchen. I was only half-surprised to find Buckner still wide-awake in the adjacent living room playing Xbox.

"Morning, sunshine," he said, keeping his eyes on the TV and steadily working through a family-sized bag of Cheetos Puffs.

"What are you doing awake?" I asked.

"Never went to bed," he said before glancing at me. "The more important question is what in the heck happened to *you?* You look like the ass end of a road kill. You get lucky last night or what?"

I wasn't sure how to answer that. The idea of "getting lucky" reminded me of the goth girls before they turned into … whatever it was they turned into. Reflexively, I looked down to see if there were any bite marks, which there weren't. Which was odd.

"Uh," I said. "I have to ask you a serious question."

He pressed pause. "What's up?"

I hesitated a moment and then sat on the couch. This was a tough subject to broach without sounding completely insane. "Did you convince some gothic-looking girls to come over and flirt with me last night?"

"What do you mean 'gothic-looking' girls?" he asked, knitting his brow.

"You know, spiked collars and boots and stuff."

"Naw, just my friend Brooke. You met her. She was that brunette you did the Macarena with. Or was that the Funky Chicken? I couldn't tell."

"Look," I said. "I need you to tell me the truth. When was the last time you saw me last night?"

"Shoot, I don't know." He scratched his head. "I remember you were at the bar pouring drinks for people. You were making a mess, too—spillin' booze everywhere."

"Right," I said. "Did anything happen after that?"

"Happen? Like what?"

"I don't know. Just humor me."

He shrugged. "Not that I recall. I did get distracted talking to a pretty little redhead though, so I might not be the best source. Why? Did something crazy happen?"

"That's what I'm trying to figure out. I think I drank some absinth last night."

"No shit?"

"Yeah. Your friend gave it to me. What happened next … I'm gonna go with 'hallucination.'"

"Hot dang, really?? I heard that stuff makes folk a little batty! What'd'ya see?"

"You wouldn't believe me if I told you."

"Well, yeah." He chuckled. "That's the point of hallucinating, ain't it?"

Yes.

Yes! That *was* the point, wasn't it? Buckner was a genius! Absinth makes human beings hallucinate. It makes them see things that aren't really there. The only conclusion to draw from this was: Last Night Didn't Happen. No gargoyle girls. No car chase. No girl with a bazooka. It was *alllllll* a dream.

"Hold on," I said and shot up from the couch. I looked out the window to my assigned parking space. It was empty.

"Do you know how I got home last night?" I asked.

"Probably Ubered it," Buckner said. "That's what we did."

"So my car's still in the Hills?"

He laughed. "That or it's getting towed. Better be prepared to pay up, buddy boy. But don't go changin' the subject now. What'd you see last night?"

I turned to him and attempted a shrug. "It's hard to say."

"Well, my question," he said and pointed meaningfully, "is how'd you get all them cuts and bruises? You get in a fight?"

I looked down at my scraped up chest. It was still highly possible that these injuries were sustained in a *normal* drunken stupor, rather than a paranormal one. Still, I needed a second opinion.

"Alright," I said, sitting back on the couch. "I'm gonna tell you what I saw. It's gonna sound crazy, and you're gonna laugh at me, but I gotta tell somebody."

So I told him. I told him about the goth girls taking me to the bedroom. I told him about them morphing into monsters and chasing me outside. I told him about the girl with the Mustang, the shotgun and the roundhouse. By the time I was done, I sounded like a guy who'd just finished a marathon.

"So you think any of that was real?" I asked.

"Doubt it." Buckner shook his head. "I mean everybody knows magic is real and all, but just the small stuff. Last I heard, there weren't any vampires or werewolves lurkin' about."

"Yeah," I agreed. "They *were* like vampires. They were drinking my blood for God's sake!"

"But you said the bite marks are gone, right?"

I nodded. "Yeah, I can't explain that."

"Well, look." Buckner leaned forward. "There's a real easy way to settle this. Hold on."

He got up and disappeared into his room for a minute. He reappeared with his laptop and sat next to me.

"If you doubt it, Google it," he said. "Let's start with something simple."

"Like what?"

"Vam-pi-ers" he spoke as he typed with two fingers. "Are, they, real, question mark. That oughta do it."

The first thing to pop up was a Wikipedia article. Buckner clicked on it.

"Go to the 'sightings' tab," I said, pointing.

"Way ahead of you, hoss. Check this out."

We both peered at the first paragraph and Buckner began reading aloud.

"Since the Reveal of 1982, thousands of people worldwide have claimed to see supernatural creatures, including vampires and demons. However, authorities have never confirmed these sightings, which are largely believed to be false. Moreover, numerous cases have been proven as elaborate hoaxes. Experts believe that all such sightings are merely designed to exploit the public's imagination and generate mass hysteria regarding the Magic Phenomenon."

He looked up from the laptop. "See?" he said. "None of that stuff is real."

"What about the government websites?" I said. "Look up the Magic Department."

"Dang, I still can't believe we have one of those."

"Type it in," I said. "I think it's under magic.gov."

"Got it."

A second later we were both skimming through the website. We both chuckled when we saw the Wikipedia paragraph had been cut and pasted verbatim.

"Here, look at this," Buckner said. "They got a whole section on monsters. It says here that the Department of Magic Affairs has conducted a thorough investigation into the existence of paranormal creatures and found no evidence that they exist. It also refers readers to the 'What is Magic?' tab for a reminder that magic is merely defined as a bio-electric phenomenon affecting less than 0.000001 percent of the world's population. It also emphasizes that this in no way suggests the existence of werewolves, zombies, vampires or aliens."

"What does it say about gargoyles?" I said.

"Doesn't mention them. I'd assume it's the same though."

I leaned back and rubbed my scalp, putting my hair into a mad scientist style.

"It seemed so *real*," I breathed.

"Well, I ain't never tried absinth myself," Buckner noted. "But I hear it can mess you up somethin' good. I'd chalk it up to that, compadre."

Just then, a text ringtone came from my pocket. It made the sound of a stormtrooper's blaster from *Star Wars* and Buckner raised an eyebrow. "That the misses?" he asked.

"Dude, she's just my girlfriend," I grumbled, digging the phone out of my pocket.

"Well don't let your future father-in-law hear that kinda talk. He might fire you. Ever think of that?"

I didn't answer. Meagan's text was angry. It began with "François!" and I could almost hear her shouting it. She also fully spelled out her words, which was never a good sign. It asked with very pointed language why I was avoiding her, why hadn't I answered, where I currently was and what I was currently doing. It also threatened a personal visit if I didn't respond within thirty seconds.

As I read, Buckner leaned over to do the same. "Sounds pissed," he said.

"That's because I'm an asshole. I should've texted her last night."

He leaned away and raised another eyebrow. "You mean before or after you got chased by demon vampire girls?"

I shook my head and started crafting an apology with my thumbs. The autocorrect wasn't doing me any favors. The message "I'm so sorry, I was asleep!" turned into "Sodium rock salt, Iowa slapped!" I actually came within a hair's breadth of sending it, too.

"Dude, that was the absinth," I said distractedly. "Anyway, I gotta get cleaned up."

A brisk shower later, I put on my freshly cleaned suit. It was stylishly dark with a skinny tie. It made me feel like I was in a Tarantino movie. Not *Reservoir Dogs,* of course, I wasn't that cool. Maybe *Jackie Brown?* Anyway, I still had three hours until the interview so I made myself a Mushroom Delight breakfast—a carton of diced mushrooms fried in real butter with three handfuls of shredded cheese—before hailing an Uber. The nearest car was three minutes away.

"What time's the big interview?" Buckner asked as I came back into the living room. He was playing *Duty Bound,* the latest in the *Kill 'em All!* franchise on Xbox. His character, Jax Bishop, was in the middle of wasting a large crowd of terrorists with a Gatling gun.

"Eleven," I said.

He glanced at the clock and then at me. "And you're leavin' *now?* It's eight-thirty."

"Traffic," I said with a shrug. "And I want to get there early."

He chuckled and shook his head. "Well *that,* partner, I believe you will achieve."

By my calculation, I'd arrive downtown by 9:30. That left me an hour and a half to get a coffee, take a little stroll, ditch my hangover, and then be in the Goodman, Sachs & Morgenstern lobby with twenty minutes to spare.

"Thanks," I said.

He paused the game and looked at me. "Well, I'd say good luck, but I'm still holding out for you comin' to your senses."

"It's just an internship, man."

He shrugged and turned back to the TV. "If you say so."

• • •

Contrary to what most people think, LA is actually a very green place. And by "green" I don't mean environmentally friendly. I mean that there are a lot of trees and bushes everywhere. (Perhaps the word "bucolic" would've been best.)

As such, my apartment building existed within a veritable jungle of dense, tropical foliage. There were palm trees, tall ferns and a dozen other types of plants that I didn't know the names for.

I was in the middle of hacking my way through them when I saw my ride parked at the curb. Now, at moments like these, people usually say things like, "he stopped dead in his tracks," or "it looked like he saw a ghost." But those phrases are overused. I can do better than that. I'll invent a new one. "He stopped like the music when Biff walks in."

Good? No good?

Alright, so when I looked up I stopped dead in my tracks. It was like a flashback or a phantasm of some kind. There, parked in front of my building like it was no big deal, was a jet-black Ford Mustang with a tall, ponytailed girl leaning casually against the hood.

I stared like I'd just seen a ghost. Then ... I reacted.

Now if I were a member of the U.S. military, I'd tell you that it wasn't me that deserved the credit for my next move; it was the training. It was the training that had sharpened me into the iron tip of a spear. It was the training that gave me the reflexes necessary to dive into the nearest bush and start belly crawling back toward the building.

I'd made it a good ten feet before a confused voice called out, "*François?*"

I stopped.

Part of being a good commando is knowing when to freeze.

I waited. I listened.

Footsteps. Drawing closer.

Run? Stay? Fight?

"What are you doing?" the voice said. It was above me now. Sounded curious.

I turned.

Black combat boots stared back at me. They transitioned into bare, toned legs that went up and up and up into an alarmingly small pair of cut-off jean shorts.

I let out a protracted "uh" sound and then blinked a few times to regain my senses.

"Are you okay?" she asked. Her nose wrinkled like she'd just witnessed a nasty fall.

I got back to my feet as casually as I could and winced when I saw my suit was covered in dirt.

"Yeah, why?" I blurted. It came out sounding a little more defensive than I intended.

"No reason." She shrugged. "How are you?"

"How am I?" I said. "First of all, you're not real. This is a hallucinogenic haze brought about by an overabundance of absinth in my system. Second of all, I've got a really important interview in a couple hours and I need to get going."

At that, I began walking briskly toward the sidewalk. She quickly caught up and kept pace beside me.

"What interview?" she asked. Oddly, she sounded genuinely curious.

"It's for an internship," I said, getting out my phone.

"A what?"

I elected to ignore her and muttered, "I need another Uber," and began tapping at the screen.

"I can give you a ride," she offered.

"That's impossible because your car is imaginary and I can't ride in it. I didn't ride in it last night, and I can't ride in it today because you're not really here right now and this is all in my head and I need some coffee."

"So you're still freaking out, huh?" she asked.

"I'm not freaking out. I'm perfecting calm. I know exactly what's going on right now. Why would I freak out?"

"Let me give you a ride," she said. "I promise I'll get you to your interview thing on time."

"Are you an Uber driver?" I asked.

"No. But I hacked your phone so my car's the only one that'll show up on your app."

"What?"

"Yeah. So come on. Let's go for a ride. I'll explain some things."

I believed her about the hacking thing. Uber wasn't showing any other cars in the entire city of Los Angeles—other than the black Mustang parked like a caged animal right in front of me. Thus, hallucination or no, I got in.

A minute later, we were speeding up Wilshire as if it were a roller coaster ride. The girl never took her foot off the gas once, which was remarkable given the bumper-to-bumper LA traffic. She avoided it all like a game of Frogger, making liberal use of the sidewalks. All I could do was hold onto the grab handle for dear life and try not to embarrass myself.

"So," the girl said. "I guess I should start with the easy stuff. My name's Cassie Chu and I'm a secret agent. I'm also a succubus. Do you know what that is?"

I tightened my grip on the handle as we fishtailed through a red light onto Sunset.

"Of course," I grunted. "It's a super hot demon chick who drains the essence out of men." (I'd played *Magic: The Gathering* a few times as a kid. Sue me.)

She scrunched her face a little in annoyance. "Well that's kind of a *guy* way of looking at it, but okay. Besides, I'm only half. My dad was human. And I don't 'drain the essence' out of anyone."

"What do you do then?"

"I kill monsters."

We were back on the sidewalk again and a guy in an Elvis costume dove out of the way. It was one of those things that if you saw it in a movie you'd probably laugh, but in real life all you can think about is whether or not the guy had a heart condition and how long your prison sentence will be.

"So you're like Blade?" I asked.

Cassie looked at me askance before swerving back onto the road. A bicyclist in full *Tour de France* gear toppled over his front wheel in shock. "Who?" she asked.

"It's a movie. Never mind."

She found a pocket of empty road and gunned it. I swallowed. The combination of booster rocket G-forces and my lingering hangover were beginning to exact a toll on my Mushroom Delight breakfast.

"The only movie I ever saw was *Cars 2*," she said with a grimace. "And it sucked."

She then yanked on the wheel and the Mustang veered onto the 101 North. (If you're not from LA, the 101 North is the opposite direction from downtown.) I pointed this out to her, but she merely maneuvered onto the shoulder and treated it like an empty lane.

"What time's the interview thing?" she asked.

"Eleven," I told her.

She glanced at her clock—which read 8:46—and then gave me a look. "I think we'll make it," she said. "Besides, we have to make a stop first. It'll only take a second."

I noticed we were heading back in the direction of the Hollywood Hills—and with them—the eerily vivid memories of every single thing that had happened last night, absinth or no. It occurred to me that hallucinations weren't usually this *real.* Usually they were more abstract. I mean, imagining your walls melting is one thing, but dipping straight into *The Matrix* and having full conversations and car chases was quite another.

Anyway, the freeway—even if we were driving on the shoulder—was comparatively relaxing next to the city, so I figured I'd take a shot at understanding some things.

"So," I began. "Let's say for the sake of argument that I'm not imagining all this. How come the cops haven't talked to me yet? I mean, my car exploded. You fired a *bazooka.* Is anyone dead?"

Cassie nodded sagely. "All good questions. First, no *humans* are dead. The vampettes, on the other hand, are toast. Second, I'm not imaginary. I'm real. Third, that was an M72 rocket launcher I fired—very different from a bazooka. Fourth, the cops haven't talked to you because none of them have any memory of last night."

Hmm.

Ever notice how some answers just lead to more questions? This was precisely one of those times. So let's start in order.

"What's a 'vampette?'" I asked.

"Well *technically*," she groaned, "the official term is 'vampire spawn,' but I like vampette. It sounds better. Plus, I made it up."

"So they were vampires?" I asked.

"Vampettes, yeah. Just be glad they weren't *full* vampires. Those guys are crazy. Much tougher to kill."

"What makes them so hard to—?"

I cut myself off. This was no time to get sidetracked.

"Why were they trying to kill me?" I asked.

"Well, killing people is kind of what they do. But why you in particular, I'm not sure. That's why we need to find out who *you* are. You're sure you're not a wizard or anything?"

"I don't think so."

"VIP? Undercover spy?"

"My parents are computer programmers who collect bobble-head dolls of Steve Jobs. There are far more varieties of him than you might think. I'm not a spy."

She glanced at me, confused. She probably didn't know who Steve Jobs was. Or what a bobble-head doll was. Or why anyone would collect them. Why *would* anyone collect them? "Either way," she said, "I know someone who can help."

"Who?"

"You'll see."

I couldn't believe I was about to ask this—especially with a straight face—but I did anyway. "Is he a wizard?"

She chuckled. "I told you," she said. "You'll see."

"Okay. So why don't the cops have any memory?"

"The BPI."

"The what?"

"The BPI. Come on, even non-magic people know what *that* is."

(I could tell she was struggling not to use the word, 'Muggles.')

"You mean the Bureau of Paranormal Whatever?" I asked with a frown. "I read about that once. It has like two employees or something. And one of them is a clown."

"Jasper's just the mascot," she said. "And it's Paranormal *Investigation*. The BPI has thousands of people, not to mention all the automata. It's huge."

"Automa-what? Actually, never mind. What does it do?"

"The BPI?"

"Yeah."

"They cover things up, mostly. Like your car. They make sure no one knows about that stuff. Their slogan is something like,"—she deepened her voice to sound overly serious—"*Guarding Against Instances of Magical Display.* Basically, they're a bunch of old guys with sticks up their butts, but mostly what they really do is wage war against YouTube all day."

"So who are *you* then?" I asked.

"Me? I don't know. I guess I'm sort of an assassin. But I'll explain more about that later. First, we have to get you to Rosewood."

"Who?"

"My boss. Don't worry. He's nice."

I sat in silence a moment to let everything sink in. I typically find that creating a little bullet-point list in my head of what I know—and what I don't know—tends to help with difficult situations. So ... what did I know?

1.) The odds were steadily decreasing that this was an absinth-induced hallucination.
2.) I was nearly killed last night by vampire spawn.
3.) "Cassie the Assassin/Succubus" was taking me to see someone named "Rosewood" at an unknown location.

As for the things I *didn't* know, that list would take up the next six to seven hundred pages. Needless to say, I still had a lot of questions—many of which were vital to my continued sanity—yet one in particular pushed its way to the front of the queue.

"How come you were wearing pajamas?" I asked.

"When? Last night?"

"You were wearing *Hello Kitty* slippers," I said.

She smiled girlishly. "I *love* those! But yeah. I was asleep when I got the call. And considering I was in Tokyo at the time, there wasn't any time to change."

"You flew here from Tokyo?"

"Well, I ran most of the way. And I know that doesn't make any sense, but you'll understand in like two minutes."

"Understand that you ran here from Tokyo?"

"Something like that."

I paused a moment and looked out the window. How does someone run to California from Tokyo? And how in the world was that going to make sense in a couple minutes?

"So are you sure you can't tell me where we're going?" I asked.

"Of course I can," she said. "The Hollywood Sign. Ever been up there?"

I added another item to my list.

4.) Hollywood Sign. *Why?*

"Uh, can't say that I have," I said. "But, speaking of Tokyo, are you Japanese?"

She glanced over at me and frowned. "Um … no?"

There was a slight, awkward pause before she suddenly brightened in understanding. "Oh, wait," she said. "You mean because I'm Asian looking? Look at you, all racist. No, I was just working there. My dad was from Hong Kong—at least I think he was—but that's kind of a sore subject. And you're really not French?"

I shook my head. "No, I just had cruel parents."

And then, for some strange reason, all conversation ceased on a dime. So I made another note:

> 5.) The succubus does not appreciate jokes about cruel parents. Reason still unknown.

"They're *from* France," I added. "They just emigrated here when I was a baby."

Still nothing.

When we stopped, I noticed we were on a dusty hillside above the Hollywood Sign. It was one of those weird moments where you see something familiar from a completely new angle and barely recognize it. (Kind of like seeing a celebrity up close. Always a disappointment.)

Cassie got out and I followed. She headed toward a chain link fence topped with clusters of angry-looking security cameras. I'd read somewhere that the city of Los Angeles doesn't play around with its most famous landmark. Trespassing on it is still punishable by firing squad, and to emphasize this, the site had a small, sturdy security booth, housing a single LAPD officer. The man inside it looked about as grim as a human being can possibly look. I'd say he had one of those patent "flat faces," but it was more like his whole head had been shaped in an upturned bucket.

As we passed him, I asked Cassie if he was going to bust us, but she explained he was an automaton working for the BPI.

"You mean like a robot?" I said.

"More like gears, spindles and magic working together, but yeah, sort of."

She walked up to the fence and touched a certain link, and the whole thing rolled aside like a carpet.

And now is as good a time as any to say that Cassie Chu was the most attractive girl I'd ever seen in my entire life. I'd noticed this earlier of course, but right now just seems like the best time to tell you about it. So ... where to begin?

Let's start with the wisdom every frat guy likes to pull out of his backwards hat when he's had a few, and is trying to sound like Don Juan. It concerns the difference between "hot" and "beautiful."

"Hot" is like a porn star or a swimsuit model.

"Beautiful" is like Audrey Hepburn or vintage Elizabeth Hurley.

However, every once in a while, a Marilyn Monroe comes around, and is *both*.

Cassie Chu was definitely both. She was a twenty-six on a scale of one to ten. And she wasn't even trying either. Right now, all she was wearing was shorts and a tank top, and yet the sight of her was almost too much to look at.

You want details? Okay. She had the tall, broad-shouldered figure of a runway model, yet with a surprisingly large bust and the nicest backside I'd *ever* seen. And in the era of Google Images, that's truly saying something.

Her hair was long and dark, with a hint of purple in the sunlight.

Her eyes were round and cat-like.

Her smile was broad and devilish.

Anyway, I've read that less is more when it comes to descriptions, so I've already messed that up enough. Let's just wrap it up by concluding that Cassie Chu was a succubus. (Or at least, half of one.) That meant that she was literally *supernaturally* beautiful. Hopefully that gives you some idea what I'm talking about.

So yeah. The fence rolled away when she touched it and that was kind of cool. I followed her to the letter "H," and watched as she took a small key from her pocket.

"This is gonna look weird," she cautioned, before pressing the key into the wood. It disappeared as if it had just entered an invisible lock, and then she turned it. A door-sized rectangle opened in the H, and there—on the other side—was *not* a view of the LA basin. Instead, there was a crowded city street.

My concerns about hallucinations returned.

"It's a backdoor," Cassie explained. "They're all over the city, but this one's special, hence the BPI guard. That's Washington, D.C., on the other side. You can walk through it. It's totally fine."

I stared a moment with a pinched face. "What do you mean, 'walk through it?'" I said.

"I mean walk through it. It's a door."

"And then I'll be in DC?"

"Yep."

I stared a moment longer. "Do you wanna go first?"

Cassie shook her head. "Can't," she said. "You're not magic. If I go through first you won't be able to follow."

"Won't people freak out when they see me?" I asked.

"Why would they freak out?"

"I'll be appearing out of nowhere," I said.

"Oh, that. No, to them it will look like you're walking out of a Coffee Bean."

"A Coffee Bean?"

"I mean, if you had a cup in your hand it would help, but no one's going to care." She looked at her watch. It had a high-tech, sci-fi look to it. "Come on," she said. "You have that interview thing in a couple hours, right?"

Somehow, staring into a magical portal in the "H" of the Hollywood Sign made me forget all about my future with Goodman, Sachs & Morgenstern. I'd been stressing for weeks about the prospect of sitting down to a formal interview with Meagan's dad, yet now, the guy seemed far less intimidating.

"So I just step through it?" I asked.

"Just step through it," Cassie said.

So I did. It was like fifth grade when I jumped off the high dive for the first time. I closed my eyes, counted to three and stepped into oblivion. The next thing I knew, I was standing on Constitution Avenue, staring at the Capitol Mall.

"See?" Cassie appeared beside me. "Nothing to it. Now we have to go through another one. It's this way."

She started walking and I trotted to catch up. I couldn't stop looking in every direction like a freshly arrived tourist. "Where?" I asked.

"Up there." She pointed. "We have to use the entrance to that giant phallus at the heart of your capital."

"The Washington Monument? Are all the backdoors inside major landmarks or something?"

"Just the special ones," she said. "It makes it so security people can stand around and it doesn't look weird."

I accepted that with a shrug and followed her across the street. I'd never seen Washington, D.C., before. It was a crazy-looking place—really spread out and solid. All the buildings looked historical, with monumental buildings of brick and limestone. Plus, the weather was terrific. It was a bright spring afternoon that fell right in the sweet spot between winter and summer. And this—combined with the fact that we were trotting across the Capitol Mall—was the most likely reason for all the tourists. They were everywhere and stuck out like a thousand sore thumbs. Which brings me to a point I've never fully understood. Why is it that when Americans travel— whether at home or abroad—they feel a powerful compulsion to dress like dorks? I don't mean that to sound harsh or anything—I'm not exactly a paragon of fashion myself—but you know exactly what I'm talking about. We've all seen it. I mean, I assume most of these people—whether they're from Cleveland or Boston or Sacramento—don't wear these clothes when they're back home. Only when traveling do they break out the pleated khaki shorts, the Mickey Mouse fanny packs, the pastel-colored hats and the oversized orange polo shirts. *Why?*

Anyway, that's what everyone looked like who was waiting outside the monument. I also saw a foot patrol cop ambling nearby and wondered if he was an automaton. He looked like a normal guy on the outside, but I found myself wondering if there were a bunch of gears and springs on the inside.

Cassie then broke my reverie when she informed me that I was staring and that my feet had stopped moving. I stammered an apology and followed her as she skipped to the front of the line.

No sooner than she did, than a middle-aged guy with socks up to his knees got angry. At that point, Cassie did something I'll never forget. She turned to him, her eyes glowing purple, and said, "You are not angry that I am cutting in line," and he repeated dumbly, "I am not angry that you are cutting in line."

"You are happy about it," she said.

"I am happy about it," he repeated.

"And you will lose those socks."

"I will lose these socks."

She smiled and motioned for me to follow. I paused, though, and waved my hand in front of the guy's face. He didn't react.

"And these are not the droids you're looking for," I said.

Cassie grabbed my arm and pulled me to an employees only door. "That's mean," she giggled. "He's gonna be totally confused now. Anyway, this is it. There's a really scary-looking guard on the other side, but don't worry. You're fine if you're with me."

"I still don't know where we're going," I said.

She looked at me and said, "To find out who you are," and then turned the key.

The door opened to a small, drab room with a gated elevator on the far wall. Beside it stood an old man in a starched conductor's uniform of red and navy with brass buttons and white gloves.

Some "scary guard," I thought and stepped inside.

Cassie followed and closed the door behind her. The moment it clicked shut, the old man gained an extra two feet in height, his head became a ball of blue fire and his uniform transformed into an oversized suit of medieval armor, complete with a six-foot greatsword. He also sprouted wings made of solid flame. I'll admit ... he was a little scary.

"Hi George," Cassie said, and pressed the button for the elevator.

George didn't say anything.

In a weird way, he reminded me of one of those British Royal Guards who don't react no matter what you do—unless of course you do something bad and then you suddenly realize they have guns.

Once we were safely inside the elevator, I asked, "George?"

Cassie shrugged. "I just call him that to give him personality. He's ... not from around here."

"What is he?" I asked.

She gave me a hesitant look. "You'll get the wrong idea if I tell you."

"The wrong idea?" I said. "In the past twelve hours I've been chased by vampire spawn, rescued by a succubus, and traveled through a mystical portal in the Hollywood Sign. I can take it."

"It wasn't a 'portal,'" she scoffed. "You went through a backdoor. Totally different. But fine. He's a Guardian Angel."

"You mean like from Heaven?"

She laughed and rolled her eyes. "See? I told you you'd get the wrong idea. There's no such thing as 'Heaven.' Don't be a weirdo. He comes from an Eternal Plane. Anyway, I don't know much more than that. I don't really study that kind of stuff."

"What stuff?" I asked.

"Wizard stuff."

The elevator traveled a solid mile underground—at least it felt like it did—before it finally stopped. Cassie opened the grated doors with a squeaky lever. "This is it," she announced. "Welcome to the Supernatural Intelligence Agency. SIA for short. Obviously."

When I stepped out, I figured I'd traveled through a time warp to the era of World War II. A large open space stretched in front of us, cluttered with old wooden desks piled with antique equipment. And by antique equipment, I mean typewriters, rotary telephones, clunky radios and men wearing tailored, three-piece suits. The walls were lined with the type of old doors you see in P.I. movies with a square of wavy glass and some guy's name written on it. The ceiling was made of solid concrete and supported by regular columns made of brick. Altogether, the place had the feel of a bunker. (Or—in an example that hits closer to home—the terrifyingly old-fashioned dentist office my parents used to drag me to as a kid.)

"The Supernatural what?" I said after a pause.

"Intelligence Agency," Cassie said. "This isn't the head-quarters, though. That's in London. This is just the American Office. My boss works here."

She led me out of the main room and down a long hallway. I noticed absently that all the doors on either side were closed and I couldn't hear a peep coming from any of them. That's weird, right? I mean, I don't have a lot of experience in office buildings, but wouldn't you expect to see at least a *few* doors open—maybe with some guy chatting in the doorway holding a coffee or something?

Cassie stopped in front of a door labeled:

Agent Thomas J. Rosewood
Deputy Assistant Director of Protective Services

She knocked twice and I heard the clinking of multiple locks and deadbolts coming undone. The door swung open and Cassie skipped inside.

"Hey boss!" she chirped happily, letting me follow behind her.

I don't know why, but I expected the office to look messy for some reason. I thought there would be stacks of papers everywhere, open file folders, dog-eared books and maybe one of those wooden globes that hides a liquor cabinet inside. Instead, the room had the scholarly opulence of a royal library. Everything was polished oak, mahogany and fine leather. Bookshelves that required a ladder lined the walls, while plush sitting chairs with emerald reading lamps dotted the immense floor space. At the far end was a large, ornately carved desk fit for a king. Behind it sat a man I assumed was Agent Thomas J. Rosewood. He wore a finely tailored three-piece suit like everyone else we'd seen, yet somehow he wore it *better*. It fit him more naturally—like he was the man who had designed the original and everyone else was a copycat. *Or ...* he was British.

Which he was.

"Ah. Cassandra!" He slapped his desk before bounding to his feet.

I put him somewhere in his mid-fifties with soft features and grey hair. He had a breezy, cheerful demeanor that made me think of Santa Claus. I liked him instantly.

Cassie seemed to have similar feelings and bounded over to give him a hug.

"My dear girl," he said as he squeezed her. "How are you?"

"Everything went great," she said, pulling back to admire his suit. "Have you put on some weight?"

"Ha! At my age it's a losing battle, I'm afraid. By this time next year, you'll have to *roll* me into this office." He stole his eyes from her a moment to look at me. "And who's this?"

Cassie skipped over and pulled me closer. "This is François Lemieux," she said. "He's why I came to see you." She turned to me. "François, this is my boss, Agent Rosewood."

Rosewood put out a hand. "Delighted," he said, giving me a firm shake. "Any friend of my dear Cassandra is a friend of mine."

"Thanks." I glanced around and added, "You have a really nice office."

"Oh, this place?" He frowned and waved a hand around the room. "It is a silly contrivance of magic, I assure you. Truth is, I always fancied myself a bit of an old-fashioned chap, you see, so I built it like this. It's modeled on an actual room in Buckingham Palace."

I wasn't quite sure what he was talking about, but I nodded. "It's really nice," I said.

"Oh, thank you, thank you. Come. Sit." He motioned to a pair of chairs opposite his desk. "Can I get you anything? Tea? Coffee?"

"Oh, no thank you," I said, taking a seat.

I realized that this was my first encounter with a real life English person. And even though we were at the Supernatural Intelligence Agency, he was—somewhat disappointingly— more *Downton Abbey* than *James Bond*. Still, there was just something about that polished accent that immediately made me want to imitate it. For example, notice how I told him,

"*Oh,* no thank you?" I wouldn't usually say "oh" like that. But now I rather feared it was only the beginning ...

"So it's kind of a weird story," Cassie began, and grabbed a handful of M&Ms from the desk. "I'd just finished the thing in Tokyo when Greta called me."

"*Greta,* you say?" Rosewood perked up. The name seemed to shock him.

"It was definitely her," Cassie went on. "She told me I had to find François Lemieux in Los Angeles. She told me where he lived and then to keep him close until it was no longer necessary. And that was it. She didn't say anything else."

Rosewood gasped. "She called you out of the blue? How did you manage to find him?"

"He showed up on my GPS."

"Hmm. Very unusual. Did you notice anything odd, or perhaps out of place?"

Cassie shot me a wary look. "Well, three vampettes were about to make a meal out of him ..."

Rosewood blanched and wheeled on me with wide eyes. "Dear me! Are you alright, François?"

"They bit me a few times, but I feel okay."

For the past hour, I'd been indulging in a panic-inducing thought that at any second I was going to turn into a "vampette" myself. I was hoping Rosewood might assure me otherwise.

"Oh, not to worry," he said. "It's not like the cinema, it's not contagious. It takes a full vampire and a long, tedious process to make another one. Still. Nasty business. I do apologize."

"He did really well," Cassie said. "Most non-magic people wouldn't have lasted five seconds."

Rosewood nodded in agreement. "I should say so. Very impressive, François."

"I owe it all to the Toasted Walnut," I said.

He stopped, suddenly bemused. "Toasted what?"

I gulped. "I feel stupid for saying that out loud. It's my car. It's brown. Or it was brown. It's gone now."

He frowned a second longer in confusion and then shrugged. "Well the important thing is that you are safe and sound. Now, Cassandra,"—he turned to her—"vampire spawn do not operate on their own, you know. They had orders. Did Greta say anything—anything at all—about who might wish to harm François?"

She shook her head. "She just said to keep him close and hung up. It was weird. She's usually cryptic, but not *that* cryptic."

I raised my hand. (Yes. I felt very stupid after I did it.) "Who's Greta?" I asked.

For the briefest moment, there was a pause—like Cassie and Rosewood were wondering if they should tell me the truth.

Rosewood spoke first. "Greta," he said, "is an astrologer."

"An astrologer?"

Cassie leaned over. "Real astrologers are no joke. When one of them tells you something, you listen. They're super rare and can actually see the future—something even the greatest wizards can't do."

"Not for a lack of trying." Rosewood smiled sheepishly. "I dare say I've tried it once or twice myself. It is quite difficult."

I turned to Cassie. "And she told you to come find me?"

"Yep."

"Why?"

She gave me a look. It lasted for a couple seconds until a cartoon light bulb suddenly appeared over my head and I snapped my fingers. "Yep. Stupid question. That's why we're here. Got it."

"There's something else," she said, turning back to Rosewood. "When I took him back to his apartment, I tried a basic enchantment, but it didn't work."

Rosewood turned on me again and furrowed his brow. "Hm. Unusual, yes," he said. "And I trust you were fully focused while casting the spell?"

"A hundred percent," Cassie said a little defensively.

"In that case, there is but one thing I can think of." Rosewood stood and made his way around the desk. "François, if you'd be so kind as to permit me, I'd like to try a little experiment."

"What kind of experiment?"

"Oh, it's quite harmless, I assure you. But if I am correct, you will most certainly thank me."

"Trust him," Cassie said. "He's the best."

"I'm not sure about all that." Rosewood grinned. "But I try my hardest. Now, François, you're going to see a little 'ball of light' in my hand and I'm going to throw it at you. Don't be alarmed. You might feel a bit of an odd tingle, but that's all quite ordinary."

I noticed that my back was pressed firmly against the chair. *What kind of "ball of light?"* I wondered. *And what "tingle?"*

Truth be told, I'd had just about enough magic for one day. Yet for some reason, in certain situations, you can't just say "no." It's awkward. Plain and simple. So instead, you mutter something like, "… yeah … okay, sure."

"Very good," Rosewood said and gave a curt nod. He held out a fist and opened it face up. A ball of light—about the size of a softball—hovered a couple inches above his palm. It was bright, but not blinding, and had a tinge of blue to it. "Now hold still," he said with a firmer tone. He then flicked his wrist and the ball shot at me like a bullet. I didn't even see it. I also didn't feel a thing. There was no tingling at all.

"Just as I suspected!" Rosewood declared. "Marvelous!"

"*What?*" I asked.

"You have been *hexed,* my boy!"

"Hexed?" My back pressed tighter to the chair. "Is that like *cursed?*"

"Oh heavens, no! A hex can be a good thing, it all depends on its nature, you see? Now if I were to hazard a guess, I'd say this hex has been with you a very long time. Perhaps since *birth.* Extraordinary."

"What does it do?"

"If my suspicions are correct," he said. "It is designed to shield you from the uncanny. No magic, of any sort, will work when applied to your person. *That* is why Cassandra's enchantment wouldn't work. I also suspect this gave you a terrific advantage against those devilish vampire spawn. None of their strength could affect you. It undoubtedly saved your life."

"That's why he was so heavy!" Cassie blurted. "I knew there was something weird going on!"

"Yes," Rosewood agreed. "However, I fear the hex works *both* ways."

"Both ways?" I asked.

"Indeed. It may very well protect you from magic," he explained, "but one might say it is 'holding you back,' as well. I trust you have never noticed anything peculiar about yourself?"

"You mean like magically peculiar?"

"Yes."

"Then no."

Rosewood sat on the edge of his desk and nodded sagely. "I would imagine that to be so. You see, François, *someone* put this hex on you as a child. Someone knew something that we don't, and they did it for a reason. Perhaps to protect you. Or perhaps not. Oh, and neither of your parents are magical, am I right?"

"My parents? I highly doubt it."

"Wait," Cassie said. She bolted upright in her chair. "Boss, are you saying what I think you're saying?"

Rosewood grinned. "François may very well be a wizard, yes."

There are certain words that have a bit of a stigma attached to them. "Wizard" is one of them. It depends on the context, but usually when a fully-grown man uses a word like wizard, he's either a.) Really into Dungeons & Dragons, or b.) He's an actor who's been paid millions of dollars to sit in a booth at Comic-Con and appear genuinely interested. I'd never thought I'd hear the word applied to me. I *also* never thought I'd say to someone, as I chuckled awkwardly, "What? Me? Oh no, you've got the wrong guy. I'm not a wizard."

"Well, there's only one way to find out," Rosewood said. "It's up to you, of course, but I can remove the hex. You see, now that I know it's there, it's remarkably easy to dispel. Plus, it's old. I imagine it would wear out on its own within the next year or two."

I looked between Cassie and Rosewood who both stared back at me expectantly. Cassie was tapping her foot and biting one of her nails.

Eventually, I said, "Um," and then clamped my mouth shut again.

I thought: *Is this really happening? Am I about to give the thumbs up to becoming a wizard? And what does a wizard even do, anyway?*

Well, as the man just said, there was only one way to find out.

"Okay. What do I have to do?"

Cassie's eyes lit up as Rosewood hopped off his desk and went rummaging through his drawers.

"Ah," he said. "Just the thing!"

He brought out an antique magnifying glass rimmed with gold. It was a little dusty, and he blew on it with a flourish. "Galileo himself made this," he said proudly. "I came across it at this little boutique in Florence. The owner had no idea what he had!"

My back was pressed against the seat again. "What are you going to do with it?"

"Oh, nothing nefarious," he said with a little laugh. "It's just to gauge the hue of the hex."

He peered at me through the lens, making his eye look triple-sized. "Hm. A light shade of indigo, I'd say. Very well."

He put the magnifying glass down before standing up. "Now François," he began, "I'm going to do the 'ball of light' thing again, only this time a bit more intense. It should be fine, although there might be a bit of a 'pressure.' Just hold still."

With that, he brought up both hands and a blue sphere of energy—about the size of a soccer ball—materialized between them. It was transparent with little filaments of lightning that sparked inside, reminding me of a plasma globe. (My parents had like six of those things.) He concentrated on it for a moment, making tiny gestures with his fingers. Then there was a flash and the ball zipped at my chest. I waited a second, completely forgetting to breathe. A moment later I realized that nothing happened. It didn't hurt. There was no pressure. I didn't feel a thing.

"Is that it?" I asked.

"Let's see," Rosewood said, picking up the magnifying glass. "Oh yes. That did it. The hex is gone."

"I don't feel any different," I said, looking myself over.

"Oh no, you wouldn't. But now that it's done, you'll need a proper teacher. I'd volunteer myself, of course, but alas I cannot. Here." He skipped over to a shelf and pulled out a small, leather-bound book. "Use this," he said, and handed it to me.

I took the dusty, dog-eared volume and read aloud, "Introduction to Magic: A Beginner's Guide to Spellcasting by Alroy

McFadden. Published 1852. New York, New York." I looked up. "This will teach me to be a wizard?"

"Oh yes." Rosewood nodded merrily. "Old Alroy is a marvelous teacher. Now you'll also need this." He went back into his drawer and pulled out a gold Zippo. It was worn and scratched like an antique. "*Solitarius Tractus!*" Rosewood announced proudly. "A vital tool for any wizard. Watch this!"

He flipped open the cap and sparked the flint.

What happened next can be described in two ways. First, his entire body got sucked into the lighter like a bed sheet into a vacuum. Second, he became an open Word Document that just got moved into the toolbar on a MacBook. Whichever helps you visualize it best.

Either way, he vanished and the lighter dropped onto the desk with a heavy thud. An odd silence ensued for a couple seconds—though it seemed a lot longer—before I turned to Cassie and asked what in the heck just happened.

Her eyes were glazed over slightly and she didn't answer right away. "Hm?" she said. "Oh, that. He's fine. He'll be back in a second."

"Where did he go?"

"Inside the thingamajig," she said.

Now, I know I already mentioned how pretty Cassie was, but I feel like I need to mention it again. The reason for this is that right at that moment, with her leering at me, I couldn't help but squirm in my seat. I actually had *butterflies* in my stomach. I hadn't felt this nervous around a girl since high school.

After a moment, Cassie asked, "You okay?"

I told her I was. She smiled back without saying anything.

Then—before things got even more awkward—the Zippo sprang into the air, snapped open, and out came Agent Rosewood.

"See?" he said. "Perfectly harmless! The *Solitarius Tractus*—known colloquially as a 'Solitar'—is where you will learn magic.

You can go inside it and create any environment you wish, so as to provide yourself with a safe, spacious '*dojo*,' if you will. There, you will learn magic spells without fear of harming yourself or others."

"So ... if I open it and then light it, I get sucked inside it?"

Rosewood laughed. "Ah, well the magical physics of it all is rather complex, I'm afraid. But yes, in effect, you will get pulled inside. In wizarding parlance we refer to it as a 'micro plane,' but you don't need to concern yourself with that now. The most important thing for you to understand is that the Solitar is a wizard's most sacred, private place where he can study the ancient arts of magic. In time, you will build a whole *world* inside, and I implore you to guard it carefully and keep it on your person at all times. In the wrong hands, it could be very dangerous indeed."

"How?"

"Ah." He chuckled again. "I'm afraid that's a lesson you will have to learn on your own, dear boy. Just trust an old chap, and keep the Solitar safe. You will not regret it. Now," he added with a sharp breath. "It just so happens, I have an important assignment for the two of you—that is, of course, if you will be working together?"

Before I could answer, Cassie told him that we definitely were.

"Very good." Rosewood then pulled a file from his desk. "This," he said, slapping it in front of us, "is of utmost importance and must be kept strictly off the books. The fate of the world depends on it."

• • •

After climbing back in the Mustang outside the Hollywood Sign, Cassie drove *way* slower than before. She was like a normal person, even using her blinkers. The time was 10:43 and we had to make it downtown for my interview at eleven. In LA traffic, that meant that getting there on time was as likely as driving to the southern tip of Argentina and then back in roughly the same time frame. Still, no one likes a backseat driver, so I kept quiet and hoped that she knew what she was doing. What amazed me most was that I actually still *cared* about the interview. Even after learning I was a wizard—and then getting handed an assignment to save the world—I was still nervous about sitting across a table from Meagan's father. I was even worried about the sorry state of my suit. It was covered in dirt from collar to cuff. How was I going to explain that? And would it even matter? There was no way I was getting there on time.

I brooded on this, trying to remember some of my practice questions. None of them came. It was like my brain was a blank sheet of paper. Then Cassie broke the silence.

"So ... do you have a girlfriend?" she asked.

Of all the questions in the universe, I wasn't expecting that one. I told her that I did and asked, "Why?"

She gave a little shrug, and with all the nonchalance in the world, stated, "Because I like you."

I honestly wasn't expecting that either. I also didn't know how to respond to it. Hence, the following:

"Um, thanks?"

It was times like these when I wished I were a "cool guy." If that sounds shallow, let me explain. To my mind, a "cool guy" knows exactly what to say in all situations. If a pretty girl tells him she likes him, he says something right back that makes her laugh, and then he laughs, and then she laughs and then everything works out. I've never been that guy. I've never known what to say. I only know what to say about twenty minutes later when she's long gone and may as well be on the moon. Which is *why*, I was all too familiar with the "look" that Cassie gave me.

"Thanks, huh?" She then gave an exaggerated sigh. "A girl puts herself out there, and all she gets is a thanks ..."

"Sorry?" I tried.

"That's worse! Jeez, how did you get this supposed 'girl-friend,' anyway?"

I had a quick flashback to when Meagan introduced herself. Everything after that was kind of a blur.

"I honestly can't say," I said.

She looked over and raised an eyebrow. "So what's her name?"

"Meagan."

"Is she pretty?"

I blinked and told her that yes, yes she was. I also mentioned that tomorrow was our 1.5-year anniversary.

"Who has a 1.5-year anniversary?" Cassie asked.

I shrugged in response.

The car was strangely quiet a moment before she suddenly blurted, "Okay fine. I lied, okay? I'm sorry, it's just … I didn't want to spook you. But you're perfectly safe, I promise."

I didn't know what the heck she was talking about, but usually when someone emphasizes out of the blue that you're "perfectly safe" it means that you're not. Thus, I found myself slowly edging away. "What do you mean?" I asked.

She paused, chewing her bottom lip, and then said guiltily, "So remember how I told you I was a succubus?"

"Yeah …"

"Well, I actually, sort of, *do* 'drain the essence' out of people. Or actually, it's not their 'essence'—that's a weird word. It's just their magic. Even non-magic people have a little of it. And without it, they die. So I guess it's like their 'life force' or something. But I can't help it. It's what succubi feed on."

"So …"

"Yeah," she said flatly. "I'm a monster."

She glanced at me again and must have noticed my hand slowly inching toward the door handle because she quickly added, "But I don't! Er ... what I mean is I hold myself back. I don't want to hurt anyone."

My hand stopped. "So what do you do then?"

"What do you mean?"

"For food," I said.

"I don't know. I eat ... food. Like, cheeseburgers and stuff. It's just that for me, sex is way, *way* better. Although chocolate ice cream comes in at a distant second."

"Oh."

"Anyway, I just told you about the succubus thing because ..." She paused again and looked at me. "I don't know. You're kind of cute. And you're a wizard, so you're immune to the whole 'dying when I kiss you' thing. And your ears stick out."

Cute. Wizard. Dying. Ears.

For some reason I focused on the "ears" part, and reached for them self-consciously.

"No they don't," I said.

"They do. But I guess what I'm trying to say is that I think you're hot. And I have ... how do I say this? Impulse control issues? Like when I see a really cute guy it makes me super hungry and I go a little crazy. But you don't have anything to worry about. I have years of practice with this."

Slowly, my non-cool brain began to put two and two together. Unless I was mistaken—which has happened in the past— Cassie was saying that because I was a wizard; that meant that somehow she could sleep with me without killing me, and that possibly she kind of *wanted to*. (Sleep with me. Not kill me.)

"So what you're saying is—" I started to say.

"We're totally gonna have sex," she finished. "It's only a matter of time."

Ever give one of those snorting, awkward laughs that makes you wish you could rewind time a few seconds so you could *not* do it? I gave one of those. "Ha ha, yeah. Maybe," I said. "I actually do have a Meagan, er … a girlfriend, and I don't think that would be such a good idea."

And yet even as I said those words, I was already imagining Cassie climbing onto my lap and lifting her top over her head and then—

"I think it would be a great idea," she said.

I swallowed. "You know my interview is in like five minutes. Do you know a faster route?"

She glanced at me. "Are you worried?"

"About the internship?" My voice cracked. "No, it's just, um …"

"You know, you don't have to be scared of me," she said. "I told you. I'm a nice succubus. And I'm only half, anyway."

"No, no, that's not it. I just can't be late."

Beads of sweat were starting to drip off my brow. Cassie noticed and looked me over with an amused smirk. "Are you always like this when you're flustered?"

"I'm not flustered," I said.

"Are too."

"It's been a crazy day," I said, then loosened my tie a bit. "It's really hot in here. Can I roll down the window or something?"

"You're asking my permission?"

I gave another snorting laugh. "Ha. It's just my first time in a Batmobile."

She giggled and made a gesture toward the door. "Go right ahead."

"Thanks."

"You're welcome."

I rolled down the window as we turned onto Hollywood Boulevard. The traffic was surprisingly light, yet I still wondered why she was taking *this* route. There were at least three others that would've been quicker.

"We're not going to make it," I muttered absently. I hadn't intended for Cassie to hear, but she did. She flashed me a wicked smile and asked, "Is that a challenge?"

"What? No. I didn't mean to say that out loud."

"I think you did. I think you want me to drive fast again."

Memories of this morning raced back into my head—the diving Elvis, the flying *Tour de France* guy, the poor souls scrambling off the sidewalks …

"No, it's cool," I said. "I can be a little late."

In truth, if I was even a little late I'd lose any chance of impressing Meagan's dad. But I didn't want any casualties on my conscience.

Cassie shrugged, disappointed. "If you say so."

Then there was an awkward silence.

We pulled up to a red light on Hollywood and Highland. I stared at it, doing my level best to look anywhere besides the beautiful succubus sitting next to me. Cassie, meanwhile, drummed her fingers happily on the steering wheel. From the corner of my eye, I saw her shoulders rocking almost imperceptibly in a little dance. It was the sexiest thing I'd ever seen. I mean, she was barely moving and yet I couldn't help but slowly turn and stare. Every curve seemed to melt into the next and my eyes traced from her midriff to the straining fabric of her tank top to her … *shoot.* She was looking at me.

"Hi," she said.

I then pulled a move that every hormone crazed eighth-grader is all too familiar with: The Sudden Look Away.

There are few things in life more embarrassing than The Sudden Look Away, but sometimes it's all you can do. It's also a matter of instinct. There's no time to think, "Gosh, this will look ridiculous when I do it." Instead, it just happens.

In my case, it snapped my gaze out the passenger window in time to see a black and white police cruiser pull up beside us. My first thought was that somehow Johnny Law had caught up to the infamous black Mustang that had been tearing across the city a few hours ago. My second thought was that there was something a tiny bit *off* about this police cruiser. Its windows were tinted. I'd never seen a cop car with fully tinted windows before. I was about to mention this to Cassie when the officer's window rolled down. I was so focused on the dark glass; I didn't even notice the face behind it. Or at least, I didn't notice it right away. Once I did, however … there was no turning back.

The cop—wearing an old-style police cap—was staring straight ahead. He then turned very slowly to look at me. Or perhaps "look" isn't the best word. He didn't have any eyeballs. He didn't have any skin either. He had a skull. A skull face.

And so he and I sat there, staring at each other for a good, long two to three seconds. Then, as if breaking from a trance, his jaw fell open all the way. What came out was a sort of roar/screech that sounded as far from human as a sound can possibly get.

Cassie suddenly took notice. "Oh, fuck," she sighed and stomped on the gas. A growl erupted from the Mustang's engine as it blasted forward like a rocket. The police cruiser—not to be outdone—screeched its tires as it shot after us. It was like a scene straight out of *The Fast and The Furious*—two cars drag racing off the line in a cloud of burnt rubber smoke.

I looked forward, feeling an eerily placid calm. "That police officer was a skeleton," I said numbly.

Cassie yanked on the wheel and sent us fishtailing through a light. "Someone really wants you dead," she grunted. "Hold on!"

She gunned the accelerator again. The police car caught back up and tried to ram us with its bumper. I whipped around to get a look at the cop again, but all I saw was the ominous tinted glass of the windshield.

Cassie pressed a button on the dash and a touch screen folded out of the stereo. Her fingers danced over the surface as she mumbled, "I got something for ya," and then jabbed her finger on a final button. A series of heavy *thunks* came from the trunk and I spun around in time to see the cop car explode from underneath. The chassis launched twenty feet in the air. When it hit the ground it tumbled into a violent roll like a giant fireball.

"Grenades," Cassie explained. "But he's not dead yet. We have to crush every bone and burn it. Otherwise he'll keep coming."

I looked around again to see the skeleton cop—now completely bare-boned—burst from the wreckage. His jaw still hung open as he sprinted after us. He could *move,* too. We were in a car and he was on foot, and he was gaining on us.

"They're very tenacious," Cassie noted with a hint of annoyance as she glanced in the rearview mirror. I got the distinct impression she'd done this before. "I have an idea," she added. "We have to find a garbage truck."

"To crush it?" I asked.

She slid into an empty lane. "We'll turn onto La Brea. We need a suburban neighborhood."

I looked around for any sign of Skeleton Cop. He was tough to miss. Tourists were screaming and diving to either side as he sprinted up the Hollywood Walk of Fame. It struck me then what an odd sight that was. Here was this animated skeleton in broad daylight booking it up the street in plain view of everyone. Before long, he was dead even with us, pumping his arms like an Olympic sprinter. He kept turning his skull face sideways to make sure he was still with us. Cassie was right. He looked very determined.

We took a sharp left onto La Brea and he followed close behind. A few twists and turns later, Cassie whooped when we saw a garbage truck lumbering ahead of us.

"First things first," she said. "Open the glove box. There should be a bunch of little discs in there. Hand me the one with the sword painted on it."

I popped the glove box and dug through a pile of discs that looked like poker chips. Each one had a different decal on it. Most were the outlines of various guns, while there were a few others showing grenades, flamethrowers, etc … Finally, I found the one that had a samurai sword on it.

"Here." I handed it to her. I didn't bother asking what it was.

"Okay, here we go," she said. "Stay in the car until I get him inside the trash compactor. When I say, 'go,' get out and press that big green button on the side of the truck. See it?"

Before I could respond, she yanked the wheel and stomped on the brakes. The Mustang slid in front of the garbage truck, bringing both to a halt. Cassie jumped out and dove for Skeleton Cop. A full-sized samurai sword had materialized in her hand—don't ask me how—and there was a flurry of slashes and boney limbs. I watched, stunned, as all the severed bones zipped back to Skeleton Cop as if attracted by magnets.

Still, the fight didn't last long. Cassie maneuvered him toward the garbage truck and shoved him inside.

"Now!" she shouted.

I stumbled out and slammed my fist against the button.

Skeleton Cop tried to escape, but Cassie kicked him back in. A couple seconds later, I heard a cascade of loud cracks and snaps.

The truck driver—apparently finding his nerve—exited the cab and started yelling. Cassie told him she was super sorry and to stay back, and then tossed what looked like a grenade inside the compactor. There was a muffled *pop* and a sudden burst of heat.

"The BPI will reimburse you!" she chirped, hopping back toward the Mustang. "Sorry!"

I followed her back into the car and we sped away.

A good minute went by in total silence. Then Cassie said, "So how do you like being a wizard so far?"

"I'm not a wizard," I said.

"Hey, don't worry about that interview thing," she added cheerily. "We'll get there on time."

I looked at her. It was 10:58. Even if the car could fly— and it probably could—we still wouldn't make it.

"I honestly don't care anymore," I stated flatly.

"Don't be silly," she said, and yanked the wheel again. It put us on a collision course with the garage door of a suburban house. I had just enough time to shield my face before we shot straight through it, hitting nothing but air. When I opened my eyes we were exiting a parking garage in the heart of downtown. Goodman, Sachs & Morgenstern was only a block away.

After casually pulling up to the curb, Cassie raised her chin. "See? And with a minute to spare."

I turned to her. "Why was that thing trying to kill us?"

She shrugged. "We'll figure it out. And don't worry. If there's another one, I'll be close by. Now go." She made a little shooing gesture. "I'll be in touch."

So I did.

The interview went worse than I'd feared. It wasn't just Meagan's father in the room; it was a whole panel of his clones. The first thing they asked was: "What the hell happened to you?"

Chapter Three

Dinner and a Carnival

AS IT TURNED OUT, Rosewood's mission of "utmost importance" was actually pretty dull. As far as I could tell it was just a missing persons case. The guy who'd gone missing was an alchemist/scientist who worked for NIMA—otherwise known as the National Institute of Magic and Alchemy. His name was Professor David Steinberg and from his photo, he bore an alarming resemblance to Albert Einstein. His area of non-magical expertise lay in something called "explosive lensing," which is used in making nuclear weapons. As for his alchemist training, he concentrated on something called "arcinology."

He'd gone missing three days ago, yet no one—including his own wife—thought his disappearance was unusual. According to her, he frequently disappeared for days at a time working on various projects. Rosewood, however, thought something was afoot. He didn't want to raise any official alarm bells yet, so he tasked Cassie—and by extension me—to see about locating him. There was no great hurry, he'd explained, but he still wanted Cassie to do whatever she could.

As for me ... it was time to return to normalcy. Following the events of yesterday, I got a nice long sleep and cleansed myself of hangovers, vampire spawn, wizards and skeleton cops. It was now late afternoon and I was getting myself spruced up for François & Meagan's 1.5 Year Anniversary. We were going to dinner and then heading to the Hollywood Bowl for a concert. It was going to be a marvelous evening.

But there were a few problems.

First, Meagan invited her *parents* to come to dinner with us. When I asked her why, she explained that "daddy insisted," and it would give me a second chance to impress him after my epic fail at the interview. She also said that we were changing restaurants to a fancier one and that it would be "daddy's treat."

Second, the performer we were seeing at the Hollywood Bowl sucked. He was a boy band member turned solo artist who Meagan still had a crush on from middle school.

Third, I was running late.

"I got the best bouquet Ralphs had to offer." Buckner appeared in the doorway to the bathroom holding some roses as I made sense of my hair. I gave them a quick glance and breathed a sigh of relief. I'd intended to pick them up earlier but forgot.

"Bro, you just saved my life," I told him and went back to frowning at my reflection,

"You know it's never too late to call this whole thing off," he said. "There's another party in the Hills. Whaddaya say? Meet some more vampire girls?"

"Can't," I said.

He gave a resigned shrug. "Just figured I'd try. So where ya'll headed?"

"That restaurant, Spago."

"The one in Beverley Hills?"

"I guess. I'm gonna Uber it."

"Oh yeah, that's right. Whatever happened to your car? I ain't seen it out front."

I figured someone would ask about that eventually. The best lie I could come up with was: "It's, uh, in the shop. Bad piston rod."

"*A piston rod?*"

"That's what the guy told me." I turned to face him and held out my arms. "How do I look?"

"Like a man before his last supper, I suppose."

"You might be right. Did I tell you Meagan's dad is coming?"

A wide range of emotions suddenly flashed across Buckner's face. Some of them conflicted and were clearly vying for supremacy. First, there was shock. Then there was laughter. Then there was concern. Then there was anger.

"I'm sorry," he said. "Did you say Meagan's dad is coming on your date?"

"Yep. He's paying for it too."

Buckner let out a long, Texas sigh. "I will be damned," he said. He ran a hand through his hair and winced. "Look, you already know my position on this matter ..."

"I do," I said.

"But I'm gonna tell ya again. That girl and her family are no good for you. Why in the name of the Lord God she would invite her daddy to your anniversary is beyond me. But I guess that's because I'm a simple kind of guy. When somethin' smells like bullshit, I don't take no bite of it. Know what I'm saying? So look, I suggest you take these here roses, walk outside, and hand them to the first girl you see. You never know what might happen."

I was about to laugh when my phone vibrated with a text from Meagan. I was supposed to meet her in front of the restaurant in five minutes.

MEAGAN: Hey, I'm here. U on ur way?

I texted her back.

FRANÇOIS: Yep. Be right there. Luv you.

"I'm in deep shit," I told Buckner and pushed past him.
"No argument here," he said.

I ran into my room to grab my shoes. Miraculously, they were nowhere to be found.

That always happens, doesn't it? On any other day, the shoes would be *right there.* Not today. Within a few seconds, I descended into one of those frantic states where I—with a straight face—checked both the microwave and the refrigerator in case somehow they'd gotten in there. I eventually found them buried under some clothes in the corner of my room. I was in the middle of yanking them on when something tapped against my window. I ignored it. No time for curiosity. Then— another tap. And another. They were getting louder, insistent.

Annoyed, I jumped up to open the blinds. I did it just in time to see a small pebble bounce off the glass. I looked down to see Cassie Chu winding up for another throw. I opened the window before she got the chance.

"Hey!" she called up.

Keeping my voice to a low hiss, I demanded to know what she was doing here. I hadn't told anyone about her yet, and for some reason I felt like I needed to keep the whole thing a secret.

"That's not very nice." She frowned, but instantly brightened. "I have an idea. Hold on." She took a few steps back and then with a running start, jumped a good twenty feet up to my window. Her hands found the frame and she did a graceful somersault into the room.

"Hey, you fixed your chair," she observed, pointing.

In a single, panicked motion, I pulled her aside and closed my door.

"Cassie, seriously," I whispered. "What are you doing here? I have to meet Meagan in one minute!"

She winced. "Oh. The anniversary thing? I forgot about that."

I led her back to the window. "Look, she's gonna explode, okay? I have to go right now."

"Wait," she said. "I think I know how to find out who's trying to kill you."

"We can deal with that tomorrow. Meagan's already waiting and she's gonna kill me before anyone else gets a chance. Plus, her parents are going to be there."

"Why are her parents going to be there?"

"All I know is that they both hate me," I said. "If I'm late, they'll hate me even more."

Cassie's nose wrinkled like she'd just smelled something weird. "Aren't anniversaries supposed to be fun?"

"Not for guys," I answered. "Anyway, I gotta go. Seriously."

"I can give you a ride," she offered.

"There's no chance. If I ride with you, a cyclops will come bounding down the street and you'll end up firing a missile at him."

"What?" Cassie looked offended. "First of all, smarty pants, cyclopes live in caves. Second of all, I'd never fire a missile at one! They're so sweet!"

I told her I was still going with Uber. "Is there any chance you can leave through the window?" I asked. "If my roommates see you, they'll start asking questions."

"Of course I can," she said. "But wait, I have to tell you something."

I looked at her, waiting. (Good God, she looked beautiful …)

"So," she said slowly. "I don't want to freak you out or anything, but I kind of have to go with you."

"What?"

"Well, someone's obviously trying to get you," she explained. "And Greta—remember my astrologer?—she told me I have to keep you close. I assume that means to protect you."

"You think someone's going to kill me at Spago?" I asked.

Her eyebrows curved upward. "Maybe?" When she saw my blank stare, she quickly added, "You won't even know I'm there! I'll go sit at another table or something."

"Cassie, you can't just walk into a place like that without a reservation," I told her. "Unless, of course, you're Meagan's father. Apparently."

"Is he rich?"

"Very."

"I can make him write you a check for a million dollars if you want? It's easy. He won't even realize it."

"No."

(I said "no," but the idea *did* sound amazing.)

"Anyway," Cassie said. "I don't need a reservation. I can just enchant the guy at the door."

I took a moment to think. It only lasted for about 0.3 seconds, as I noticed I was already two minutes late and hadn't even left yet.

"I can't talk you out of this, can I?" I said.

"Nope."

I exhaled and ran a sweaty palm down the length of my face. "Alright. I'll meet you outside. But look, no stops along the way. Deal?"

She snapped a quick salute, saying "Deal," and then bounded out the window.

• • •

To the city of Los Angeles, Spago is more than a restaurant; it's a forum for the city's elite to see and be seen. Mostly, that means movie stars and other famous people—but there are also a lot of behind-the-scenes players with fantastically beautiful dates. In fact, that's a good way to tell who's who. If there's an overweight, old guy with a twenty-two-year-old model sitting across from him, odds are he runs a movie studio. Anyway, I was only ten minutes late when I walked in and found Meagan already seated with her parents. Cassie had agreed to wait a few minutes before following me in.

As I approached their table—seeing them all sitting and chatting together as a unit—there was this tiny voice in my head saying, "What in the world are you doing? You don't belong here." It was odd. I'd been with Meagan for a year and a half, and I'd spent plenty of dreadful evenings with her family. And yet, this time was different. This time they looked like strangers. I couldn't quite believe I was about to sit at *their* table, and make small talk. It didn't feel right.

Also, I forgot the roses.

I announced my arrival with a jovial, "Hi everyone!" and Meagan stood up to give me a weak hug. She looked terrific in a red sundress with her blonde hair freshly curled. It fell in soft waves over her shoulders and practically glowed.

"I'm so sorry I'm late." I smiled at her. "Traffic was crazy."

"It's fine." She smiled back and took her seat.

"What route did you take?" Mr. Goodman asked.

"I actually took an Uber, sir. My car's in the shop."

A gasp came from Meagan's mom and she put a hand to her mouth. "Oh no! Did you get hit?"

Mrs. Goodman was basically Meagan fast-forwarded twenty years, minus ten for easy living, so when people mistook them for sisters, it wasn't just a faux compliment. She was tall, blonde, and had very good posture.

"Nothing like that," I said with a light chuckle. "The guy at the shop said the piston was bent."

Mr. Goodman scowled like he knew that that was complete and utter bullshit. He was a smart man—in spite of everything else.

"So François," he said. "Now that we have a moment, what happened yesterday?"

"Sir?" I asked.

"Your interview with my firm," he answered. "You embarrassed me in there, not to mention yourself."

Before I could saying anything, Meagan put a hand on my shoulder and said, "Daddy, let's talk about something else, okay?"

He shook his head. "No. I'm curious. He couldn't even wear a clean suit? He was covered in mud."

Meagan shot me a sideways glance that demanded, "Is that *true?*"

"Again sir, I'm really sorry about that," I said. "This lady's dog got away from her and jumped on me outside the building. There was nothing I could do."

Mr. Goodman gave me a hard look. "A dog? What kind of dog?"

"The big kind, sir. I'm not sure what breed."

"*Anyway,*" Meagan said sharply. "I thought maybe you two could talk *after* dinner? We don't have to be at the concert until nine."

Mr. Goodman shrugged. "Fine with me. Though I'm not sure what there is to talk about. I ... oh! Justin!"

He shot to his feet and shook hands with one of his star clients. He was a pop star turned movie star and I ... I didn't have an opinion. He was alright. I guess.

"You've met my daughter?" Mr. Goodman said.

Meagan blushed and stuck out her hand. "Oh my God, you're so amazing!"

"Ah, thanks!" The pop star smiled back. He looked profoundly uncomfortable, as if he'd been trying to sneak past but got caught.

"Well hey, I gotta go," he said abruptly. "Someone's waiting for me."

"See you in the office next week," Mr. Goodman said. He then added with a mock scolding, "Don't be late."

"Ha! I wouldn't dream of it. It was nice to see you all!"

After he hurried out the door, Meagan's dad retook his seat.

"Hell of a guy," he said with a nod. "A real worker. You know, François, you could learn a thing or two from a man like that."

After ordering we struck up a conversation about future goals. I—like an idiot—mentioned my Film Studies major, which drew a sharp rebuke from Mr. Goodman and a stony glare from Meagan. (I'm not sure why; it's not like this was new information.)

I was just beginning to wonder if Cassie had arrived yet, when I caught her grand entrance. It was one of those cinematic moments where my jaw literally fell open and I dropped my fork with a loud clatter on the hardwood floor.

I'd only seen the succubus three times so far. The first time she was in pajamas and it was dark. The second two times, she was dressed casually in shorts and a tank top. This time, however, she wasn't playing around. She wore a slinky, black cocktail dress with thin straps at the shoulders and a hem that didn't quite make it halfway down her thighs. Her hair was done up, exposing a long neck and broad shoulders. And her smile … *oh man*. It was truly something else. And I won't even try to describe all the other points of interest. I'll end up sounding like a total sleazeball. All I'll say is that I wasn't the only one staring. The entire restaurant took notice. Patrons froze with forks hovering above their plates. Waiters bumped into each other. Busboys tripped and fell.

Plus, she wasn't alone. Some guy was on her arm. I recognized him, too. He was about my age and I'm pretty sure he was an actor on a TV show. Yet it was quite clear that next to Cassie, he was all but invisible. And short. In her heels, she towered over the guy. Somehow this made her even sexier.

"What is wrong with you?" A voice asked to my left.

Meagan.

I spun around, guilty. "What? Oh, nothing. Will you excuse me a second? I'm gonna use the restroom."

I was out of the chair in a flash, and the next thing I knew I was splashing cold water on my face. I took a long, hard look at myself in the mirror. I *wanted* Cassie. Like *a lot*. I couldn't get the image of her out of my head.

I blinked and splashed some more water. After I was done, I grabbed a paper towel. This whole thing was so wrong. I shouldn't be thinking about another girl with my girlfriend right outside. Heck, I shouldn't be thinking about Cassie at all. She was half succubus, which meant she was only half human.

The Wikipedia article on succubi wasn't pretty. They were *demons* that quite literally screwed men to death and dispatched their souls to Hell. Sure, they were beautiful and charming on the outside, but that was just part of their craft. Suckers like me didn't stand a chance. And yet … *did you see her in that dress?!*

I couldn't go back out there yet. I stepped over to one of the urinals to buy myself some time. No sooner had I unzipped, than a man's voice echoed through the empty room. "You're a piece of work, Lemieux."

A second later, Mr. Goodman appeared beside me, shaking his head.

"How's it going, sir?" I asked.

I knew from his tone he was about to be an even bigger jerk than usual. He always was when no one else was around. He stood there for a second, staring down until he got a stream going.

"The thought of you with my daughter sickens me," he said. "I want you to know that if you're after my money, you won't get a dime."

I frowned. "You know Meagan introduced herself to me, right? She asked *me* out, not the other way around."

"She's trying to piss me off," he said bitterly. "'Daddy issues.' Ha. What a bunch of crap." His eyes suddenly narrowed. "You know why a star like Justin trusts me with his fortune,

Lemieux? Because I'm a man. I make lots of money and I buy lots of shit. Good shit. Big house. Nice car. A fifty-foot yacht. You, on the other hand, are a pussy. When I see you talk, all I see is a big pussy flapping around. *Film Studies?* Go fuck yourself. What do you have to say about that, Lemieux?"

"I'm also majoring in Finance," I said.

"Another pussy move," he answered. "Hedging your bets like a frightened turtle. You think I got to where I am by playing it safe? Do you?"

I finished and gave myself a little shake. "So you want me to drop the Finance major?"

"I don't want you to do a damn thing," he said. "I want my daughter to come to her senses. You could fall off a cliff for all I care. In fact, I'd like to help you with that."

I zipped. "Well, Mr. Goodman, it's always a pleasure."

"I bet it is," he said, and followed me to the sinks.

Now, I know what you're thinking. You're thinking I should take a swing at the guy, right? But that's only because you don't know Robert Goodman III like I do. He's exactly the type of guy who would provoke somebody just so he could sic his pack of lawyers on them. I wasn't about to do him the favor. Plus, it would probably destroy my relationship with Meagan.

When we got back to the table Mr. Goodman was all smiles. He kissed his wife on the cheek and gave a little wink to his daughter. The food came shortly thereafter, and I did my best to seem pleasant. What struck me as particularly crappy was that I hardly said anything to my girlfriend. This was supposed to be our anniversary. But instead of talking to her, I spent the whole time auditioning in front of her parents.

Meanwhile, at Cassie's table, the world was a much brighter place. She was holding court, telling a funny story to a *group* of guys—all completely held in thrall. It made me miserable. And jealous. She was there, and I was stuck here. I felt like someone studying for a midterm while a party raged next door. She looked so light and genuine, wildly gesturing with her hands and smiling as new bouts of laughter burst from her companions.

It was then that I realized Cassie Chu wasn't just pretty. She was—for lack of a better word—*cool.* I know that sounds really "high school," but it's true. She was charismatic. She was fun. And *that* was what made her so beautiful. High cheekbones and a terrific figure only go so far. You have to have something behind all that to truly make it special. Cassie had that—whatever it was. Confidence? *Joie de vivre?* Who knows.

"François? *Hello?*"

Shoot. It was Meagan again.

"You have the tickets, right?" she asked.

The whole table was staring at me and I gulped. This is a nightmare that sits near the top of the list for every guy. It's your anniversary. You're going to a concert. You're supposed to have tickets. You don't have the tickets.

It's made even worse when it's not just your girlfriend staring expectantly, but her disapproving parents as well. Now, in my defense, I'd had an extraordinary thirty-six hours. You can't blame me for letting a few things slip. My problem was that I couldn't explain anything about vampettes or wizards to my present company, so all I had was the ability to sit there like a total schmuck and say, "Uh, the tickets?"

"Oh my God. You don't have them, do you?"

I noticed a gleeful glint in Mr. Goodman's eye.

"I can get them," I said quickly. "They'll be at Will Call. No problem."

"Are you kidding? The lines will be huge! You were supposed to get them yesterday!"

Mr. Goodman's look of delight hardened to one of pure hatred. "You better make this right, François. It's my little girl's anniversary for God's sake!"

"This is very disappointing," Mrs. Goodman added.

My shoulders slumped as Meagan fumed. "What did you even do yesterday?" she asked.

I searched for an answer. The truth was that I went to sleep. But that wouldn't do.

On a side note, I'd like to point out how incredibly deflating it is to fight with your girlfriend when her parents are sitting across from you. It's the ultimate no win situation because even if you're right, you're still wrong. And in my case, I wasn't even right. I'd screwed up and everyone knew it. Absently, I glanced over at Cassie's table, but was startled to see no one there. Did she leave? With that *guy?*

And that's when I felt a light scratch on my shoulder. I turned and looked up to see Cassie smiling excitedly. "I knew that was you!" she said. "Oh my God, this is so crazy!"

She had changed her tone slightly, sounding more like a teenager.

My heart skipped a beat. I had no idea what she was up to, and quite honestly, I wasn't sure I wanted to find out. Still, I didn't have much choice but to play along. "Ha, yeah," I said. "How are you?"

"François Lemieux!" She clapped her hands excitedly. "I can't believe it's really you! Give me a hug!"

I stood and nearly got a face full of boobs as I awkwardly put my arms around her. In those heels of hers, she must have been like 6'4". My heart was pounding in my ears and my face was probably red as a turnip. When I sat back down, Cassie noted the questioning looks around the table.

"François and I went to high school together," she explained. "We haven't seen each other in like,"—she looked at me—"what? Two years?"

"Yep. Almost," I said, then gulped and added, "Cassie, this is my girlfriend, Meagan."

Cassie leaned forward to shake her hand and one of her breasts—spilling from her dress—lightly pressed against my forehead. It produced an effect that made it difficult to keep my voice level.

"And these are Meagan's parents," I said/squeaked. "Robert and Amanda Goodman."

Cassie gave them both a radiant smile. "Nice to meet you," she said, and then focused on Mr. Goodman. "You, sir, look like a big shot movie person. I can tell. That's a really nice suit, by the way."

I never thought I'd see the day, but Robert Goodman III blushed. "Oh no," he chuckled. "Not me. I just handle all their money!"

"Even better!"

"François's never mentioned you," Meagan suddenly said. Her tone was noticeably icy.

"Oh really?" Cassie raised an eyebrow. "We sort of used to have a thing together, but that's all. Anyway, how did you two meet? Er, wait. You guys are eating, huh? I don't want to intrude."

"Nonsense!" Mr. Goodman said. "Cassie, was it? Why don't you pull up another seat? I'm sure the restaurant won't mind."

"Really?" she asked. "I don't want to be a bother ..."

"Impossible."

Mr. Goodman had switched into friendly mode, which could only mean one thing—he thought he had a shot at getting Cassie out of that dress. If I didn't think he was a scumbag before, now I *really* did. What was he, like fifty?

"So, Cassie, do you live in LA?" Mr. Goodman asked once she'd pulled over an extra chair.

"Nope," she said. "I go to NYU."

"That's a great school. What are you studying?"

She giggled. "Acting."

"Well, you certainly have a star quality. Whenever you're ready to get started, give me a call. I know people."

"Can we get back to the tickets please?" Meagan said.

"Tickets?" Cassie asked.

"For a concert tonight," I explained. "I forgot to pick them up yesterday."

"François dropped the ball," Mr. Goodman added. "It's very disappointing."

Cassie looked at him and frowned. "I don't think so," she said. "And neither do you."

Her voice had quickly switched from playful and girly to flat and even. I recognized the tone and looked at her eyes. Sure enough, they were glowing purple.

"It is not disappointing at all," Mr. Goodman said with a shrug.

"And you're gross," Cassie added.

"I am gross," he repeated.

Meagan suddenly leaned forward, her mouth agape. "What did you just say to my father?"

Cassie turned her eyes on her.

"You don't feel well and you need to go home early," she said.

I put up my hands. "Whoa," I cautioned. "Don't—"

Cassie shushed me with a sideways look. "There is no concert tonight," she continued. "And François is a great boyfriend."

"He really is," Meagan agreed.

I glanced at Mrs. Goodman and she seemed to be in a trance as well. "Cassie, are you crazy?" I whispered. "You can't just hypnotize them."

"Of course I can, it's easy," she said. "Besides, why are you even hanging out with these people? The dad's a total perv!"

I glanced at Mr. Goodman who silently mouthed the words "total perv," while staring blankly.

"I'm not 'hanging out' with them," I said. "These are Meagan's parents."

Cassie looked at the pair of them and scrunched her face. "I don't think Meagan likes you very much."

"Right now, I'm sure she doesn't. Anyway, stop hypnotizing her. It's not cool."

"Oh, come on!" she pleaded. "I need you to come with me to the Ghost Carnival. I promise it will be so much more fun than this." She made a gesture toward the restaurant in general.

"A what carnival?"

"Ghost," she said. "And it's only open a couple more hours. We have to go soon."

I thought a moment. It was *so* wrong that Cassie had just entranced my girlfriend. I mean, where's the line on something like that? If you can truly do the Jedi Mind Trick on anyone, isn't that a little too much power?

"We can't just get up and leave," I said.

Cassie smiled and turned back to Meagan and her parents. She made them repeat a few more things—including something about Mr. Goodman toilet papering his own house before going to bed.

"TPing?" I said. "Really?"

Cassie shrugged. "I never got to have much of a childhood. You ready to go?"

I took a final look at Meagan and her parents. "So, to them it will look like we disappeared and they won't even care?" I asked.

"Yep."

"Cassie, we can't do that. It's wrong. I'm not sure why, but it is."

She frowned a moment in thought. "I guess it might be a little messed up," she admitted. "But think about it like this: First of all, I was raised by a full succubus, so the fact that I'm not completely evil is a miracle. Secondly, everything we do is to protect people like them. Do you know how many dark sorcerers or death priests have tried to wipe out the whole planet in the past few years? It's wizards like you, and friendly succubi like me, who stop them. And right now we have important stuff to do. In the grand scheme, a little enchantment isn't so bad, right?"

"I don't know," I said, still waffling.

But the truth was I didn't really have much of an argument. Besides, the prospect of getting the hell away from Meagan's parents and this catastrophe of an anniversary held a certain appeal. I took a final look at my girlfriend. She was still hypnotized, but other than that, she looked fine. She probably wouldn't even miss me. In fact, at this point, I *knew* she wouldn't.

Thus, a few minutes later, Cassie and I were going a hundred and twenty down the 10 toward Santa Monica—straight into an LA sunset.

• • •

By the time we reached the Santa Monica Pier—which is where the Ghost Carnival was apparently—it was mostly dark. After we parked, Cassie put on the parking break and told me to look away.

"What do you mean?" I asked.

"I mean look away," she said. "I have to change."

She was still wearing the cocktail dress.

"Oh," I said. "Yeah. Sure."

I shifted in my seat and looked out the window.

"It'll just take a second," she said, and I heard the distinct sound of a long zipper coming undone. Her seat reclined flat and there was a low rustle of fabric slowly slipping down her thighs.

I thought about baseball.

I'd heard that line used once before when I was a kid. It was in *The Naked Gun,* with Leslie Nielsen. Ever since—even though I'm not a baseball fan—I think of fly balls, line drives and home runs every time I'm in serious danger of embarrassing myself. I also leaned forward in my seat a little. Just in case.

"You okay?" she asked.

"Yep."

She giggled and I shut my eyes tight at the rustle of more fabric. From the way she was shifting around, I figured she was shimmying into a new pair of shorts. Or panties.

Ball three, bottom of the 8th ...

Eventually, Cassie gave me the all clear. When I turned around, she was just pulling her top on. It was a cruel thing to do. I caught the briefest glimpse of side-boob before it was gone.

"Sorry 'bout that," she said. "You ready?"

"I was born ready."

It was another warm, spring night as we made our way up the pier. And just in case you don't know, Santa Monica Pier is a small theme park catering to tweens and tourists. It's one of those LA landmarks, like the Walk of Fame or Madame Tussaud's, that locals seldom visit. It has brightly lit carnival rides, a roller coaster, and the world's only solar-powered Ferris wheel. (I guess it had batteries, though, since it was nighttime now.)

We were readily approaching said Ferris wheel when I asked Cassie where the Ghost Carnival was.

"Up there," she said, pointing.

I stopped. "You mean the Ferris wheel?"

"The entrance is kind of tricky," she explained, "but once it goes around a few times, we'll be in the carnival. It's magic stuff."

I took a heavy breath. Now was probably a bad time to explain I was afraid of heights.

And don't laugh at that either. We've all got certain things that freak us out. Some people are afraid of snakes. Some people are afraid of tall buildings.

Anyway, I decided to pretend I was fine with it. My heart was beating up in my nose and I was breaking into a flop sweat, but I was fine with it. After all, the voice of Meagan's dad still echoed in my ears. What did he call me again? A pussy? Screw that. I was going on that Ferris wheel if it killed me.

We waited in a short line, my nerves growing increasingly rattled, before getting into a tiny, rickety, squeaking gondola. It could fit about five or six people in a circle, but Cassie and I had it to ourselves. Her hip pressed into mine as she scooted next to me. I forced an image of Babe Ruth into my head. It worked like a charm.

Then we were off, climbing higher and higher and higher—and what kind of a sick jerk thinks that this is fun? The gondola was probably hanging by a little rusty screw that no one's bothered to check in like six years. Any second now we could drop off like an overripe piece of fruit.

Then, as if the gods were mocking me, the wheel stopped abruptly when we reached the top. An ominous squeak came from the tiny screw above.

Now, I thought I was doing a good job of keeping all these concerns from my face, yet Cassie still leaned forward and asked, "You're not scared of heights, are you?"

I told her no, but she wasn't convinced.

"So you won't mind if I …" her voice trailed off as she started rocking back and forth, swinging the gondola.

"Please stop," I said. Unconsciously, my eyes had glued themselves shut. I also realized I hadn't taken a breath for quite some time.

"You really are afraid of heights, aren't you?"

"There's no shame in it," I said tersely. "Napoleon Bonaparte was terrified of cats. He conquered half the world."

Cassie's arm suddenly looped under mine and she pressed closer. "You know what scares me?" she said. "Pancakes."

I peeked an eye open. "Like with syrup?"

"Oh my God. If you took me to an IHOP, I would go completely ballistic."

I wasn't quite sure if she was messing with me or not but I chuckled anyway. "I used to get weirded out by unicycles," I said. "Still do."

I then went on to explain my reasons why—which was mostly a long string of incoherent babble regarding a birthday clown when I was six—and as I did so, I felt the gondola swing slightly as Cassie leaned over the edge to look below. She let me keep talking until I heard her make a light gasp.

"What?" I said.

"Hm? Oh, nothing. Keep telling me about the unicycle thing. That's really random."

"It's broken, isn't it?" I said, panicking. "The wheel's coming apart at the screws. Tell me the truth, is the Fire Department here? Jesus Christ, I should've stayed at the restaurant. How did you talk me into this, anyway?"

I felt her shoulder shrug against mine. "I don't know," she said. "I told you it'd be fun?"

"I shouldn't be here," I said. "I should be with Meagan. She's my girlfriend. It's our anniversary. And you shouldn't have enchanted her like that! That was messed up!"

"Why?"

"Because it is. You can't turn people into puppets whenever you want. And she's my girlfriend!"

"Well jeez, sorry for trying to help. You were getting your ass kicked."

"I wasn't getting my ass kicked," I said.

"You were totally getting your ass kicked. Which I don't even get, by the way. Why are you going out with her?"

"What do you mean 'why am I going out with her?'" I said. "She's my girlfriend, that's why."

"François, seriously, you don't even like her!"

The wheel suddenly jerked and started moving again. A little cheer erupted from the other riders.

After a few seconds, Cassie said, "See? All part of my plan."

I opened both eyes and looked at her. She was grinning sheepishly and I smirked. "Bullshit."

"It's true! I'm not afraid of pancakes. Who's afraid of pancakes?"

"I still shouldn't be here," I said.

"Yes, you should!" she insisted. "Besides, it's about time I had a plucky sidekick. I've been doing this gig solo for way too long."

"I'm not a plucky sidekick," I said. "And why do you care so much about me going out with Meagan, anyway?"

She cocked her head, confused. "I told you already. I like you."

The wheel jerked to a halt again and there were a handful of screams. My best guess was that emergency crews were scrambling to evacuate the passengers below because the whole thing was about to explode at any moment. My eyes clamped shut again.

"By 'like,' you mean like in a friendly way, right?" I asked.

"Nope."

A long pause.

"Oh."

"Yep."

Then there was a *really* long pause. My eyes were still closed, of course, but I got the distinct feeling that Cassie was staring at me.

"You don't have to be so nervous," she finally said.

"I'm not nervous."

As soon as I said that, I realized how stupid it sounded. I was stiff as a board with my knuckles white on the edge of my seat.

Cassie laughed. "Yeah, you look pretty relaxed."

"Shut up," I said.

She then shifted around, trying to get a view of whatever was happening below. I wanted to ask her about it, but I didn't. I just did the old "Count to a Hundred" trick in my head. It was the only thing I could think of to distract myself. Baseball wasn't working anymore. Every time I tried, I got an image of Cassie instead.

"I think it's going to be a while," she eventually said.

"This better be worth it," I muttered, and Cassie scooted closer.

"You just need a distraction," she said softly.

I frowned and drew in a deep breath. "Unless an alien starship suddenly appears overhead and starts firing at us, I don't think anything is going to distract me right now."

I then felt a single fingertip start to slowly trace its way up my thigh. Cassie shifted and pressed closer. "We could make out?" she suggested.

That got my eyes open.

"The thing is," she went on, "I can't kiss you until you ask me to. It's a succubus thing. Kind of like inviting a vampire into your home."

"Cool," I said.

And yet it wasn't "cool." The truth was I was still pretty nervous about the whole succubus thing. I mean, if I kissed her, what would happen? Would it hurt? Would I die? I didn't know.

"Or you could kiss me," she said quietly. "That'd work too."

"Cassie, is there any way we could talk about this when we're not fifty feet in the air and about to die?"

"Are you really that scared?" she asked.

"The wheel's going to explode any second," I said firmly. "You may not know it, but I do. I can feel it."

Yet right at that precise moment, the ride started moving again and a loud cheer erupted from the other gondolas.

"You were saying?" Cassie asked.

"Shut up."

And so the Ferris wheel continued to go around as we sat there in silence. It seemed to last forever. Finally, though, we came to a stop and Cassie told me to open my eyes.

I half expected we'd be staring out over the ocean again, but no. We were on the ground. And Santa Monica Pier was nowhere to be found.

• • •

When Cassie pitched the idea of a "Ghost Carnival" earlier, I believe her exact word to describe it was "fun."

This place wasn't fun. It gave me the creeps. It was like the Tim Burton's nightmare version of a carnival. It was full of empty, decrepit kids rides that were falling apart and covered in slime. Or blood. It was hard to tell in the dark. The only light came from a few sickly bulbs tinted in a shade of puke-like green. The ocean was gone too. It was as if this place was in a little bubble all on its own. (I learned later that this wasn't far from the truth. The Ghost Carnival was what magic people called a "Transient Plane," and could only fit a small amount of space within it. It hopped around from place to place, and only people in the know knew where it would pop up next.)

"So why are we here again?" I asked as we made our way up a deserted walkway. I was finally beginning to calm down despite the ridiculously unnerving surroundings.

"Information," Cassie said. "Ghost Carnival is where shady people come to do shady business. It's weird, right? It's always the shady characters who seem to know all the important stuff."

"Not true," I said. "I'm a shady character and I don't know anything."

She laughed and poked me with her elbow. "You're the least shady character I've ever met," she chided. "It's one of the reasons I like you so much."

"So who are we looking for?" I asked.

"His name's Tom. He's a werewolf."

I stopped. "Do you mean that literally, or …?"

"What do you mean?"

We were really hitting every item on the "Things François Is Afraid Of" list today. Of all the monsters out there in the movies, something about werewolves has always scared the living crap out of me. I couldn't even watch *Underworld* with Kate Beckinsale without closing my eyes at strategic moments.

"Is he,"—I wasn't sure how to put this—"*angry?*" I asked.

Cassie frowned. "Well, he's not very nice."

"Yeah but is he a … wolf thing? Or a guy who can turn into a wolf thing?"

"He's a wolf thing."

"I see," I said. "Well, listen. I don't *technically* need to be here for this, do I? I can just go hang out by that,"—I looked around—"that incredibly creepy cotton candy machine with a blood stain on it over there. Or you know what? I'll just go back to Santa Monica. It's no problem."

"You don't want to talk to Tom?" she said.

"No it's not that, I just, um—"

"He's not an animal, you know," she said defensively. "Werewolves come from the same plane that succubi do."

"Oh."

"Besides," she said with a grin. "I thought you were tough. You're not scared, are you?"

"Here?" I asked, gesturing around. "Not at all."

"Good. Let's go then."

And so we went looking for Tom. We found him outside the world's most disturbing Fun House. All I'll say is that it had a giant, angry baby face with a yawning maw that served as its entrance. There were other points of interest too—including singed doll heads dangling from one of the rope bridges—but I'll spare you the details. As for Tom—he was a werewolf alright. The best way I can describe him is this: Whoever designed the Chewbacca costume for *Star Wars* started with a basic werewolf template, and then made it less scary. Tom looked like he'd been caught somewhere in the middle of that process. He wasn't terrifying—but he wasn't cuddly either. When he saw Cassie, I noticed a flash of recognition in his bright yellow eyes.

"You're not welcome here," he said in a gravelly voice. It took me a second to realize it sounded "gravelly" because there was a low growl behind every word.

"Yeah, but I'm here," Cassie said. Her tone was harder now. I figured she was in battle mode.

"I won't say a word if the human remains," Tom said.

Cassie kept her eyes locked on him. "He's with me. And unless you want me to kick your ass again, Tom, you're going to tell me everything you know about that skeleton attack yesterday."

Tom remained silent. He swayed slightly, eyeing us both like he was considering an attack. His hands were tensed, and I noticed long, curved fingernails sharpened into points.

After a moment, Cassie shrugged. "Have it your way," she said, and took a step forward.

"He stays outside!" Tom growled.

Cassie paused and looked at me. Her eyes formed a question. "He doesn't like humans," she explained. "Just stay out here a minute while I talk to him? If anything happens, give me a shout."

Obviously, I had no desire to kick it by myself in this place, but for some reason I didn't want to embarrass myself in front of the werewolf. (It's strange the things people get self-conscious about.)

I said, "cool," and watched Cassie disappear behind him inside the baby face.

Now it was just me and …

"Hey! Psst! You!"

I whipped around to see who was talking but no one was there.

"You dumb shit. I'm right here!"

I followed the voice and looked down.

Standing at my feet was a … *dwarf?* Or you know what? Not a dwarf. He was a gnome—less than two feet tall, bearded and red-faced. He wore a pointy red hat that gave him some extra height, but still a little fella.

"How's it going?" I said, not knowing what else to say.

"What are you doing with my girl?" he asked.

"Who?"

"What do you mean 'who?'" he barked. "The girl with the tits! What are you doing with her?"

By now he'd raised his fists and was glaring. Part of me wanted to stifle a laugh, but another part of me got that skittish sensation you get when a Chihuahua comes after you with everything its got.

"She wanted to talk to Tom," I said.

"Well, she's mine!" the gnome said. "If you touch her, you're a dead man."

I raised an eyebrow. "Oh yeah? Who's gonna stop me? You?"

I'll admit, I was surprised I said that. I'm not usually a confrontational guy, but something about the gnome irritated me. His voice was like the verbal equivalent of someone repeatedly poking you in the forehead. His reaction to my taunt, however, I didn't see coming …

"Oh, yes!" he cried, and a swift uppercut from his tiny fist caught me right in the wrong place. The little bastard was strong, too. I keeled over like a fallen tree and landed hard.

He immediately pressed his advantage. He moved to my face and started kicking savagely. He got in a good three shots before my survival instincts started to cut in. I took a hand from my groin and caught his leg. He almost wrenched it free, but I pulled, knocking him over.

"Bastard!" he shouted, scrambling to his feet. I tried to do the same, but he got me with a solid jab in the nose. I toppled over. More kicks and punches followed. It suddenly dawned on me that I was thoroughly getting my ass kicked. I attempted a wild punch to turn things around and got lucky. It got him in the chest. I jumped forward to put my weight on him. We tumbled a couple times until he landed on top, alternating one fist for the other as he went to work on my face.

So when I was fourteen, I joined the wrestling team in high school. I'm not sure why, but I did. The coach was this ex-NFL player, named Coach Lloyd. He was a giant of a man whose career had taken a serious dive. Anyway, there weren't enough students on the team to fill out a full roster. That was how I—a late bloomer weighing in at a mere ninety pounds—found myself wrestling on the varsity team's 132-weight class. Needless to say, I didn't fare too well. In fact, I lost every single match—except *one*.

It was against a girl.

Now I'm not saying that I won because she was a girl. I'm positive there are a lot of girls out there who could beat me up. What I am saying, though, is that I won because I fought *so much harder* to win. I gave it everything I had. And it was a battle, believe me. She and I went the full three rounds, and I only won by a single point. It was the proudest moment of my life. Because I'll just say this: I know in the movies it's a common sight to see Scarlett Johansson beating the daylights out of men five times her size. But in real life—if you're a guy—it still sucks to get your ass handed to you by a girl. It just does.

And right now, something similar was happening with Me vs. The Gnome. I mean, he was only two feet tall for God's sake. I *had* to win this. I got hold of his arm and remembered some of my old wrestling tricks. I needed to pin him down, isolate his arms or legs—keep him still. I managed to get him in an awkward half-nelson and push his face into the pavement.

"You give up?" I shouted.

He grunted. "You think this is over? I'm just getting started!"

Then, like a magic trick, he *cloned* himself. I was still pinning the original, but the new guy was fully free to attack. I threw an elbow at him. He dodged, and copied himself. Now there were three. Then there were five. Then ten.

A good man knows when he's beaten. He also knows when to run for his life.

I scrambled to my feet and sprinted up the dark pathway past crumbling Tilt-a-Whirls and Magic Tea Cup rides. A small army of gnomes followed. A few of them dove for me, but I shook them off. I kept running. It was only a matter of time till I got caught. The situation had just gone from mildly comical to completely terrifying.

Then a loud gunshot brought us all to a halt. I looked over and saw Cassie holding a heavy revolver. She was pointing it at one of the gnomes.

"Don't make me do it, Howard," she said.

The gnome—I'm pretty sure he was the original from the scuff marks on his face—dipped his head and shuffled his feet.

"Sorry," he mumbled.

Cassie looked up at me. "You okay?"

No. No, I wasn't okay. I just got the shit kicked out of me by a garden gnome. I thought I was going to die.

I told her I was fine.

Cassie kept the gun pointed meaningfully. "Come on," she said. "Let's get out of here. Tom was a bust. He didn't know anything."

And it was all for nothing.

Back in Cassie's car driving up Santa Monica, I became a man of few words. I didn't know what to say. Meanwhile, she winced yet again as she checked my face for the hundredth time.

"I'm really sorry," she said. "I can get something that will fix the swelling."

"Is it that bad?" I asked, gingerly touching a swollen cheek.

Another wince. "Kinda."

I let out a long breath. Truth be told, my pride hurt a lot worse than my face. This was something that couldn't happen twice. I wasn't going to let another garden gnome get the drop on me. I knew what I had to do. It was time to crack open that spellcasting book from Rosewood. It was time to learn magic.

Chapter Four

Everyday Objects

AFTER POURING A BOWL OF CORNFLAKES the next morning, I got out *Intro to Magic: A Beginner's Guide to Spellcasting.* The first twenty pages were written in a strange script that didn't look entirely human. (Think: "Elvish" from *Lord of the Rings.*) I studied each page, trying to make sense of it, but nothing looked familiar. Starting on page twenty-one, though, the book became shockingly normal. The writing was flat and utilitarian, while the print itself looked old, like something you'd see in a historic newspaper.

The introduction was only a couple pages. It explained that learning magic is like learning a musical instrument—it's tedious and frustrating in the beginning, but gets easier as time goes on. It also explained that there are nine Disciplines of Magic. They are, in no certain order: Abjuration, Conjuration, Divination, Enchantment, Evocation, Illusion, Necromancy, Transmutation, and Alchemy. For each discipline, there are twelve levels of mastery. A full wizard is expected to achieve a minimum of Level Eight for each.

Once I was finished with the intro—and my cornflakes—I flipped to the first chapter. It was titled, *Forming a Spell: The Basics.*

As I started reading, I remembered Rosewood telling me to do all my practicing inside the Solitar—that little magical

Zippo he gave me. I retrieved it from my room and turned it over in my hands. It was real *gold.* Not brass. I'm not sure how I knew, but somehow the human brain just knows real gold when it sees it. There's a reassuring heft that's unmistakable.

Anyway, I figured this was something I needed to do with my door securely locked. I laid out all the necessary materials on my desk. I had the spellcasting book, the Solitar, and a small fire extinguisher from the kitchen.

Then I sat there for ten minutes procrastinating. The memory of Rosewood getting sucked into the Zippo like a bed sheet kept flitting through my head. He hadn't looked like he was in any pain, but wouldn't the laws of physics/biology insist that he was?

I picked up the book as well as the Solitar and gingerly opened the cap. Nothing happened. I needed to spark the wick first. I put my thumb on the little wheel, took a deep breath, and flicked.

It's hard to describe what happened next, but I'll give it my best shot. I flicked the lighter, my room turned into liquid, and then all of it—including me—swirled into the Zippo like water down a drain. The next thing I knew I was standing on the fifty-yard line of a football field. I recognized it, too. It was the field at my old high school, complete with modest bleachers along the sidelines and bright yellow goalposts at both ends. The sight of it triggered some distant memory of Becky Altman and the way she looked when I caught her eye that one time during the homecoming game. And then, there she was—standing in front of me in her cheerleading uniform. She smiled brightly and said, "Hi!"

"Becky?" I asked.

"That's me."

"What are you doing here?"

She shrugged. "I guess you want me to be."

I stared at her a moment and slowly turned, doing a full three-sixty. By the time I returned to Becky, she was gone. Now there was a fire hydrant. I recognized it as the exact same one that was near the house where I grew up. It had a faint, ethereal glow to it, which I noticed was on everything inside the Solitar. It wasn't much, but enough to tell the difference between here and the real world. I blinked in surprise until eventually I figured out what was happening. If I thought about something, even for an instant, it appeared. It was like being *inside* my imagination. Every thought became a reality, and every reality could change at any moment. There was a strange, slippery sensation to it all. Being inside the Solitar was like ice-skating. If I couldn't control my thoughts, then the world would keep shifting until nothing made sense at all. And then the tank from *Indiana Jones and the Last Crusade* appeared and a German soldier popped the hatch and shouted, "*Er kommt weg! Lass uns gehen!*"

I wasn't sure which was weirder—the tank or the fact that I understood the German guy perfectly. He said, "He's getting away! Let's go!"

I almost took him up on his offer, but I shook my head and he was gone. I had to stay focused. I brought up the spellcasting book, and a big, lavish desk—like an Oval Office desk—appeared in front of me. I took a seat and opened to Chapter One.

As soon as I started reading, I noticed an abundance of Latin words like *Formatio, Cantus* and *Imago*. The writing was even more formal than the introduction. Plus, there were precious few explanations on how to do anything. It seemed like the book was meant to accompany a class—not be used on its own.

Either way, I read through the Latin terminology until I got to the first, introductory spell. It was called, "Firelight."

The first order of business was to bring my hands into *Formatio.* (Fortunately, there was a little picture that demonstrated this.) It simply meant to bring my hands even with my chest, keep them a foot apart, and have my palms face each other. I remembered that Rosewood had made the same gesture back in his office. The next thing to do—and this was the magic part—was to form the *Imago.* The *Imago* was that soccer ball-sized sphere of light that reminded me of a plasma globe. The problem, though, was that the book didn't tell me how to do it. It just said to "make it." Nothing more. So—taking my best guess—I tried to picture the ball in my mind.

Nothing happened.

I flexed and squinted and did everything I could think of, but there was nothing.

I tried for a good ten minutes, and had a quick flashback to when I was a kid trying to move the TV remote with my mind. I had the same realization back then that I was having right now: *Damn. Perhaps I'm not a Jedi ...*

I was about to give up, when a wooden cane smacked the desk in front of me. I looked up to see a tall, bespectacled man with a long, severe face and thinning red hair. He wore a coal-grey, Victorian suit, complete with coat tails and a checkered waistcoat.

"You are doing it wrong," he said, giving me a stare. His accent was a strange brand of New England American—yet very old-fashioned with a snooty, academic air to it.

"Who are you?" I said.

"Alroy McFadden," he announced proudly. "I wrote the book that you are presently mangling. You do not 'imagine' the *Imago.* Although, I suppose you could make that leap of course if you were never schooled in Latin, which I see that you were not. You form the *Imago* by doing precisely the opposite of what you were doing. You think of *nothing.* You clear your mind, which in your case will be easily accomplished, and what remains is magic. Do you understand?"

"Nothing. Clear mind. Magic," I repeated.

"Very good." He nodded crisply. "I see that you have reverted to your natural state of ape-like communication, and I recommend you continue to do so until you learn to speak properly. Now,"—he smacked the desk again—"clear your mind and form the *Imago*."

I nodded and raised my hands back into *Formatio*—a.k.a. Evil-Wizard-Lurking-Above-A-Crystal-Ball Pose. I had plenty of questions for McFadden—like how he was suddenly inside my head—but I figured that could wait. He was exactly what I needed right now—a tutor.

So, without further ado, I closed my eyes and tried to think of nothing. At first, I thought of a large, empty white space and me hovering inside it. (I was slightly influenced by *The Matrix.*) I thought it might be working until I opened my eyes and saw that I was hovering inside of a blank white space with McFadden floating in front of me. He didn't look pleased.

"Ah. This is your conception of nothing, I take it?"

I looked around. Endless white in all directions. I shrugged and gave him a weak smile. "Sort of?"

With the speed of a viper, his cane smacked me on the shoulder.

"I suggest you try harder," he said. "Nothing means *nothing,* do you understand? Not 'large empty white space.' Now try again."

I thought of the football field first, bringing us back to the fifty-yard line. This time, however, it was night with the game lights on. My brain apparently thought it looked cooler that way. I went back to concentrating on nothing. It was hard to do with my shoulder smarting from the blow. Or at least, so I thought. It took several seconds, but I came to understand why McFadden hit me with the cane. By focusing on the pain, I stopped thinking about anything else. So when I opened my eyes …

Bingo.

Hovering between my hands was a brilliant *Imago*—a blue-tinted ball of light with wispy lightning bolts twisting inside. My jaw dropped as I stared at it like I'd just discovered fire. In fact, I felt a unique kinship with whoever the guy was who discovered fire. He and I were equals now. You see, even after all I'd witnessed—after Vampettes, Rosewood, Cassie and slipping inside the Solitar—I still had my doubts. I mean, *me,* François, a wizard? There was no way. Yet nothing erases doubt like a glowing ball of electricity between you hands. It was the coolest thing I'd ever seen. It also meant that yes, yes I was. I was a freaking wizard.

"Hardly," a voice said sharply. It was McFadden.

I looked at him blankly and he gave an exasperated sigh. "I'm in your *mind,*" he explained. "I can hear your ridiculous thoughts. The 'guy'—as you say—who discovered fire no doubt appeared infinitely more intelligent than you do. Would you care to see your face?" His cane morphed into a large mirror and he showed it to me. "Look at that," he said. "That is the face of a baboon doing a crossword puzzle."

"Hey man," I said. "I've got a glowing ball of light between my hands. I'm good."

"Clearly," McFadden snorted. "But if you are quite done congratulating yourself on a feat fit for a two-year-old, I suggest we get on with forming the spell."

I'd already read the basic concept of spell formation at the beginning of Chapter One. Basically, it was just like playing a musical instrument. I pressed my fingers—like pressing piano keys—to manipulate the patterns of lightning bolts inside the ball. Each finger movement was called a *Cantus* (the plural was *Canti*), and the lightning bolt thingies were called *Fulmen*. So, to use the proper spellcasting Latin, I performed a series of

Canti to manipulate the *Fulmen* to produce a specific spell. The easy spells were like remedial piano songs with only a few simple notes. Firelight was, apparently, the easiest of all spells— like the magic equivalent of Chopsticks.

The book assigned a roman numeral to each of my fingers and then provided a letter from the Greek alphabet to each number. The Greek letters denoted the strength with which I was supposed to use each finger. Easier notes used lots of strength while harder notes required a more delicate touch. Each note caused one of the *Fulmen* to adopt a fixed point inside the *Imago*. (Just like when you touch the surface of a plasma globe.)

Anyway, the point is that each spell had its own version of sheet music. Firelight looked like this:

$$IV\Omega \ X\Psi \ III\Psi \ II\Psi \ VII\Omega \ II\Psi$$

Confusing, right?

I thought so. I set to work on pressing my fingers but I could never get the strength right. After a few minutes, I sensed the growing frustration of McFadden as he watched in horror. Eventually, he let out a long sigh and told me to take a break.

"Watch as I do it," he said testily.

He raised his hands in *Formatio* and easily formed the spell. He moved his fingers slowly and deliberately, giving me a chance to imitate him. He did it over and over, but it was hard to follow. It reminded me of learning to play a song using a YouTube tutorial. I kept wishing I could rewind McFadden's movements, but I couldn't. I had to watch the whole thing over again.

At least an hour had gone by and I still couldn't make it work. When I suggested we stop, McFadden slumped in relief.

"The best idea you've had yet," he said. "Perhaps you'd care to leave the Solitar altogether and never return?" The idea seemed to brighten his mood a little.

"I'm gonna get it right," I said. "But first, how'd you get in my head? I've never seen you before."

His eyebrows shot up as he adjusted his cuffs. "Dear me. I would've thought that to be obvious. But then again, I suppose when conversing with the hoi polloi, one must never assume any level of intelligence. Very well. As you may recall—and don't strain yourself trying—when you first opened my book, you found twenty pages written in Endruvian, did you not? Those twenty pages contained—"

"What's Endruvian?" I said.

For a split second, I caught a spark of confusion in McFadden's eye, but then it was gone. Its replacement—Massive Irritation—let it be known that it was here to stay.

"As rude as you are imbecilic," he said flatly. "What is Endruvian, you ask? It is the script you mistook for '*Elvish*,' which is not even a real language. To say so, would be like saying you wrote something in '*human*,' which of course no one does. The Endruvian script is an ancient form of magic created by an elder race in another realm. Every one of its letters contains more information than all the libraries on Earth. Thus, the twenty pages you read contained the memories of my former self, as well as a small percentage of my vast knowledge regarding the uncanny."

"So ..." I said slowly. "It's like I downloaded you into my head?"

"I suppose you could say so, yes. Much to my joy."

"Then why can't I do the spell?" I asked. "If you know so much, how come I still don't know anything?"

McFadden shook his head, and to my surprise, gave a light snort that almost sounded like laughter. "Your condition, François, as a man who doesn't know anything, is, I'm afraid, irreversible. The reason you don't have access to my knowledge is the same reason you can't recall every single word of a novel you read two years ago. Technically, the knowledge *is* in your brain, but you can't get at it because you're dumb."

"Can *you* remember everything you read two years ago?" I asked.

"Two years ago I was dead. Just as I was dead a hundred years before that. But in answer to your question—yes. I could. We didn't have *The Food Network* back then, nor Facebook. When a man read something, he remembered it. He didn't fill his head with senseless pap."

"Hey, you can learn a lot from *The Food Network*," I said. "Nothing impresses a girl more than a guy who knows how to cook. Just the other day, my girlfriend was upset and I made her this—"

He leaned forward and interrupted. "Women," he said importantly, "are impressed by a man's intelligence and good character. The rest is a sideshow. Now, if you're quite finished, I suggest we get back to practicing. It is my sincere hope that once you succeed, we shall 'call it a day,' so to speak, and I shan't see you again for some time."

So I got back to practicing. And you know what happened then? I got it right on my first, mother f-ing try. *Booyah. Firelight.*

This is how it happened: I formed the *Imago,* I did the *Canti,* the *Fulmen* stuck to the sides, and on the last "note," the *Imago* flashed and disappeared. What remained was a teardrop of flame hovering a couple inches above my palm. It was about the size of an apple and the most beautiful thing I'd ever seen. (Besides Cassie Chu in that dress.) ((Or Cassie Chu wearing anything at all.))

"Cassie who?" McFadden asked. "Ah. You're lusting after a succubus. Why am I not surprised? Now I understand why your brain is barely functioning. You're thinking with the wrong part of your anatomy. I suggest you—"

McFadden suddenly disappeared as I noticed Cassie skipping toward me. She was wearing Becky Altman's cheerleader outfit, except ... *sexier.* On Cassie, it looked more like a slutty Halloween costume. And right as I thought that, her outfit became a Cat Woman costume, which was even better. She halted with a stomp right in front of me and grinned.

I knew she was just my imagination, but I still turned red. She was standing so close ... I mean, her breasts, good God, were about a millimeter from my—

Okay stop. Close your eyes and think of anything else. Anything else. Anything else. Anything else.

When I opened them, Cassie lay supine in black lingerie on a pool table that had materialized out of nowhere. Her fingertips lightly toyed with one of the balls and she gave me a suggestive look.

I closed my eyes again.

My first thought was of a bulldozer moving large mounds of earth. I focused on it until I heard the telltale beeps of it backing up. I opened my eyes and Cassie—still wearing the lingerie—was driving it. Then there was a massive thunderclap to my right and a mushroom cloud blossomed into the sky.

Then I thought: *Getting weird. Time to exit the Solitar.*

And just like that, I was in my room again. The lighter fell with a heavy *thunk* on my desk as I reappeared in a swirl of liquid. As soon as I did, a familiar voice chirped, "How'd it go in there?"

I whipped around to see Cassie lying on my bed with her head propped on an elbow. She was wearing her usual outfit of jean shorts and a tank top with her hair loosely pulled into a ponytail. I jumped in fright and did my best to sound righteously outraged as I demanded to know how long she'd been there.

"A few minutes." She looked at me with a smirk. "Why? Were you fantasizing about me?"

"*What? No!*"

"It's okay if you were," she said. "I'm very pretty."

Jesus Christ, did she know? Could she see inside the Solitar somehow? The lingerie? The bulldozer?? Fuck. Fuck, fuck, fuck.

"I was learning a spell," I spat angrily. "That's all I was doing."

"Okay, okay. Jeez." She looked like she was holding back a laugh. "So what are you doing today?"

"I don't know," I said. "Maybe go to the gym?"

What the hell did I just say *that* for? I never went to the gym. Why would I say that now? Was I really that lame?

"I have a better idea," she said, and sat up on one arm. "How about a tour of LA's Magic Community? You'll need it if you're going to help me track down that Steinberg guy. Oh, and I also brought this for your face." She pulled a tiny vial from her shirt and held it up. "It'll fix the swelling."

"What is it?" I asked.

"I don't know. Some kind of alchemist thing that heals bruises." She tossed it to me. "Try it."

Ordinarily, I would've been a little hesitant, but given my current state, I was happy for any distraction. The liquid inside the vial was thin and clear like water. I rubbed a few dabs on my cheeks. At first, I felt nothing. But then it grew steadily warmer until it was hot—really hot. Suppressing a horrified shriek, I jumped toward the nearest mirror. It's always a very disquieting thing to see magic being done to your face. The black eye, the swollen cheeks, they were all deflating like day-old balloons. Before long, they were entirely gone and everything went back to normal.

When I turned to Cassie, she flashed me an enthusiastic smile. "See?" she said. "Good as new. Now you owe me a favor."

I raised an eyebrow at her. "What could *I* possibly do for *you?*"

"A lot of things, actually. But I'll keep my favor in reserve. So." She bounded to her feet. "Are you ready for your tour of LA's magic side?"

• • •

There was a time when downtown Los Angeles—DTLA—was the lamest part of the city. All it had were banks and a bunch of old warehouses. Now, it's one of the coolest parts of LA. My own personal theory for this is that Los Angeleans have a strange obsession with New York. There are examples of it everywhere. West Hollywood is called WeHo, mimicking New York's Soho. (North Hollywood goes by NoHo as well.) And when you visit DTLA, it looks like a miniature version of Brooklyn, with artsy loft apartments in converted warehouses with lots of rusty, fire escape charm. I'm not sure why, but I think the obsession stems from the unique layout of LA, which is distinctly un-city-like. It's more flat and suburban, with no central spot that everyone can point to and say, "That's where the action is." Thus, the idea of New York as a *real* city, with skyscrapers and history and dark alleyways, holds a certain appeal—and a bit of jealousy.

Thus: DTLA.

I'd only been downtown a few times for parties, yet Cassie clearly spent a lot of time there. She navigated its overcrowded streets like a native. Before long, we found ourselves in one of the back alleys still untouched by gentrification. The buildings on either side were crumbling brick and had the aforementioned fire escapes dangling overhead. They also had something else— something I wouldn't have seen if Rosewood had never removed that hex. Certain bricks, as well as certain objects on the ground—like half-broken crates, trashcans or a stray penny—*glowed*. Not bright enough to be distracting, but definitely enough to notice. The colors were all different, too. One of the bricks to my left was bright violet. A discarded shoe to my right was muted yellow. Cassie explained that everyday objects like these were called "imbued." Imbued meant that they had some sort of magical quality that could be used for a variety of purposes. Some of them, like the violet brick, opened a doorway to another part of the city. (In this case, it led to the ladies' room on the tenth floor of the Capitol Records Building.) Other objects, like the shoe, didn't do anything—unless they were mixed with other imbued objects, which was the province of an alchemist.

"It's why I like to think there's sort of a city within the city," Cassie explained as we left the alley for a crowded street. "Imbued stuff can lead to all kinds of places, and only magic people can see it. Does that make any sense?"

I nodded, still thinking about the violet brick and the ladies' restroom.

"So who put that there?" I asked.

"Who put what where?"

"That brick," I said, pointing to the alley. "Who decided they needed to go from there to Capitol Records on short notice?"

Cassie shrugged. "Could've been the other way around, you know. It could've been a rock star looking for a quick getaway. Anyway, it's always been there as far as I know."

A rock star ... I thought.

That made sense.

I got a mental flash of a young Mick Jagger getting caught in the ladies' room with an adoring fan and making a frenzied escape. It made me chuckle for a second until something hit me. There were imbued objects all over the place. If people created them, then they were like little echoes of the past dotted across the city. And in thinking about that, I suddenly understood the layout of magic on Earth. It left little imprints everywhere, like snapshots of tiny histories. Mick Jagger making a hasty retreat. A magician levitating a penny. A shoe … well, I'm not sure what happened with the shoe. Either way, the glow of imbued objects told the untold story of magic in Los Angeles. It's hard to realize something like that and not feel like a part of it. I wondered what violet bricks my life would eventually leave behind. Perhaps someday in the future, some young wizard might find a secret doorway to the broom closet of the Sriracha hot sauce factory, and say to himself, "I wonder who did this? And *why?*"

"So check this out," Cassie said, pointing ahead to a broken down Honda perched on the curb. It was missing half its wheels as well as most of its paint. I didn't see any imbued glow, but as she later explained, not every magic thing is imbued. (It was complicated.)

"What does it do?" I asked.

"I use it all the time," she said. "It's one of the entrances to the Magic Bank. Which is kind of boring, but it's a good example of a Secret Room. You wanna go inside?"

Cassie had just explained that Secret Rooms were a big part of the Magic Community, and one of the main reasons they were able to stay off society's radar. They were little planes of existence, sometimes no bigger than a bedroom, that were separate from the rest of the world. My Solitar was *sort of* like a Secret Room, but not exactly, according to Cassie.

"The Solitar is a wizard thing that you can carry around with you. Secret Rooms stay put. And you can't do whatever you want in them. They have rules," she'd said.

When she opened the door to the Honda, the metal groaned in protest like it hadn't moved in a hundred years. Cassie hopped inside and the moment she crossed the threshold, she disappeared. It was just like the cornfield in *Field of Dreams.* So just like James Earl Jones, I cautiously tested the waters a few times with my fingertips before following.

Once I did, I didn't feel a thing. I sat down on the worn upholstery, and the next thing I knew, I was sitting on a gilded chair in the enormous, vaulted lobby of a bank. It had a serious Roman Pantheon vibe with lots of marble and columns holding up an impressively domed ceiling. A row of tall countertops lined the walls with only a few employees standing by. The rest of the place was totally empty, giving it the hushed ambience of a library.

"It's actually really dangerous in here," Cassie whispered. "This is just the lobby, but if you go through those doors,"— she pointed to a huge set of them across the room—"you enter the maze. It's endless and if you get lost, you'll never get out."

"What's in it?" I asked.

"The maze? Everything," she said. "Valuables and money and whatever you want. Like me, for example, I have a bunch of ready cash and weapons stored there. It comes in handy when I'm on the run."

"So it's like a Jason Bourne type thing," I said.

"Who?"

Damn. I really needed to show Cassie some movies. They were practically the only subject I knew anything about.

"Anyway," she said. "I just wanted to show you a Secret Room. There's all different types. Some are shops, others are hideouts—a bunch of stuff."

"Are we going in the maze?" I asked.

The idea seemed to shock her. "No way. I mean, I can't show you any of my stuff—it's all top secret—and if we go in there without a direction we'll never leave. The whole thing is like an endless set of hallways with safes lining the walls. And no numbers. Everything looks the same."

"Sounds kinda creepy," I said.

"That's because you've never seen a Larva Mage before. *That* is creepy."

After we left the Magic Bank, we got back in Cassie's car and headed for Silver Lake. If you're unfamiliar with LA, Silver Lake is like the Hollywood Hills, but for young people who aren't millionaires. It has the same narrow, winding roads, which snake their way through a series of steep hills. The houses, however, are less "mansion-like" and more "gentrified-like." This is because the neighborhood mostly caters to LA's dwindling supply of hipsters.

We were there to visit Cassie's friend, Quentin, who was also her personal alchemist. Now, if you're anything like me, when you hear the word, "alchemist," you think of a guy playing with a chemistry set. Yet in the real world of magic, alchemists are more like inventors, dreaming up new technologies and gadgets. They can't perform magic like wizards, but they *can* manipulate imbued objects to create crazy stuff.

Quentin's house was a standard Silver Lake home, built on a steep slope and ensconced in thick foliage like it was trying to hide. Out front, there was a tiny driveway that led to a red-painted garage that opened automatically for Cassie's car.

"I'm on his list," she explained.

Once inside, the garage floor descended like an oversized elevator. There was total darkness for a few seconds until we emerged in a *second* garage that was the size of an aircraft hangar. It had tons of empty floor space, but there were also a dozen different workbenches scattered throughout—all littered with heavy tools and strange machines.

When we got out, I discovered that Quentin was a lot younger and better looking than I would've liked. (I was picturing an old guy for some reason.) Basically, he was a cooler, much tougher-looking version of me. He was medium height, which still put him several inches below Cassie, had dark wavy hair and wore a faded black T-shirt that drew attention to his rippling biceps. After a second, he looked up from welding something that looked like an *Iron Man* suit, and broke into a broad grin.

"Back for more?" he asked.

The cockiness in his voice made the innuendo unmistakable.

Cassie, I noticed, blushed. "Shut up," she said and brought me up beside her. "Q, this is François."

"Hey," I said.

He frowned and gave me a once over. "So you're the 'wizard,' huh?"

"I guess," I said. "Yeah?"

He raised his eyebrows like he wasn't impressed. He then turned to Cassie with a scowl. "So," he said. "You just wanted to show off your new boyfriend or what?"

"Come on, it's not like that," she said. "I actually need some stuff."

In a flash, Quentin's good humor returned. "In that case, come with me. I've got some shit that'll rock your world. I was thinking of you when I made it."

"Really?"

"No. But you're still gonna like it."

We followed "Q" to another workbench along the far wall of the garage. Along the way, I was thinking two things: 1.) This guy is an asshole, he's obviously had a thing with Cassie, and I don't like him. 2.) His nickname is *Q???* He builds high-tech gadgets for an attractive super agent and his name is *Q???*

A veritable blizzard of *James Bond* references was coming to me, but Cassie with her "I've only seen *Cars 2*" wouldn't understand!

Q reached the workbench and picked up a sleek metallic case. "So the first thing," he said, "is a new watch. Check this out. It's got a grappling hook and a laser."

I had to stifle a snort as he continued with his demonstration, but eventually I couldn't help but ask if the watch could also detonate explosives.

He turned to me. "What explosives?"

"Never mind."

It was one of those times where if I tried to explain myself I'd just sound even stupider. Q gave me a look like I'd just succeeded anyway.

"Moving on," he said, picking up a new case. "I've got some next generation Ice Grenades—totally new design. Even the latest protection charms won't be able to stop these bad boys." He took one out of the case. "You throw one of these at a villain and he's gonna be an ice statue no matter who he is. Guaranteed."

Cassie immediately snatched the case and stared at it wide-eyed. "I've been after you for a year to make these."

Before he could answer, she pounced on him, giving him a massive hug. It lasted a long time and Q's hands wandered south a bit. He then gave me a happy look over her shoulder.

"Thought you'd like that," he said.

I grimaced at him.

Once Cassie let go, he told her he had one more surprise and that he'd been saving the best for last.

"I call it a micro disc," he said, picked up a small square of clear plastic. It had a tiny black dot in the middle that I could barely see. "It works just like your standard holding disc," he explained, holding it up to a light. "It can store one small-sized weapon at a time. My recommendation is a Walther PPK."

Before I could stop myself, I asked, "What's a holding disc?"

Q turned, looking annoyed, but before he could say anything, Cassie said, "Remember that little poker chip thing you handed me with the sword painted on it? That's a holding disc. Each one can store a piece of gear. Mine are all full of weapons."

"Yes," Q said. "Only this one is much smaller." He indicated the tiny dot. "You can stick it anywhere on your skin and it will look like a freckle. Plus, it's invisible to any magic detection technologies. If you need to sneak a gun into a really secure place, then this is the tool for you."

Cassie took the micro disc and gazed at it admiringly. "It's so small," she whispered. "I could stick it anywhere."

"That's the idea," Q said.

She examined it a moment longer before her eyes flicked back to Q. "Can I try it on?"

"Be my guest."

Cassie skipped off, disappearing through a nearby door. Right before she disappeared though, she chirped, "You two be nice!"

And that was how I found myself standing awkwardly next to Q in a giant empty room. It took several seconds of tense silence before I said, "So, uh, how long have you known Cassie?"

He looked at me with a resentful glower. "You're not hooking up with her, are you?"

I did my best to look shocked. "What? No. Hey man, no. I have a girlfriend."

"Then what are you doing with her?"

I told him that it was a long story, but he didn't buy it. He just stared at me until I started speaking again.

"Apparently her astrologer told her to find me," I said. "And then this guy Rosewood lifted a hex off me and now I'm a wizard. Beyond that, I really don't know. I'm kinda new to this whole 'magic thing.'"

"You don't say?" he said.

Right then, Cassie skipped back into the room. "This thing is awesome!" she declared. "I dare either of you to find it!"

There was an awkward pause.

"Uh, I'm good," I said.

"Yes," Q agreed.

Cassie frowned. "You two are no fun. Anyway, Q, I'm taking it. Just put it all on my tab."

"Already done," he said. "I only have one micro disc for now, but I'll start making more. I'll give you a call."

Cassie hugged him again, kissing his cheek. "Have I ever told you that you're the best?" she said.

Q gave me another look over her shoulder. "I believe you have," he said. "Many times."

Once they separated, he surprised me by saying, "François," and stuck out a hand.

I shook it. "Quentin."

He gripped my hand a split second longer than necessary. Then—with a heavy sigh—he said, "Alright, hold on," and walked off to a nearby workbench. He plucked an old, leather bound book from a pile.

"Here," he said, handing it over. "Read this and you won't be so new to magic anymore. If you're going to be hanging around Cassie, you better know what you're doing."

I looked at the book. There was nothing written on the cover. "What is it?" I asked.

"It's what wizards used before smart phones and the Internet. It's called a *Vicipaedia,* which is just Latin for encyclopedia. It has a thousand volumes inside it, each one giving you information on magic, foreign realms, types of creatures, hidden histories, etc … It'll get you up to speed."

"Whoa," I said, and turned the book over in my hands. "I don't know what to say. Thanks."

Q gave Cassie—who was beaming at him—a brief look. "Don't mention it," he said. "And in case you're worried about reading a thousand volumes, it has a photo-memory spell attached to it. You'll be able to read each one in a matter of minutes."

• • •

After leaving Quentin's place, Cassie said she had one last thing to show me. We dipped back onto Sunset and she pulled the Mustang into the back parking lot of the Guitar Center. She pulled me over to the rear exit and took a small key from her pocket. I recognized it from earlier. She'd used it with the backdoor in the Hollywood Sign. Instead of putting it in the door, however, she handed it to me.

"This is yours," she said. "It's really easy to use. Watch." She took out her own key, and said aloud, "Paris." When she opened the door, there was Paris—a nice view of the Eiffel Tower and a guy in a beret playing an accordion. (No shit.)

"So this is a basic key," Cassie explained. "This will take you to any major city. All you have to do is say the name aloud."

I continued to stare at Paris until she closed the door and I was looking at the back of the Guitar Center again.

"So I just say any city?" I asked.

She nodded. "Give it a try."

I put the key in the lock and said, "Boston," and the door opened to a field-level view inside Fenway Park.

"Wow," I gasped.

"I know, right?"

Cassie then took out another key—this one bright pink— and told me to close the door.

"This is a special one," she said. "But you have to be a total badass like me to get it. Watch this." She twisted the lock and the next thing I knew I was staring at Wilshire Boulevard a block from my apartment.

"See?" she said with a grand gesture. "Total badass."

I stared a moment before asking, "So that one can take you *anywhere?*"

"Sort of," she said. "There's like a million backdoors all over the world. Most of them are 'restricted access,' unless you have a key like this one. It's from the SIA."

I was impressed. "Membership has its perks," I said and she beamed.

It was late afternoon as we stopped in front of my apartment building. I couldn't help but wonder if I should invite Cassie up, or at least ask her to come get a coffee or something. It just seemed like the polite thing to do. Plus, it seemed a shame to waste a good magic hour.

What's a "magic hour," you ask? It's that time of day that everyone on Earth can't get enough of. It's that little window of pink-grey light that arrives right after sunset. I suppose the proper word for it is, "twilight," which *was* a really cool word, until a certain series of novels ruined it. Then there's the word, "dusk," which sounds vaguely Klingon, and doesn't have much romanticism to it. Thus, magic hour.

Cassie studied me a moment like she was waiting for me to say something. A few options ran through my head. 1.) "So I guess this is it." 2.) "Hey, thanks for showing me around!" 3.) "Hey, wanna come up to my room?"

Sadly, I went with Option One.

"So I guess this is it," I said.

She frowned a little and cocked her head. "You mean you're not gonna give me a ride?"

Now it was my turn to frown. "Uh, my car blew up, remember? Besides, isn't the backdoor thing faster?"

She shrugged and shuffled her feet. "I guess," she said. "But I thought you might like to take her for a test drive ..."

"Her?" I asked.

Cassie stepped aside theatrically.

I'd seen it parked on the curb when we walked up, but now I was coming to realize it was for me.

And you're probably thinking that I was about to receive a Ford Batmobile of my very own. That would be the logical choice, right? Wrong. Waiting for me on the curb and glittering in the pink-grey light, was a brand new, powder blue Vespa.

That's right. Like a scooter.

When my eyes widened, Cassie jumped and looked ecstatic. "I picked her out myself," she said, skipping over to it. "I call her *Mary Lou*. Isn't she cute?"

She *was* cute. Very cute. I could easily picture a high school girl riding her through the streets of Rome with her best friend and having the time of her life. A dude doing the same, however, not so much.

"How did you get it?" I asked.

"The BPI did," Cassie said. "It's to help with your cover story. Just tell people you traded in your other car."

"For a Vespa?"

She shrugged. "It's better for traffic."

I stepped closer to admire my new ride. She had sleek lines, chrome trim, and a vintage design. "I don't know what to say," I said.

Cassie leaned forward to rub *Mary Lou's* seat in little affectionate circles. "She's really comfy. So whaddya say? Give a girl a ride?"

There was something in Cassie's eyes that made me feel like I'd give her a ride *anywhere*. Besides, who could refuse a little scooter ride during magic hour?

A minute later, we were cruising up Sunset with Cassie's arms wrapped around my waist. The night was warm with a cool breeze and *Mary Lou* purred like a kitten.

Now, to an outside observer, I might have looked like a dork riding a baby blue Vespa with an inexplicably hot girl on the back. But in my head, I was anything but. I was Lancelot returning home from a great victory. And *Mary Lou?* My trusted stead.

Chapter Five

This Is How You Dance

OVER THE COURSE OF THE NEXT WEEK, I learned a lot of things. None of them had anything to do with my college classes—which I mostly skipped—and everything to do with my brand new *Vicipaedia.* The thing was a marvel. I was fast on my way to becoming the biggest magic nerd on the planet. The book started with the longest Table of Contents in human history. It had a *thousand* titles listed in chronological order, and if I picked one, the *Vicipaedia* morphed into the original book. Some of the books, I noticed, were highly useful, like Thaddeus Kroeber's *Introduction to Dark Creatures: Where to Find Them and How to Destroy Them,* whereas other titles were more obscure, like *A Magical Interpretation on the Evolution of Horsemanship in the Mongol Empire: 1236-1307.* (Which I've now read, by the way, and it was surprisingly good.)

But the number of titles inside the *Vicipaedia* wasn't the cool part. As Quentin briefly mentioned, the book came with a "photo-memory spell," and with that spell came the granting of a wish held by every student since the dawn of time. I could now *Good Will Hunting* every single book inside the *Vicipaedia* within a matter of minutes. I could literally read each page faster than I could turn it with my finger.

As a result, I was now rapidly making up for lost time. I was learning everything that I *should've* been learning for the past twenty years—instead of filling my head with algebra and *Ethan Frome.* I mean, who cares about stuff like that when you can learn the secret history of goblins in World War II? Or perhaps the Treaty of Trolls that ended the American Revolution?

By the following Friday, I was a veritable expert on all things Magic. However, I still sucked at being a wizard. I'd spent hours inside the Solitar practicing spells, and so far, I had only mastered two: Firelight and Firebolt.

Firebolt was my first "offensive spell." I could fling a small bolt of fire at things and set them alight. But don't get too excited about that. The Firebolt wasn't a Fire*ball,* which apparently is a much more destructive thing to be used by badass wizards only. Think of it like this: A Fireball is like a Molotov cocktail the size of an oil drum. A Fire*bolt* is a Molotov cocktail the size of one of those little whiskey bottles you find in the mini-bar of a hotel room. Plus, it only had a range of about ten yards. (See? My football field was coming in handy.)

Either way, I practiced both spells to the point where I could do them in my sleep, which, according to Evil McFadden, meant it was time to learn the spells as "cantrips." A cantrip is an easy, low-level spell that a wizard can cast automatically, skipping the whole "forming the spell" phase using the *Imago, Canti, Fulmen,* etc …

"I would like to inform you, François, that in my living days, I taught *hundreds* of potential wizards the art of spellcasting. Some of them were quite gifted, while others took a bit longer to master the craft. You, on the other hand, are like nothing I've ever seen. I dare say that if I took up the challenge of teaching a mongoose to play the cello, I would find quicker success than I am presently. Your sheer lack of talent is so severe as to be fascinating. Truly!"

I'd learned not to pay attention to McFadden while learning anything new. He was clearly of the old school when it came to techniques of instruction. Or actually, he was old school when it came to everything. No one wore a suit like his who was born in the last century and not attending a costume party. I was actually quite surprised he didn't smack me with his cane more often.

"It's hard," I complained, failing for my ten thousandth time. "I need to use both hands."

(By definition, a cantrip needed to be done one-handed.)

"Ah," McFadden said. "A keen summation of your difficulties. It's 'hard.' You should have said so earlier. With feedback like that, I know exactly what you need."

I looked up at him hopefully. "What?"

"A new brain. Yours is clearly defective."

I winced and went back to practicing. It really *was* hard, too. It wasn't just that I sucked. The best way I can describe doing a cantrip is with a piano analogy. Everyone knows that song Heart & Soul, right? (It's the one Tom Hanks plays in *Big*.) If you recall, it has a bass clef part and a treble clef part. Most people who've never taken piano lessons play the song as a duet, with one person playing the left hand, while the other person plays the right. If you take some lessons though, you'll learn to play both hands at the same time. It's not easy to do. Each hand is playing a separate melody. Doing a spell one handed—i.e. a cantrip—is the same principle. It's like you have to teach yourself to stop thinking if you want to have any hope of getting it right.

I'd been at it for hours—a fact which McFadden reminded me of every two to three minutes. Eventually, I gave up.

"Perhaps you're not as dumb as I thought!" McFadden exclaimed. "Quitting is clearly the most sensible course. And if, perchance, you decide to quit magic altogether, well then I applaud you, sir. From the bottom of my heart."

I told him I'd see him tomorrow and caught the beginning of a heavy sigh before I exited the Solitar. I looked at my alarm clock and sure enough, the readout was a surprise. I'd discovered earlier in the week that time moved at a different speed inside the Solitar than it did outside. By my calculations, it moved at roughly *half* of normal speed. That meant that for every two minutes I spent inside the little Zippo, only *one* minute passed outside. So in a way, I could literally double my lifespan. Twenty-four hours in a day was for chumps. I could have forty-eight hours. (Although the sleep deprivation thing would catch up to me eventually.)

Anyway, the clock said it was only 11:23 am, even though I'd been in the Solitar for half the day.

A quick shower and a bowl of Fruit Loops later, I was riding *Mary Lou* to Ralph's to buy Meagan some flowers. I hadn't talked to her since our anniversary debacle and I figured it was time for a romantic gesture. I wasn't sure how mad she was—but if I had to guess, I'd go with Level Five. (Five is the highest number.)

The trouble was that Meagan lived in a sorority house.

Now, contrary to what National Lampoon movies might tell you, large gatherings of attractive coeds in one spot is *not* paradise. In fact, it's one of the scariest environments on Earth. These girls knew a thing or two about solidarity, and if Meagan was pissed at me, then they were *all* pissed at me.

I scootered up to the pink-trimmed Beverly Hills mansion and parked outside the main door. I freed the roses from an impromptu bungee cord knot and straightened my clothes. I patted down my hair. I took a deep breath. And I entered.

Now as any wise man will tell you: Sometimes in life you get lucky—sometimes you don't.

Today was one of the lucky days. The sorority house was empty. All the girls were probably on campus. As for Meagan, she only had one class on Friday at four, so there was a good chance she'd be home. I headed up the winding stairs to the second floor where she shared a room with a girl named Krista. Krista was a dark-haired Southern belle with a thick accent and a powerful hatred for yours truly. (Come to think of it, *everyone* in Meagan's life hated me.)

I'd just rounded the stairs when I heard a familiar giggle. It was a sweet sound—and Meagan made it whenever she was feeling frisky. I smiled involuntarily until I stopped, frozen in place ...

When I was eight years old, I caught my dad red-handed delivering Santa's presents. He wore an angry scowl as he labored at assembling a red bicycle while drinking a beer. I remember how the sight of him like that turned my whole world upside down. See, I was a sucker. I genuinely believed in Santa Claus. Other kids at school were skeptical, but I *believed*.

Well, catching my girlfriend making out with Jake O'Malley—the star quarterback for the UCLA Bruins—made me into a sucker *twice*. The other kids at school had tried to warn me, but no ... I refused to see that Santa Claus was a fraud.

And so Meagan and Jake continued to go at it. They were standing in her doorway as she leaned up on her toes with her hands pressed to his chest.

His hands were firmly placed on her butt.

I slid backward a couple steps down the stairs. For some reason, the big thought in my head was: *Is this the first time? Or the hundredth?*

"Babe, I gotta go," I heard Jake say to the sound of another giggle from Meagan. "I'll be back for Round Two in a few."

The best way to describe Jake's voice would be to say it sounded like Keanu Reeves doing an impression of himself. It was that bad.

"More like Round Two *Hundred*," Meagan purred. "I can't believe you kept going like that!"

"What can I say? I've got stamina and you've got that ass."

There was then the distinct sound of a meaty paw slapping a girl's bare butt cheek.

I chose not to listen to anymore. I know it makes me sound like a wimp, but I slunk away instead of charging in. There are probably a number of reasons why—but all I can say is that emotions are funny things. Sometimes they're not what you'd expect. Like, for example, you'd think "anger" would be the first emotion upon seeing your girlfriend getting groped—and liking it—by Jake O'Malley. Instead, I felt an irrational need to hit the Burger King drive-thru for a Whopper. See? Random.

I didn't do it, though. I just went outside and stared at *Mary Lou's* handlebars for ten straight minutes in a dumb stupor.

The next thing I knew, I was walking heavy-footed up the stairs to my apartment. Buckner and Brian were playing Xbox in the living room and offered me a controller. I trudged right passed them in a daze. I was moving like an ape, with my arms hanging limp while I took small, dragging steps.

Did Meagan say, "Round Two Hundred?" I thought. *Like just counting today or ...?*

When I got to my room, I locked the door behind me. Buckner called out something about a girl stopping by, but it was muffled. I looked to my bed and shuffled toward it. It was time to go to sleep—the best way to solve any problem. Before I got to the edge, however, my phone rang. I dug it out of my pocket and saw that it was a blocked number.

"Hey!" a familiar voice exclaimed when I answered. "We have an assignment!"

I blinked. "Cassie, this isn't a very good time."

"Yeah, but there's something big going down. I just talked to Rosewood. He thinks there's a connection between Professor

Steinberg and whoever is trying to kill you. I can't say anything more on the phone. I'm parked outside."

I peaked through my window and saw Cassie's Mustang. It looked inviting. Perhaps a little magical jaunt would do me good. I needed something to get the image of Meagan and Jake out of my head. And the sound of that ass slap.

"What kind of assignment?" I asked.

"The big leagues," Cassie said. "Now get your cute butt out here! We have to hurry!"

Damn. Did she have to say it like that?

• • •

Apparently Cassie had the Presidential Suite at the Ritz-Carlton in San Francisco on permanent standby.

"It's useful," she pointed out, dropping a pair of large duffel bags on the parquet floor. They hit the wood with a disconcerting heaviness that would've made any hotel manager wince in sudden pain. "It has lots of space."

"Cassie, I still don't get what we're doing here," I said, checking out the massive balcony through the sliding doors. It was late afternoon and I squinted against the Sun. We were in the middle of downtown with a view that swept across the entire city, including the Golden Gate Bridge.

"We're here for *this*," she said, pulling a rocket launcher out of her duffel bag.

From my extensive action movie knowledge, I knew it was a Russian-made RPG-7. It looked brand new and gleamed in the fading sunlight. No sooner did I admire it, though, than it disappeared inside a holding disc the size of a poker chip.

And *now*, my friend, comes the point where I actually know things. At some point over the past week, I'd read Pedro Villamizar's *Notable Inventions of Alchemy in the Twentieth Century,* and I knew everything there was to know about holding discs. First off, they were originally called "Discs of

Holding," because someone had played Dungeons & Dragons a few too many times. (And you'll only get that joke if you've played Dungeons & Dragons a few too many times.) Second of all, they could only hold a limited amount of stuff—roughly twenty pounds. Cassie's, however, were state of the art HD-320s, which meant they could hold thirty-two pounds. The catch—if you could call it that—was that holding discs were highly volatile. Once something like an RPG got put inside, the little poker chip became like a ticking time bomb. They usually blew after about twenty-four hours.

"You're a big fan of bazookas, aren't you?" I said.

"It's not a bazooka," Cassie answered while giving me a look. "And who *isn't?*"

"So I guess we're here to kill something big?" I asked.

She pulled one of those massive grenade launchers with six barrels out of the second duffel bag. (It's called a *Milkor MGL*, if you wanna Google it.)

"Nope," she said. "It's an extraction job. Much tougher."

She zipped the grenade launcher into a holding disc and then reached for an AK-47 from the same bag.

"Does extraction mean 'kidnap?'" I asked.

She stood and wrinkled her nose. "Why do people always say 'kid' nap? Like even if it's an adult? I don't get it."

She slipped a thin file from a nearby bag and slapped it on the suite's dinning room table. "This is who we're after," she said, opening to the first page. It had a glossy photograph of the target paper-clipped to the corner. "His name is Aeroth," she said. "He's a Vampire Lord. He's also the one who sent those vampettes after you. We're going to 'kidnap' him from his nightclub and deliver him to the BPI. They'll handle the interrogation. They're really good at that sort of thing."

As I looked at the photo, I couldn't help but smile a little.

Why did I smile, you ask? Well, you know the guy in the picture, "Aeroth?" I *knew* him. Well, okay. Not personally or anything. But I'd *read* about him.

"Aeroth was created by a Venetian Vampire Lord named Daemon in 1432 in Madrid," I said matter-of-factly. "Since then, his most recent accomplishment was as a Nazi scientist during World War II. He led the charge in human experimentation and was decorated by the Führer himself. He went by the name of Baron Von Traubel back then. His hair was shorter, but that's definitely his face."

I was kind of showing off, but I couldn't help it. Cassie just squinted at me a moment before she continued.

"Anyway," she said. "He owns a nightclub in Chinatown called *Vio*. It's for Magic Community only, which means security is going to be tight. Our mission is to get inside, look like we belong, and then when ... what was his German name again?"

"Baron Von Traubel."

"Yeah. When Von Traubel makes an appearance, we take out his guards and snatch him up. A BPI convoy will be waiting for us."

I nodded, doing my best to appear serious and confident. Like a Navy SEAL. Ever notice the stance those guys always take when receiving a mission briefing? Feet shoulder-width apart, arms crossed with one hand on the chin, an intense scowl of concentration? Well, that's what I was going for: Navy SEAL pose. I even gave a little frown, like I'd already been there and done that, and none of this was anything new.

"Right," I said. "Got it."

I noticed a slight simper from Cassie as she then proceeded to show me a layout of the nightclub, including interior photos and several escape routes in case things went pear-shaped. (She used the word "pear-shaped," not me.)

"Anyway, you don't have to do much," Cassie noted as we headed out to the balcony. She had just finished attaching several holding discs to mini-drones and was cradling them awkwardly before setting them on the pavement. I counted about a dozen of them. "Your main job is to stand there and look pretty."

"Pretty?"

"I didn't mean it like that," she said. "I'll explain in a second. Hold on."

She took a tablet from her backpack and tapped open the controls to the mini-drones.

"I'm gonna drop the discs along the escape routes," she explained as she drew her finger across the screen. "They'll come in handy if there's trouble."

All twelve drones zipped off like a swarm of bees before they vanished from sight. Cassie concentrated for a few minutes; tapping at the screen until eventually she looked up. "Done," she said.

"Do I get a gun?" I asked.

She gave me a look that left little doubt as to her rejection of that idea. "Come on," she said. "Let's get you something to wear."

The Presidential Suite had a wide array of men's formal wear hanging within a walk-in closet the size of my apartment. There were suits, tuxes, ties, polished leather shoes … and all of it was in my size.

"I called ahead," Cassie noted. "Anyway, you're my date tonight. My recommendation is the tuxedo. Your cover story is that you're a spoiled rich kid and I pulled you out of some stuffy dinner party your parents were hosting."

"Okay," I said, examining a diner jacket. "What's my name?"

"It's François. Just go with exaggerations instead of lies. If you try to memorize a bunch of stuff, you'll forget it. Trust me."

With that, she spun on her heels and left. She was clearly excited about the mission and it was actually a little infectious.

A few minutes later, I was fastening the cuffs of my new tuxedo and thinking to myself: *You know what, François? You really do look like James Bond. No bullshit.*

"Hey." Cassie interrupted my reverie as she came back into the room and I caught a glimpse of her in the mirror.

There's this stereotype that women take a long time to get ready, yet Cassie was clearly the exception. She'd gotten ready in the space of a pop song. And what she was wearing … *good God*. It put the dress she wore to Spago to shame. That dress had been classy, yet this one was tailor-made to make your jaw hit the floor. For starters, there wasn't very *much* of it. It was a glittery "Girl Going Clubbing" dress and it wasn't making any apologies. There was something about the way it hugged her figure yet barely grazed her skin that made it hard not to stare. Now, some people might say that a dress like that leaves little to the imagination. I strongly disagree. A dress like that sends the imagination into *hyperdrive*.

"How do I look?" she asked.

I gulped. "Incredible," I said breathlessly, but then caught myself. "I mean, okay. Or good. Or beautiful. Beautiful and okay. That's what I meant say. Hey, what's the capital of Mongolia?"

Her eyes narrowed.

I swallowed again and went back to straightening my bow tie. (Yes, I knew how to tie it.)

"You look handsome," she said after a pause, stepping closer.

"Thanks," I said.

"Like James Bond."

I turned to her, surprised. "I thought you never saw any movies?"

"I've seen posters," she said defensively. "Anyway, the important question is: Can you dance?"

I'd worried this would come up. I'd had a sick feeling in my stomach since the moment Cassie first mentioned we were going to a nightclub.

"I actually don't dance," I said.

"But you have to."

"Trust me, it's a bad idea. I'll blow your cover and we'll be screwed."

Cassie rolled her eyes. "Don't be stupid. Come on, I'll teach you." She then grabbed my hand and led me into the living room.

"It's really simple," she said. "Dancing with a girl in a club is all about letting her do her thing. Know what I mean?"

"No."

Cassie frowned a moment. "It's like ... caviar," she said.

"What?"

"Yeah. When you eat caviar you put it on a cracker, right?"

"I think it's called a 'blini,'" I said. "The little cracker."

"Yeah, well when a guy and a girl dance in a nightclub, he's the cracker and she's the caviar. You can't have one without the other, but the caviar is definitely the special part. *Your* part is to let it do its thing."

"Cassie, seriously," I said. "The last time I danced, I did the Macarena. You don't want me to do this. I'll just stand in the corner somewhere. I'm good at that."

Her face turned deadly serious. "That would be really dangerous," she said. "Some other succubus, or possibly a vampire, would scoop you up." She shook her head. "No, you have to dance. Honestly, François, your life depends on it."

I studied her a moment and saw that she wasn't joking at all.

Then I thought to myself: *Fuck.*

• • •

In all my twenty years, I'd never been to a proper nightclub before. There were a couple reasons for this: 1.) I wasn't twenty-one. 2.) I wasn't cool enough.

Nightclubs were for other people—people who I imagined spent their days on yachts and their nights in places I didn't get invited to. That being said, I'd seen plenty of swanky clubs in rap videos, so there was nothing too surprising. This particular club had a real VIP ambience to it, with blue floor lighting and white leather sofas along the walls. A giant dance floor dipped in the middle and was presided over by a raised dais— reminding me of a cathedral—where a DJ spun his tunes.

Cassie led me to a reserved table and slid next to me. A waitress on roller-skates—?—emerged from the crowd and smiled. "Hey!" she shouted over the music. "What can I get you?"

She had a distinctive "Harley Quinn" look to her, and I noticed absently that she didn't look at me—only at Cassie.

"I'll take an Ambo for my little friend here," Cassie said.

Roller-Skates answered with a wicked grin. "Coming right up!"

Once she skated away, I turned to Cassie. "My little friend here?" I said.

She cringed slightly and leaned into my ear. "I'm in character, that's all. Also, don't get mad, but you're not really my 'date' tonight. You're more like my ... *prey.* Sort of."

"Prey?"

"Yeah. It's easy. You're a gullible human and I'm an evil succubus and I lured you here to take advantage. And then, you know ... drain your soul. And by the way, that drink I just ordered is kind of like a magical roofie. Don't drink it. Things will get weird if you do."

A moment later, Roller-Skates returned with a single shot glass on a round tray. The Ambo was bright pink and steamed off the top like dry ice. "Enjoy!"

I looked at Cassie again. "What now?"

"We get in character," she said casually and handcuffed me to a railing along the back of the sofa. She did it so fast I didn't even see it.

"What are you—?" I started to say but she cut me off.

"Shut up!" she yelled harshly. (Then gave me a little wink.) "Stay here," she ordered. "I'll be back for you later. Bitch."

She got up without another word and melted into the crowd.

I—meanwhile—sat there with a stupefied look on my face.

Did she just handcuff me to the table? I thought. *And where did she get the cuffs?!*

Anyway, that's how I found myself sitting alone in a crowded, paranormal nightclub, wondering what in the hell was going on in my life. I thought of Meagan suddenly, and pictured her with Jake O'Malley. How long had *that* been going on? My friends had been insinuating that Meagan was cheating on me for a while, but I'd always figured they were joking.

Then another thought occurred to me: *What do I do now?*

It might sound strange, but I wasn't sure what the next step was. Should I break up with her? Should I talk to her? Should I leave a burning bag of feces on her doorstep? I didn't know. Technically speaking, Meagan was my first real girlfriend, so this would be my first real breakup. I wasn't sure how to do it. Absently, I picked up the shot glass and came within a hair's breadth of actually drinking it. It was weird, like something was compelling me to put it to my lips.

With an effort, I managed to set the drink back on the table. Right as I did, a tall, olive-skinned woman in a red dress sidled up to my side. "Hey there, handsome," she said in a low, smoky tone. "Are you alone?"

She was absolutely stunning, and I was having trouble getting my mouth to work.

"Uh, no," I said.

She raised an eyebrow. "No? You look alone to me. How about I keep you company?"

A chill ran down my spine as I realized this woman was definitely another succubus. She had an unsettlingly predatory look in her eye that made me scooch back a little. She looked a bit older than Cassie, too—like maybe a woman in her late twenties. Cassie, as far as I could tell, looked my age. Maybe that had something to do with the half-succubus vs. full-succubus thing. Who knows.

"How about you don't!" a voice shouted, emerging from the crowd.

I breathed a sigh of relief when I saw it was Cassie. She looked pissed. Really pissed.

The dark-skinned woman turned and regarded her coolly. "You shouldn't leave your human alone," she cautioned. "A morsel like that is hard to resist."

"He's mine," Cassie said, staring daggers at her. "Touch him and you'll regret it."

The other succubus put up a hand in surrender. "Don't worry," she said with a broad smile. "I'm not here for a fight. Enjoy him. He looks delicious."

Cassie continued to glare at her until she was fully out of sight. She turned back to me and sat down with a scowl. "That bitch. I've seen her before. She didn't do anything to you, did she?"

"I almost drank the Ambo. It was weird."

Cassie winced. "Compulsion," she said. "Crap. I should've thought of that. It's a type of enchantment. She can do it to you from a distance. Sorry."

I shrugged. "Did you see Von Traubel anywhere?"

"Not here yet. Anyway, we can't just sit here." She suddenly straightened and put her hands on the table. "So are you ready to dance with me?"

"Maybe I *should* drink the Ambo ..." I said. I was genuinely considering it. Roofie or no.

Cassie laughed and produced a small key from her dress. "It'd turn someone like you into a total loon, trust me."

"Someone like me?" I asked.

She undid the cuffs and smirked. "Someone with way too many inhibitions. Speaking of which ..." She stood and held out her hand.

I took it and once again found myself being dragged onto a dance floor. It was the moment I'd been dreading for the past several hours, and before that, my entire life. And as a side note: I don't think my reservations about dancing were unfounded. I'd had way too many bad experiences to have anything approaching confidence when it came to my moves. I'll give you some highlights: Seventh Grade—I asked Lara Peterson to dance during a slow song and she punched me in the face. True story. Tenth Grade—I attempted my first official "grind" with Sarah Pope who promptly screamed and then punched me in the face. Last Thursday—I did the Macarena with Buckner's friend, although I guess she didn't punch me in the face. Still, the memories of all these failed dances swirled through my head as Cassie looked at me through the blinking strobe lights and asked if I was ready. Her eyes were glowing purple again, and her voice cut straight through the pounding music as if it weren't even there.

"How are you doing that?" I asked.

"Magical powers," she said. "Now we're going to have to get closer." She stepped forward and pressed herself against me. Before I could react, she took my hand and placed it on the small of her back. I looked up at her, highly conscious of her breasts pressing into my chest.

Then she started moving. Slowly at first, just with her hips, and then more and more. Her shoulders picked up the beat and it was all I could do to stay upright. I fought to remember what she told me earlier. I thought: *Be the cracker, François. Be the cracker. Be the cracker!*

And so I did.

"Move your hips," Cassie instructed, guiding them softly with her hands. "That's it. Now find the beat. You feel it?"

I felt something alright. "I think so," I said.

I caught her smile as her hands traced up my back and around my neck. "See?" she said, twisting suddenly and pressing her backside into me. "Not so hard, right?" She took my hand again and pressed it against the flat of her stomach, pushing her thin dress up off her hips.

I got an erection.

It wasn't the first time this had happened. At my Junior Prom I had a very similar experience with Tiffany Garcia. It was a slow dance, I had a huge crush on her, and there was nothing I could do. She punched me in the face. (Just kidding. She just looked really awkward for the remainder of the song and then never spoke to me again.)

Cassie, however, didn't seem to mind in the slightest. She spun back around and pulled me close again.

"Having fun?"

"Yeah," I said.

"Then grab my ass," she ordered and her body moved harder against mine.

Now, in life, there are certain things that feel really good— an ice-cold drink on a hot day; a fireplace on a cold night. Yet as Cassie's dress rode up in my palms, I learned that a girl's bare backside on the dance floor is a feeling like no other. We were both sweating in the crowded heat, and I noticed Cassie's eyes half-lidded as she moved to the music. Her body felt incredible, writhing against mine, but it was her eyes that truly got me. She looked right at me, but didn't smile. At first I thought she was angry—like maybe I was doing something wrong. Then her hand snaked up my neck and her fingers entwined with my hair. Her mouth was slightly parted, breathing hard.

So I kissed her.

It was a small kiss—it was practically just a reflex. Our lips barely grazed, but she pulled back immediately, studying my face in wonderment.

I was about to apologize when she broke into a broad grin. "Took you long enough," she said and pulled me back in. Her kiss was deep and slow and she pulled me against her with an inhuman strength. It reminded me that she was a succubus and not just a normal girl, and a brief wave of panic shot through me. The fear was quickly overshadowed, though, by the softness of her lips and the thrill of her tongue. My hands traveled south again and she mewled softly.

"We better not," she said, pulling back a fraction. "If we keep going, I won't be able to stop."

I almost brought my lips back to hers anyway, but caught myself at the last second.

"Sorry," I said.

She grinned and put her forehead to mine. "I forgive you. Besides, Von Traubel just got here. See him?"

We had discussed the plan for nabbing the Vampire Lord for several hours back at the hotel. Cassie would do the heavy lifting, taking out his bodyguards and then knocking him out with a hypodermic garlic shot. She had several micro discs on her body concealing a variety of small weapons. I—meanwhile—was to use my newly acquired wizard skills to create a distraction. And since I only knew two spells, Firelight and Firebolt, my options for doing so were limited. We both had decided that a well-placed Firebolt at one of the guards' feet would do the trick. Cassie said she only needed a half-second to get close enough to do her thing.

"You remember where the back exit is, right?" she asked, still moving sensually against me.

I had to think a moment. She could've asked me my name and I would've had to think about it.

"Uh, yeah," I said.

"Good. Give me a second to get in position. Then after you do the Firebolt thing, run straight for the exit. I'll meet you outside."

With that, she broke away and disappeared into the crowd.

I caught my breath and then moved off the dance floor. Von Traubel was sitting at a large VIP table with two slave girls at his side and four bodyguards surrounding him. They were unquestionably the biggest guys I'd ever seen. They were all wearing expensive suits, yet I noticed a slightly green tint to their skin. I wondered what kind of creatures they were. Not human, that was for sure.

I waited a few more seconds until I figured Cassie was ready.

I looked side-to-side, checking to see if anyone was watching. It was probably a stupid thing to do. The *Imago* from my spell was going to draw plenty of attention anyway.

I drew another breath, glanced at the guard I intended to target, and formed the spell. The *Imago* was even brighter in the dark nightclub than I'd feared. The guard instantly turned to me and shouted. I made the *Canti* so fast, it was practically a cantrip. (I felt a brief moment of pride in that.)

The next thing I knew, the guard was nearly on top of me. He yelled, "wizard!" and lunged. I flicked my wrist and hit him in the shin with the Firebolt. It burst into a small flame and set his pant leg alight. It didn't slow him down, though—not even a little. He reached for me and I managed to duck out of the way. He stumbled and slapped at his leg, extinguishing the fire. I ran.

By now, the other club goers knew something was wrong. A mad stampede was beginning to bottleneck at the front exit, while I pushed toward the rear.

Green-Tinted Bodyguard was still on my heels. He bowled people out of the way like a wrecking ball. A heavy hand landed on my shoulder and spun me around. Without thinking, I did my first, official cantrip. I flung an instant Firebolt right in his face. He bellowed in sudden pain and slapped at the flames.

I continued my dash for the exit. Now that I'd seen him up close, I noticed he had a distinctive underbite with little fangs pointing upward. Definitely an orc. Then the red-dressed succubus from earlier planted herself directly in front of me with a snarl. She raised a fist, but I tagged the hem of her dress with another Firebolt and kept moving. She didn't give chase. And I'll admit—at that moment—I felt like kind of a badass.

When I got to the exit, I found Cassie waiting impatiently with a slumbering Von Traubel slung over her shoulder.

"Where were you?" she demanded, and kicked open the door.

"There was an orc and I did a cantrip!" I exclaimed. (I couldn't help the enthusiasm—I'd been practicing the damn thing for an eternity.)

"You should be proud," she said and rolled her eyes. We then ran down the back alley behind the club. We only made it a few steps before a dark SUV pulled into view and barreled toward us.

"Is that the BPI?" I asked, skidding to a halt.

"No."

Cassie dropped Von Traubel without ceremony and I heard a *crack* when his arm hit the pavement. She snatched a holding disc from behind a discarded crate. All of a sudden, she was balancing an RPG on her shoulder. She shouted for me to plug my ears and then fired. The rocket hissed and collided with the windshield of the SUV, blowing out its insides in a flash of fire and smoke.

"Come on," she said, slinging Von Traubel back over her shoulder. She did it so easily it made me wonder just how strong she really was. Definitely superhuman. That was for sure.

I followed her past the flaming wreck of the SUV onto the street where I could hear police sirens approaching. We ran down the road until we burst through the doors of a noisy Chinese restaurant still bustling at one a.m.

I caught several baffled stares as we ploughed through the narrow spaces between tables. Cassie moved like she was on a mission. (No pun intended.) She kicked open the double doors to the kitchen and quickly apologized to the cooks as we ran past.

"It's in here," she told me, taking a sharp left down a narrow hall toward a janitorial closet. She fished a key from her dress and unlocked the door. It opened into a parking garage— definitely not connected to the small restaurant—and we ran through. A line of black Escalades pulled up and the doors swung open. This time it *was* the BPI. A flock of men in dark suits and sunglasses descended on Von Traubel and told Cassie they'd take it from here. She handed him over, and in a screech of tires, the convoy was gone.

Cassie looked at me and announced that the party wasn't over yet. She burst into a full sprint to the other side of the garage. She opened the door there, which took us to another garage and then another and another. She explained as we ran—somehow she was able to talk and breathe at the same time—that we were jumping between "Transit Points," covering our tracks in case any of Von Traubel's people were following. Finally, we exited one of the garages into another back alley. I had no idea where. We could've been in Shanghai at that point and I wouldn't have known the difference. Cassie tapped an imbued yellow brick. It opened a pitch black hole in the wall and she told me to jump through it.

"Where does it go?" I panted, bending at the waist and resting my hands on my knees.

She urged me forward with a gentle shove. "Just do it," she said.

I climbed through the hole and fell onto a hard, parquet floor. Cassie landed next to me and the hole vanished behind her.

I looked around. "Holy crap," I said, still gasping for breath. "How did *that* happen?"

We were back in the Presidential Suite of the Ritz-Carlton. The room was bright and air-conditioned, and the cool air felt incredible. I was absolutely drenched from head to toe.

"I'm a good little girl scout." Cassie grinned. "I always plan ahead."

We lay there for a few minutes catching our breaths. Cassie probably didn't need to, but I sure did. I hadn't run like that since I was on the track team in high school. Without thinking, I closed my eyes and rolled onto my side. I didn't plan on falling asleep, but the next thing I knew, I was waking up to familiar surroundings. Someone—probably Cassie—had moved me back to my own bed in Los Angeles.

Chapter Six

You're a Wizard

HERE'S A FUNNY THING ABOUT COLLEGE: No matter what is going on in your life, there's no escaping the ever-looming need to study for midterms. For example, even if you just helped kidnap a Vampire Lord the previous night, the fact that you have a Statistics 13 midterm on Monday still fills you with dread. It was my least favorite class this semester, and unless I studied, I was going to fail it.

But before I could do so—and this was more important than anything else—I needed coffee. Good coffee. Not the emergency reserve stuff in the kitchen. I needed a fresh, professionally brewed cup of Joe, and I needed a lot of it. There was only one place in a thousand locations where I could get such a thing: Starcups. (Not to be confused with Starbucks.)

I headed outside in shorts, flip-flops and an old t-shirt, and hopped onto *Mary Lou.* There was a nice breeze as I puttered up Wilshire, enjoying the sunny Saturday morning. When I got to Starcups, I found it packed to the gills with people who'd had the same idea that I'd had—coffee and lots of it. Still, it only took a few minutes until my order was up. As I walked outside, my brain was consumed with how I was going to carry my precious cargo back to the apartment while piloting the Vespa. My plan was to jerry-rig an impromptu cup-holder from the bungee cord dangling off the back.

I was in the middle of trying to turn that dream into a reality, when a silver Rolls Royce pulled up beside me. It was brand new and sparkled under the early morning sun. The passenger door opened slowly and Agent Thomas Rosewood appeared, complete with immaculate, double-breasted suit and silver-topped cane.

"François," he said, smiling pleasantly. "Dear me. It warms the heart just to see you! You are well, I trust?"

I gave a furtive glance from left to right to see if anyone was watching. The only culprit was a teenage girl filming us—although I'm pretty sure she was hoping for a celebrity to emerge from the Rolls.

"I'm great," I said.

I found myself strangely happy to see him. There was something about that cheerful, British demeanor that put an involuntary smile on my face.

"Marvelous! I tell you, François. I heard about your exploits with Cassandra last evening and I must say! My hat—as it were—is off to you, sir. I am most impressed. Most impressed indeed."

"Thanks," I said. "I did a cantrip."

"So I heard. You know, it took me six *months* of practice before I did my first? You have a rare talent, François. Truly."

"The orc was about to punch me in the face," I noted. "I think that helped."

"Ha! Well I am most glad it did! So listen. I don't wish to intrude upon your morning, but I was wondering if I might have a word? It won't take long." He gestured toward the open door of the Rolls and gave a little bow.

"Is it about Professor Steinberg?" I asked.

"Partially," Rosewood answered. "But it is best we discuss these matters inside the vehicle. The inside is well guarded against prying ears—including the young lady filming us."

I chuckled. "I think she's hoping to see Justin Bieber."

Rosewood glanced in her direction and frowned in thought. "Well, I suppose I could conjure an image of the Biebs, if she wished." He turned back to me. "Did you know he's actually a hobbit? It's a rather marvelous disguise he wears—it's nearly impossible to tell."

The Rolls Royce had a uniformed chauffeur up front wearing a visored hat and white gloves. Once we were underway, I noticed his skin looked vaguely plastic. Rosewood told him—in a surprisingly curt tone—to take us back to Westwood and then circle the UCLA campus. The driver gave a jerky nod that made me suddenly wonder if he was an automaton.

"So François," Rosewood began, setting his cane aside. "I apologize again for kidnapping you this morning, but it will only take a moment. We need to discuss our mutual friend, Cassandra. You may have noticed already that I care for her very much. I dare say, she's like a daughter to me."

"She's really great," I said.

"Oh, indeed. She's a very special girl—much more so than you know. Are you aware that succubi, by their very nature, are intrinsically evil? Yet Cassandra—for reasons unknown—is *good*. In all my years wizarding, I've never come across her equal."

"She mentioned she was only *half* succubus," I said. "Does that have something to do with it?"

"Yes. Her father—dead upon her conception, I'm afraid—was a normal human. Her mother, however, was something else entirely. She was the most powerful succubus to ever enter this realm. And she was, quite unfortunately, very mean. She raised young Cassandra to follow in her footsteps. Yet something rather remarkable happened instead."

I noticed I was literally sitting on the edge of my seat. "What?" I asked.

"Young Cassandra rebelled. And while such behavior is quite common for a *human* teenager, it is most certainly not common for a succubus. Now I don't wish to burden you with the sad details, but let us just say Cassandra's mother was not pleased." Rosewood paused a moment, stiffening. "She tortured the poor girl," he said quietly. "And that, François, is when I found her. She was fifteen and nearly dead. It took all my skills to revive her. To this day, she remains my greatest accomplishment."

I felt a sudden pang in my stomach. The thought of Cassie being tortured by anyone—let alone her *mother*—made me sick.

"What happened to her mom?" I asked.

"Banished," Rosewood said sharply. "I sent her back from whence she came. It was a rather nasty battle, too. She didn't go willingly."

"So what happened to Cassie after that?"

Rosewood looked at me. "I took her under my care. I trained her as best I could, until she was ready to 'leave the nest,' as it were."

"You *raised* her?" I asked.

"For two years, one month and six days. I dare say I miss having her around the flat. She's quite funny, you know."

"She is," I agreed with a small grin. "Very."

"Yes. And so, François, we get to the heart of why I've come to see you. Cassandra told me what happened last night. She told me *everything* that happened last night."

For a split second, I didn't understand what he meant until a pile of bricks fell on my head and I remembered my epic make-out session with Cassie on the dance floor. The memory made me shift in my seat.

"Oh," I said. "Yeah. I, uh ..."

"There is no need for embarrassment, dear boy. I'm not angry. Quite the contrary, in fact. Cassandra likes you. She likes you a great deal. I knew as much the instant the pair of you walked into my office. Which is why I must ask you a favor. It is very important."

"Anything," I said.

"I need you to look after her for me. I fear for her safety. Now more than ever."

I had to stifle a snort. *Me* look after *Cassie?* That didn't make any sense.

"Mr. Rosewood," I said.

"Oh, call me Thomas, I beg you."

"Thomas," I said awkwardly. "How could I possibly look after Cassie? She's a total badass. She's the one looking after *me.*"

Rosewood suddenly chuckled with an unmistakable hint of pride. "Oh, she's quite formidable, I know. Yet you are new to the world of magic, François. There are many things you still need to learn. As for Cassandra, she's more vulnerable than she appears. Her 'tough girl' persona is mostly an act."

"I find that hard to believe," I said.

"Oh, she can fight," Rosewood said. "And if you drop her in front of a villain, she will most certainly 'kick his butt'—of that, I have little doubt. But François, listen to me." He leaned closer. "There is more to this game than fighting. Cassandra is very strong, it's true. But strength isn't everything, especially when confronting magic. You are a wizard, my boy. Untrained, yes, but a wizard all the same. And when you're ready, you will need to protect her. Just as I have done."

It occurred to me that Rosewood still hadn't reached the *real* reason he was here. I didn't doubt that he wanted me to help Cassie, but he knew as well as I did that it would be a long time—if ever—until I was ready to do so. He had another motive. And if I had to guess, he was *scared* of something.

"Mr. Rosewood," I said. (There was no way I was calling him Thomas.) "What's going on? Did something happen?"

Rosewood paused a moment, regarding me. When he let out his next breath, his whole body seemed to deflate. His shoulders slumped, and for a brief moment, he looked like a truly old man. And not the cheery, dapper one I'd come to know. There was a deep weariness in his eyes that I hadn't noticed before.

"It's Steinberg," he said heavily. "Something sinister is brewing, François. Something big that threatens us all. I don't know what it is, and none of my colleagues will listen, but I feel it in my heart. I have a rather good sixth sense about these matters, and I am certain Steinberg's disappearance has something to do with it. We *must* find him. I know I told you earlier that there wasn't any urgency. I fear that is no longer the case. The professor is either a villain himself, or someone else is using him for nefarious purposes. Either way, this could be a very troubling development. With his expertise in both nuclear science and alchemy, it is quite possible he could be a dangerous man—one way or the other."

At that moment I had the strangest thought that ten days ago my biggest worry was interviewing for a summer internship with Meagan's dad. Now, I was sitting in a Rolls Royce with a wizard who was telling me about a plot for world destruction and that I needed to do something about it. Therefore, I asked the only logical question that came to mind. I asked him what I—a twenty-year-old college student—could possibly do to help.

"I told you," he answered. "I need you to watch Cassandra's back. She isn't safe—not against forces like these. I'll do what I can from afar, but François,"—he glanced over and his eyes twinkled—"I'm afraid I'm a bit of an old man under this suit. I won't be around forever. I need to know that Cassandra has someone she can trust. I would very much like that person to be you."

I promised him I'd do everything I could. I felt a little cheesy when I told him that, like I was a medieval knight or something. But more than that, I feared I was making a promise I wouldn't be able to keep.

A minute later we pulled in front of my apartment building. Just as I made to get out, Rosewood put a hand on my elbow. "François," he said. "I would appreciate it very much if we could keep this chat between us. Cassandra gets rather cross when she feels I'm being overprotective."

I chuckled. "I can definitely picture that. I won't tell her. I promise."

"Good." He nodded crisply. "Very good. I thank you."

"No problem," I said, and opened the door. I was halfway out when I stopped and turned. "Cassie's really lucky you found her," I told him honestly. "You're a good guy, Mr. Rosewood. For real."

He grinned and gave me a wink. "It takes one to know one, François. I'm glad you are with us. Until next time." He touched his forehead in an old-fashioned gesture of farewell. The Rolls' door closed on its own and the car sped off, disappearing in a blink. I looked to my right and *Mary Lou* was parked on the curb with my coffee balanced perfectly on the seat. I stared, dumbstruck.

How the heck did he do that ...?

• • •

When I got up to my apartment, I was greeted with an unwanted surprise. As I walked through the front door, Buckner—who was playing Xbox on the couch—saw me first. He pressed pause and winced. "Brace yourself, buddy boy," he said. "The future misses is here and she don't look happy."

"Shit," I said. I still hadn't told anyone about Meagan cheating on me. "Where?"

"Your room. I tried to tell her you moved to old Mexico, but she didn't buy it. She's waitin' in there. Sorry, partner."

I really didn't want to deal with this right now. I still wasn't even sure about what to do. Should I break up with her? Get mad? Talk it out?

All I knew is that I didn't feel like doing any of those things right this second. Yet apparently I didn't have a choice. It's one of the major pitfalls of any relationship—you seldom get to choose the time and place of your battles. Thus, with a sense resignation, I trudged back to my room where I knew an epic argument awaited.

I found Meagan, wearing a short skirt, lying on my bed. She was on her stomach, reading a magazine with her feet swaying in the air. Her face instantly brightened when she saw me. "Hey!" she chirped, and hopped off the bed to give me a hug. I stood still as a statue as she put her arms around me and rested her cheek on my shoulder. "I'm so sorry about the other night," she said. "I know you're pissed. I should've called earlier, but ... well, I want to make it up to you."

I didn't know what to say. My inexperience with getting cheated on and what to do afterwards left me completely mute as Meagan kept talking. She pushed back to look up at me. "My dad can be a total jerk sometimes," she said. "If it makes you feel better, I'm not returning his calls anymore."

After a moment's silence, I found my voice. "Meagan," I said, but she quickly continued.

"I was thinking we could go out again," she said. "Just you and me. It was so stupid to have my parents come, but my dad insisted. I feel horrible about it."

She truly had no idea that I knew about her and Jake. In some weird way, it made it hard to accuse her of anything. I knew that the moment I did, the cat would be officially out of the bag. Who knew what would happen after that? Would we break up? Would she start throwing things?

Plus, the instant I said anything out loud, it would turn the whole thing real. For the moment, we were like those last bits of sunshine before nightfall—Meagan was still my girlfriend and we could still talk and kiss and touch each other without it being weird. But it couldn't stay that way. It was already over even if she didn't know it yet.

"I saw you," I finally said.

Her brow furrowed. "Saw me? Where?"

"I came to patch things up," I said. "Yesterday. At your sorority house."

Meagan didn't skip a beat. "Really? I wasn't home. My friend Kaitlin had this emergency with her boyfriend so I had to—"

"I saw you with Jake O'Malley," I said.

She stopped cold.

It's a funny thing watching a person up close after they've received startling news. A whole kaleidoscope of thoughts and emotions flashes across their face before they decide on a course of action. Meagan—after about a second—decided to go with outrage.

She let go and took a firm step back. "*What?*" she said.

"I saw you making out with him."

She paused another second as her face turned the color of a pomegranate. Then she said accusingly, "Were you *spying* on me? Jake's my *friend*. He came over to borrow my sociology notes!"

"His hands were on your butt."

"Oh my God. *Really?* I came here to make *you* feel better and you accuse me of *cheating on you?* I mean, do you even have any proof?"

"Proof?" I said.

Meagan's hands moved to her hips. She'd now taken to laughing in that scary way that people do when they're a combination of embarrassed and livid. "Yeah, proof. And by the way—if you really think I cheated on you, why aren't you more upset? Most guys would be furious. Maybe I *should* be with someone like Jake."

"For round two hundred and one?" I asked.

Her face suddenly contorted, reminding me somehow of a squeezed lemon. "What does that even *mean?*" she barked. "And why are you always so insecure?!"

As odd as it might sound, she actually did have a point about me not being more upset. I mean, not a *huge* point, obviously, as she was essentially getting mad at me for not getting mad at her for cheating on me. Still, it was probably revealing that I wasn't very angry. If I truly *loved* her, I would've been going crazy right now. Instead, I felt an odd sense of calm. Or perhaps it was *relief.*

"Um," I said after a pause. "How long are you going to keep this up? I *saw* you with the guy."

"Well, *yeah.* He came over!"

"Meagan, there was no mistaking it. You were kissing. His hands were all over you. And *proof?* What are you talking about? This isn't a murder investigation. I saw you hooking up with him. Case closed." I noticed that now I actually *was* getting upset—kind of like a delayed fuse. "And another thing," I said. "You're calling *me* insecure? Jesus Christ. Round two hundred, Meagan. That's what you said to him. Two *hundred!* No one can screw that many times in a day! You've been banging the guy for months! Probably all semester! Or longer! Was it longer?! Good God, look at me right now, I'm shaking! I feel like I'm gonna throw up!"

"You would. I can't believe what a wimp you—"

"And I feel so much better," I continued, "that you're not returning your dad's calls. I mean, what a sacrifice. And who invites her *dad* to her anniversary? Especially when she knows that her dad *hates* her boyfriend? Who does that?"

"I was trying to help you!" Meagan screeched.

"Help me? What the fuck! The guy threatened to kill me last week. And you convinced me to get an internship with him! Meagan, honestly, why did you even go out with me in the first place? Was your dad right? Were you just trying to piss him off?"

She snickered and it was infuriating. She then stared at me a long moment as if deciding to tell me something. "François, you really don't get it, do you?" she finally spat.

"Get what?"

Another pause.

"You were my *reserve* guy. Didn't you realize that? Did you honestly think you were good enough for me? If anything, *Jake* was my real boyfriend, you idiot!"

Huh.

Well that shut me up. Hell, I couldn't even move. I just stared numbly until she continued.

"I hate to break it to you, but every girl has that guy who's the 'safe option,'" she said. "You know why? Because the types of guys we're actually *attracted to*, just end up cheating on us. So we grab a guy like you—just in case. It's harsh, but this is the real world. I have plans. I'm not going to let some Neanderthal like Jake ruin them. You were my contingency and you were lucky to be *that*. Only now, you've screwed it all up!"

Again … *huh*. Talk about a bombshell.

So imagine this: One day you're walking down the street and you receive a phone call. On the other end is Morpheus, explaining that the Matrix is, in fact, real and that everything in your life has been a giant lie. You ask him what to do about it, only he says—a bit embarrassed now—"Well, there's not much you can do, I just, uh, figured I'd tell you. Good luck!"

That's pretty much the best way I can describe how I felt at that moment. I'd been with Meagan Goodman for a year and a half—thinking the entire time that she actually liked me, when in fact, I was merely part of a calculated plan to ensure she never got left without a chair when the music stopped. I'll tell you, something like that doesn't do any favors for a person's sense of self-worth. It hurts about as bad as anything can hurt.

Eventually I said, "Meagan," and then paused, studying her face as she glared back at me. "I honestly don't know how to respond to that."

"Of course you don't," she snorted. "And for the record, I was totally planning on breaking up with—"

"Except to say this," I said, feeling that odd calm again. "I actually feel sorry for you." She erupted into a mirthless laugh, but I kept going. "Meagan, a minute ago you called me insecure. I just realized you were talking about yourself. You're the most insecure person on the planet. Which is weird, by the way. You're smart, you're beautiful and you're rich. And *still*, you're insecure. I believe the word for that is 'cowardice.' You think I'm a wimp? I'm *Hercules* compared to you. So yeah. I *do* feel sorry for you. I feel sorry for Jake too. Not, like, a lot or anything, but a little. You do realize you were so worried he'd cheat on you that you cheated on him first? And not just with sex, but with an entire relationship? With me? Christ, Meagan. I had no idea you were this messed up. And now that I think about it, today might be the best day of my life. I didn't just dodge a bullet with you. I dodged a freaking apocalypse."

There was a loud *hoot* from outside the door, making both of us jump. I recognized the voice. Apparently Buckner had been listening, and I fought to suppress a tiny grin.

Meagan, meanwhile, pulled a disgusted face. "Bunch of five-year-olds," she snarled. "I can't believe I'm even here right now." She then looked directly at me, her eyes like a pair of laser beams. "So that's it then? We're breaking up?"

I got myself under control. "No," I said. "*We're* not breaking up. I'm breaking up with you. That's right. Me. François. Your 'safe option.' Now get the fuck out of my apartment."

Yeah, okay. I know. That last bit was a little harsh. Even Meagan, who was steaming out the ears, looked shocked. A better man wouldn't have said it like that. There was no need for an F-bomb. But sometimes in life—and this is an incontestable truth that everyone learns eventually—it feels really, really good to be a dick.

● ● ●

After Meagan left, Buckner was waiting in the living room with a free Xbox controller and—I kid you not—an open bottle of champagne. It put an instant smile on my face. I think he was even happier than I was.

I'd always figured my first break up would be a more heart-wrenching experience. I thought I'd end up like those poor saps in the movies—not eating or sleeping and trying to call her, only to keep getting her voicemail. Instead, I wound up playing *Halo* for the next hour until I got a text from Cassie telling me to meet her in New York. "Use the Hollywood Sign," the text said. "It'll take you right to me. P.S. I got you something!"

Just thinking of Cassie put an even bigger smile on my face. I imagined her grinning, typing the text with her thumbs, and it was like she was standing right in front of me. It honestly made me a little embarrassed. I was downright *giddy* to see her again.

"Gotta go," I said abruptly to Buckner who attempted to protest but I was already out the door.

I jumped on *Mary Lou*, and puttered at full throttle up into the Hills. I hadn't forgotten about my Statistics test, of course, but I figured I could study for it tomorrow.

Roughly twenty minutes later, I was squinting at the angry security cameras along the fence. I also waved to the automaton police officer a few yards away. He was staring at me with a lazy brand of mechanical menace from his little booth.

I thought: *If I wasn't allowed, he'd say something, right?*

I took a few cautious steps forward, but he didn't flinch. I turned from him and I saw that a single link in the fence was glowing yellow. *Imbued.* I realized that *that* was what Cassie had used to make the fence roll away. I glanced at the guard again before reaching out and tapping the link. Sure enough, the fence rolled away like it was the secret door in a video game. The automaton cop remained still. I guess I was on his list.

Slightly proud of myself, I climbed down the dusty hillside toward the "H." This time, when I looked at it, I saw a small metallic knob. I fished my keys from my pocket and inserted the magic one. I said, "New York," and opened the door. On the other side was Manhattan. The impressive visage of the New York Public Library stared back at me from across the street. I stepped through the threshold and noticed I'd just exited an office building.

The weirdest thing about using these "backdoors,"—aside from the whole teleportation thing—was the time change. I know that doesn't sound like it would be too weird, but it is. One second, it's noon. The next second it's three o'clock. And while the numbers don't matter too much, it's the *sun.* Its new position in the sky just looks off.

Anyway, I headed toward the tall, marble steps of the library, figuring that's where I'd find Cassie. She was waiting near the top and stood when she saw me.

"Hey," she said.

"Hey."

She was clutching a small paper bag, from which she produced an extra flaky croissant. "I saw this and thought of you." She grinned and held her hand out. "Here."

I had one of those delayed-reaction laughs, where at first I didn't get it, but once I did, I couldn't help myself.

"So," she said. "While you were sleeping, I did some snooping. I think I have a lead on that missing professor guy."

I swallowed a bite of croissant but my mouth was still full. "Wha' 'id 'u find?" I asked.

"I'll show you," she said. "Come on."

I followed her through the library until eventually we had descended down two different sets of elevators to a bleak-looking basement made of solid concrete. Cassie had to use a special key to get us there. Its bare floor was completely empty, save for a stone well—like the type that pulls up water—sitting at the center. Cassie dragged me by the hand to look over its edge.

"*La Grande Bibliothèque de Magie et l'Alchimie,*" she announced in perfect French.

"I don't actually speak French," I said.

"The Grand Library of Magic and Alchemy," she said. "It's right down there."

I frowned into the dark depths of the well, which seemed to go on forever. "Let me guess," I said. "We have to jump in to get there, right?"

"Yep."

"You know, a fear of heights includes jumping into wells," I said.

"Yeah, but it's a short drop. Trust me. You'll be fine."

So I did. I climbed up and jumped in. (Okay, I made that sound extra casual right there. It actually took several minutes to psych myself up to it.)

Once I did, however, I discovered Cassie was right. The fall couldn't have been more than a few feet. And not only that, but I landed on an oversized beanbag. It was bright red. The ones next to it were yellow and green. Cassie landed on a blue one a few spaces over.

I looked around. The place wasn't what I expected at all. When I heard the words "Grand Library," I pictured something more like Rosewood's office, with tall mahogany shelves, great stacks of dusty volumes and high-backed leather chairs. This place looked more like the headquarters of Google. Everything was modern, brand new and brightly colored. *And,* there were people everywhere. Or actually ... *some* were people. A wide assortment of magical creatures lounged throughout the giant reading space. A cluster of Elves were whispering amongst themselves at a nearby table. A garden gnome, just like the one who beat me up, was reading an ancient tome twice his size. A centaur—an honest to God *centaur*—was resting on his haunches and reading a magazine.

"It's a magic-free zone," Cassie explained as she led me toward a row of shelves. "If you do magic here you get banned for life. *And* some Guardian Angels swoop down and beat you up."

"I won't do a thing," I said, only half-listening as I gawked at a mermaid lounging in a hot tub with a romance novel. (At least I *think* it was romance novel. It had a picture of a shirtless merman on the cover wearing a fire helmet.)

Cassie found us a secluded table near the back and took a seat on a bouncy ball. I sat next to her.

"Okay," she said. "Even though we could totally make out back here, I'm gonna show you something else instead."

I gulped.

"So it's not much," she continued, taking a small scrap of singed paper from her pocket, "but I snuck into Steinberg's house and went through his study. It was actually really tough. The whole place was covered in defensive wards." She then gave a little impish smile. "But I have my ways. Anyway. I found a trash can where it looked like he was trying to burn some documents. The only thing I could salvage was this."

She placed the blackened scrap on the table. As far as I could tell, it didn't look like anything. It didn't even have any writing on it.

"Does it do something?" I asked, and tentatively poked at it with my finger.

"It took me an hour to figure it out," she said. "It's not magic. He used a *human* technique. Look." She pressed a button on her watch and a small violet light shined from the dial onto the paper. The letters A, R and X appeared in a strange, archaic font.

"A, R, X," I read aloud. "Does that mean anything to you?"

Cassie grinned. "*That* took me another hour. It's a word. It spells '*arx*,' which is Latin for 'fortress.' Or 'citadel.' Google had several options."

I studied the letters a moment longer. "So what does 'fortress' mean?" I asked.

"I don't know," she said with a shrug. "But it's a start, right?"

And so we spent the next couple hours brainstorming what arx—i.e. fortress—could mean. By the end, neither of us came up with anything remotely plausible. My guess had been that arx was a codeword for a new type of alchemist super shield like the one guarding the Death Star in *Star Wars*. Cassie's guess had been that arx was the name for a new battleship designed to sail through realms as a movable fortress.

It was highly unlikely that either of us was correct.

But I guess that's not really important. The important part is that as we sat there together, I couldn't help but think of what Rosewood had told me earlier. Cassie wasn't safe. I wasn't sure how that could be possible, but that didn't stop me from worrying. What did Rosewood say again? Her strength wouldn't help against "forces like these?" The thought sent a chill down my spine. Every time she looked at me with those cat-like eyes, I got a little butterfly in my stomach. I wondered if when the time came—would I be capable of protecting her?

Chapter Seven

Desperate Spells

SO OVER THE NEXT FEW DAYS, several things happened. First, I aced that Statistics midterm. How, you ask? Well as it turned out, inside the *Vicipaedia* was a book entitled *A Treatise on the Empirical Study of Magic: 1632-1812*. It contained all the information I'd ever need to understand basic statistics, and it only took two minutes, ten seconds to read it. Second, I deleted Meagan from my phone and my Facebook page. Third, I learned two new spells—Basic Levitate and Force Bubble. They were both Level One, yet a lot tougher than my old repertoire of Firelight and Firebolt. Nevertheless, I had a new motivation to get better at this whole wizarding thing. If I was going to keep hanging out with Cassie, I needed to pull my own weight. (Or at least, some small portion of it.) McFadden, meanwhile, was duly impressed by my new work ethic.

"Ah! Your speed astounds me, François! I did not know it was possible to learn at such a glacial pace! It almost makes me wish I were still alive and could conduct a study on the anomaly of your 'slowness.' Remarkable!"

"You don't have to pretend," I told him as I practiced the *Canti* for Force Bubble. "You think I'm amazing."

"Ha! I'll admit a small part of me has warmed to you a bit—much the same way it might if a dull-witted pigeon kept appearing at my window. Although, I suppose the pigeon would be more intelligent. It might get the hint after a few weeks and bother someone else."

I grinned and asked, "Can you show me the *Canti* for FB again?"

I asked that question for two reasons: 1.) I'd recently discovered that McFadden—no matter how much crap he gave me—had to do what I said. This simple fact bugged him to no end and he knew that I knew it. 2.) He strongly objected to calling Force Bubble, "FB." He was a purist, after all, but I explained to him that we now lived in the age of acronyms—to which he expressed a profound sense of relief that he was dead.

So with a sour face, he showed me the *Canti* for FB.

"Any chance you could show me again?" I asked.

His face pinched even more. "Well, of course," he said. "I should've guessed. We'll be here for the next century and a half as you learn this basic spell, won't we? Very well. I'll do it *slowly* for you. Try not to pass out from the information overload."

And so we continued practicing for a few more hours. Eventually, I could do both spells about ninety percent of the time. The remaining ten percent, I'd screw up a note or two, and the spell would pop like a soap bubble.

Still, I'd had enough for one day. Practicing magic was just like piano practice when I was a kid. It was really draining. Not because it was physically tiring—but because when you did it, you were actually concentrating the entire time. It wasn't something you could do on autopilot.

I left the Solitar and headed back out to the living room where I found Buckner playing against Brian in a split-screen of *Kill 'em All!* From the sound of things, it seemed like Buckner was winning.

"You're a little bitch!" Brian shouted, angling the controller and hammering his thumb on the trigger.

I flopped down on the couch and watched. I winced as Brian got hit with a tank shell. "Ouch," I said.

"I'm taking Tupac here to school," Buckner declared.

"You're a little bitch," Brian said again. (He stuck with the classics.)

I decided to egg him on a little. "Brian, you *suck*," I said.

"Yeah? Why don't you step into the ring, Frenchie? I'll take your goddamned head off with a chainsaw."

"I think François's got plans today," Buckner said.

I raised an eyebrow at him. "I do?"

"Well you'd be crazy if you didn't, homeboy. Who was that off-the-charts hottie who stopped by the other day? I'd've asked ya about her sooner, but I didn't wanna jinx nothin'."

I knew he was referring to Cassie, of course, but I couldn't resist playing dumb. "Who?" I asked.

"*Who?* Shoot, hoss. Don't even try to play that game with me. You know exactly who I'm talkin' about. She was like six feet tall, way hotter than any guy deserves—except me of course—and kinda Asian-looking, but not quite. Ring any bells there, Casanova?"

"Oh, her," I said. "Yeah, she's cool."

Buckner snorted. "Looks like I ain't the only one tryin' not to jinx things. See that, Shakur?" He nudged Brian with his elbow. "François here's dating a supermodel and he's cool as a cucumber. You could learn a thing or two from that."

"You're a little bitch!" Brian shouted.

I laughed and watched for another half hour until I got a text from Cassie. I was mildly surprised that it was all business. It said: "URGENT. Death priest in NY. Meet me at H sign ASAP."

Whoa …

I had another delayed reaction as I stared at the screen. *A death priest?* I wasn't totally sure what that was, but it didn't sound good. Plus, the fact that Cassie didn't seem excited about it put the hairs on the back of my neck to full attention. Did she mean that she and I were supposed to *fight it?* Crap, I only knew four spells …

"Shoot, that's her, ain't it?!" Buckner exclaimed.

I looked up. "Uh, I gotta go," I said. I started to stand, but paused mid-crouch. I looked at Buckner. This could be the last time I ever saw him. "Hey man," I said. "I love you."

"You're a little bitch!" Brian screamed at the TV.

Buckner raised an eyebrow at me. "Well I'll be damned. She's brought out your sensitive side, amigo. Love you too. Now go get 'em."

I took the familiar route to the Hollywood Sign with *Mary Lou* puttering at full speed. (In case you're wondering, that's about forty-five miles per hour.) I got there in record time using some of Cassie's driving techniques.

When I arrived at the hilltop overlooking the sign, I saw her car, but not her. It seemed a little odd that she wasn't waiting for me. Usually she did, but this time I figured she must have gone through the door already. Maybe she was waiting on the other side. I trotted down the hillside to press the yellow link and roll aside the fence. I didn't even look at the guard. Once I was through the backdoor, I found myself exiting the same office building in Manhattan and staring up at the Public Library. Nothing seemed amiss—no dark, swirling clouds gathering overhead or anything like that. The only thing that *was* weird was the absence of Cassie. I got out my phone and texted her. After a minute of waiting and not hearing back, I decided something was wrong. I went back through the door and returned to LA. I noticed that the guard was gone.

Crap.

I didn't know what that meant, but it definitely wasn't good. I did the only thing I could think of. I called Rosewood.

"Ah, a pleasant surprise, François. Is everything well?"

"I can't find Cassie," I told him in a rush. "She texted me a half hour ago to meet her at the Hollywood Sign but she's not here. She said something about a death priest."

Rosewood's tone changed immediately. "Her vehicle, François. Is it there?"

"It is," I answered.

"Damn. Listen to me carefully. Do you have your Solitar with you?"

I checked my pocket. "I do," I said.

"Good. I need you to go inside it and learn a new spell. It is a Level Three. Time is a factor so you must do it quickly. Do you understand?"

"What's the spell?" I said.

"It is called *Vigilia Temporis.* McFadden will explain the rest. Go *now.*"

I didn't say another word but popped open the Zippo and sparked the flint. McFadden was already waiting for me on the football field. He held up a dismissive hand. "No need to explain," he said. "I know everything. Flip to page two-thirty-one and keep your head on straight. You only have minutes, so we must make every second count. Is that clear?"

I nodded and opened *Intro to Spellcasting.* My space inside the Solitar had already become populated with a number of desks, workbenches and random other stuff in my own version of an outdoor Bat Cave. I settled at one of the desks and peered at page two-thirty-one. This is what I saw:

Vigilia Temporis
IVΩ IVΦ IIIΨ VIIΣ ΧΔ IIΓ VΦ ΧΨ IIΓ VIIΩ IIIΔ
IIΣ IΧΓ IIΨ IIIΦ IIΔ IIIΣ IVΦ IIIΨ

Shit, I thought.

"That is of no use to anyone," McFadden said and smacked the desk with his cane. "Focus. Look at each *Cantus* and 'play the note.' It is very simple. Take one at a time."

I formed an *Imago* and made the gestures with my fingers. I'd never even attempted a spell like this. It was like playing Mozart when all you know is the theme from *Top Gun.* It had all kinds of Gammas, Phis and Deltas that required a far more delicate touch than I was used to. Still, I made it about a third of the way through before my first screw up.

"Damn," I breathed. "What does this spell even do?"

I restarted with a fresh *Imago,* as McFadden said, "It allows you to peer into the past by a period of twenty-seven minutes, thirty-eight seconds. And before you ask, the odd time allotment was conceived by another race. Now hurry. Thirty seconds have already passed outside the Solitar. You may only have thirty seconds more before it is too late."

Too late for what? I still didn't know what was happening. Had Cassie been kidnapped? By who? Or by what? And how was *Vigilia Temporis* going to help?

I refocused on the spell. I made it about halfway through. It was those damn Deltas that were the hardest. They were like pressing a piano key with a feather.

"You're getting closer, François," McFadden noted. "But you're thinking too much. Let your fingers do the work. Not your head. Understand?"

I nodded, thinking: *No head. Fingers only.*

I made another *Imago.* The first few *Canti* went by in a breeze. Then I made my first Delta and it worked. I kept going. I made it through a couple more Gammas and Phis and even a Delta, and then—like a miracle—I was within two *Canti* of completing the spell.

Now, as any big league pitcher might tell you, this is where the pressure lies. It's those last few pitches that really get your heart going. Everything is on the line. Success is only a split second away, and the game is yours to lose. I paused to take a breath. My right ring finger made a Phi. The *Fulmen* stuck in place. I exhaled. Then my right middle finger made a nice, easy Psy.

Boom.

Vigilia Temporis.

Once or twice in my life, I've felt pretty proud of myself for a few of things. Winning that one wrestling match. Doing my first hangman with a yo-yo. But learning a Level Three spell in less than a minute topped them all.

McFadden tapped his cane on the desk again. "Quickly now," he said. "Cast the spell outside the Solitar. Use your mind to rewind time and then watch the proceedings on 'fast-forward.' With any luck, you will discover what happened to your friend. Good luck."

I told him, "Thanks," and zipped back outside. I didn't waste any time looking around. I cast the spell and a small, misty cloud appeared in front of me. It swirled into a spiral until its center was clear as glass, like the eye of a hurricane. Through it, I saw a fisheye view of the very spot where I was standing. No one was there. I remembered McFadden saying to "fast-forward" with my mind. Once I did, little bugs started zipping across the image while blades of grass vibrated unnaturally. It lasted a few seconds until I saw her. The view instantly slowed to normal speed. Cassie rolled the fence aside and headed down to the H. She waited outside it, staring at her phone. A full minute passed with nothing happening. I was about to fast-forward again when I jumped in shock.

There are some things that are just flat out *scary.* Public speaking. The little girl from *The Ring.* And a certain species of spider called a "trapdoor spider." It doesn't use a web. It digs a little hole in the ground, hides in it, and then jumps out and drags you inside when you walk past. And by "you," I'm referring to its typical prey of crickets and small mice. Unless of course *magic* is involved, in which case, the trapdoor spider is the size of a car. And also—unless I was seeing things—it had the upper body of a human female attached to its the front, kind of like a "spider centaur." Or something.

It jumped out in a spray of dirt and grabbed Cassie before she could react. Her body went limp as soon as it touched her. It then pulled her back underground. The whole exchange only took about a second.

I dropped the spell and looked to the spot where it grabbed her. The ground looked totally normal. There weren't any telltale signs of a recently dug hole.

My first instinct was to call Rosewood again, but my feet—already moving toward the spider hole—vetoed that plan. I was going after Cassie and I wasn't waiting another second. When I reached the spot, I stared at the dirt. I kicked it a few times, but it was solid. Then I saw it. It was so tiny I easily could've missed it. A pebble, about the size of a pinhead, glowed in a muted, olive green. I poked it with my finger and the ground opened up beneath me.

Sometimes with the benefit of hindsight, you realize you should've done certain things differently. Like for example, I could've stood back a little or kicked at the pebble with my toe. Instead, I bent over at the waist, peered directly at it, and *poked*. The next thing I knew, I was tumbling face-first into darkness before crashing through a tangle of sticky cobwebs and landing on a rock. I groaned and rolled onto my feet to get my bearings. I was in a large cave and it was nearly pitch black. I made a Firelight to get a better view.

I'd never felt more like Indiana Jones in my entire life as I pushed my way through giant spider webs by torchlight. And—just like Indiana—it didn't take long before I found what I was looking for. A long, human-sized cocoon dangled from a stalactite in the ceiling while the spider woman crawled creepily nearby. She was working intently on another web. She was so focused, in fact, that she didn't even notice my Firelight for a full second and a half until she spun around to hiss at me.

Now at this moment, I'd like to point out a very critical difference between men and women. You see, as a guy, there are certain things that I can't help but notice—no matter the circumstance. In this case, it was the fact that the spider woman was bare-breasted and surprisingly attractive. Her hair looked to be dreadlocked in thick rows while her features belonged to those of a high fashion model. Now if the situation were reversed, of course, a girl probably wouldn't have noticed these things. But I sure did. Spider Woman's boobs were quite bouncy.

Anyway.

The point is that she saw me. Her eight legs moved deliberately along the walls, while her eyes remained pinned on mine. I edged closer to Cassie—or at least what I assumed was Cassie in the cocoon—and ditched my Firelight for a Firebolt. I tossed it at the thin strand of webbing fixing her to the ceiling. I did my best to catch her when she fell, although I didn't really *catch* her. It was more like I broke her fall with my torso and got the wind knocked out of me. When I got back to my feet, Spider Woman was only a few yards away. Her spider body was sideways, but her human torso was bent to face me.

I took a step back and told her I didn't want any trouble. (I honestly couldn't think of anything better to say. It was a weird situation.)

She hissed in response, opening her mouth a little too wide for comfort. It revealed rows of long pointy teeth. Any thoughts I had about her being attractive vanished immediately. They were replaced with the very deep, profound and primal fear of getting eaten. I scrambled to lift Cassie's cocoon over my shoulder and backed away a few more steps. It occurred to me that if Spider Woman decided to move quickly—especially in this environment—she could be on me in a heartbeat.

I formed a plan. It might not have been a *good* plan, but it was a plan. I crouched slowly to set Cassie down and formed an

Imago. Spider Woman hissed at the sudden brightness. Her legs tightened, almost imperceptibly, but I could tell she was about to strike. I quickly did the *Canti* for Force Bubble. It popped up right as a yawning maw of razor-sharp teeth lunged for my face. They clamped upon a transparent barrier a few inches from my outstretched palm. The impact made her reel back with a howling screech. I made a quick Firebolt and threw it at her. She dodged it easily, moving sideways like a crab. I threw another and another until I got her right in the seam between her woman torso and spider thorax. It made her screech and sent her scrambling a few yards away, slapping at the spot with her hands.

Now was my chance. I popped the Force Bubble and grabbed Cassie. I dragged her with one hand, while I made a Firelight with the other. We quickly reached the spot where I first fell through. Then the clicking of too many legs came up behind me and Spider Woman lashed out with her claws. They caught my shirt as I rolled away. There was a small sting, but nothing serious. I attempted to form Basic Levitate, but screwed it up. Still, I had just enough time to throw a last-second Firebolt at Spider Woman's face. She ducked but one of her dreads caught the flame and ignited. This made her even more frantic than when I got her in the torso.

I ran back to Cassie and tried BL for a second time. It worked and I cast it between her cocoon and myself. Then we were both drifting upward like a pair of astronauts in space. The speed was infuriatingly slow—but then again, this was *Basic* Levitate. The faster stuff took practice.

Spider Woman made a final lunge, but I got her with another Firebolt. She hissed in rage before a sudden explosion of earth brought us back above ground. I grabbed Cassie and trudged up the hillside as fast as my legs could carry us. When we got back to the road, I leaned her against the Mustang and started tearing the webs from her face. Underneath, she was breathing but unconscious. I didn't see any bite marks. Frantically, and with an eye on the spider hole, I called Rosewood. He answered within a millisecond.

"I've got her," I panted, still huffing from the run.

"Is she conscious?"

"No. She's breathing, though. The thing that took her was like a giant spider with a woman's body. It's still down there. Can it crawl back up?"

There was a pause. "Dear me," Rosewood breathed, sounding a little surprised. "You are describing a Drider. Very dangerous indeed. François, listen to me. You must get Cassandra to the hospital. There is no time to lose."

"Which one?" I asked.

"There is a magic hospital nearby. Its backdoor is located within the Magic Castle. Do you know where that is?"

The "Magic Castle" that Rosewood was referring to, ironically, had nothing to do with real magic. It was a famous mansion in Hollywood designed to be the world's premier venue for magic shows—i.e. card tricks and disappearing coins. It had a fabled history, opening in the early 1960s, and every magician of note from Blaine to Copperfield had at one point performed there. Also, it had a very exclusive membership. No one could enter without an ID pin, and I—unfortunately—didn't have one.

"I'm not a member," I said, already hoisting Cassie up and dragging her toward the passenger door.

"I will call ahead, do not worry about that," Rosewood said.

I starting ripping more webs off Cassie's body and managed to fish her keys from her pocket. A quick thrill jolted through me at the thought of driving her car.

"When you arrive, there will be someone to greet you," Rosewood continued. "He will lead you to the hospital's backdoor. Is everything clear?"

I told him I understood and trotted around to the driver's side. I pulled the door closed and twisted the ignition. The engine came to life with a deeply satisfying rumble. I gunned the accelerator and wound down the hill like a race car driver. I could suddenly understand Cassie's unique driving habits—it was hard to drive the car any other way. A few minutes later, I skidded to a halt next to the Magic Castle's valet parking stand and jumped out. A short, middle-aged man in a white coat bounded over to greet me.

"Where is the patient?" he asked with a sense of urgency. He had a slight accent that I couldn't place.

I opened the door and started to pull Cassie out. He gave her a quick once over and declared, "Drider bite. We must get her to the ER. Quickly now."

He grabbed her feet and helped me carry her inside. Once we were in the mansion's main entryway, a bookshelf along the sidewall slid open to reveal a hidden door. We carried Cassie through a short hallway until we reached another door. The man—who I assumed was a doctor—jangled a set of keys from his pocket and undid the lock. The door opened into what I now recognized to be a completely new location. The walls were bright white—almost blinding—while doctors and nurses rushed in all directions. I figured this had to be the emergency room. A trio of red-faced gnomes arrived pushing an empty cart. They told us to hand her over and we gently set her on the thin mattress. They wheeled her off in a flash. The doctor who had helped me turned and took me by the elbow.

"They will take good care of her," he assured me. He then stopped when he saw the small scratch from the Drider's claws on my shoulder. He peered at it a second, lifting my sleeve to get a better view. "Stay here," he said curtly and then disappeared into the knot of commotion criss-crossing the room. He reemerged a minute later with a tiny vial pinched between his fingers. "Drink this," he said, nearly shoving it toward my lips. I did what he said, and as far as I could tell, it didn't have any taste. Or at least, it had the same non-taste that water does. Either way, I asked him what it was.

"You'll be fine," he said. "Just a precaution."

"What about my friend?" I asked. "Is she going to be okay?"

He shook his head. "I didn't see any signs the poison had taken root. Our team should be able to extract it without any issues. If all goes well, she'll be good as new in a few hours." He then cocked his head and gave me a strange look. "You're not familiar with Driders?" he asked.

I told him no.

"But … you're a wizard, are you not?" He seemed strangely confused.

"I guess I'm sort of a recent arrival," I explained. "It's a long story."

He looked at me a moment longer and then shrugged. "Well, you're free to wait here if you wish. Otherwise, we will be in touch. I suggest you call Thomas. I know he'd appreciate knowing you got his girl here safely. Tell him that Alexander told you she will be fine."

With that, he blended back into the chaos of the ER. The place was *crowded.* I noticed that plenty of the patients looked human—although there were lots of pointy ears for Elves. There were also a number of creatures that I didn't recognize at all. Perhaps if I'd taken a Greek mythology class at some point, I'd have been better equipped. I stared at them all in perplexed silence until I collapsed backward into a chair. I got out my phone and called Rosewood.

"Well done, François," he said, sighing in relief after I'd told him everything. "You have saved Cassandra's life. I cannot tell you what this means to me. I am forever in your debt."

"You did all the thinking," I said. "I'm in *your* debt. Seriously. Thank you."

"I only wish I could've gotten there in time myself. A Drider is no small foe. They are most dangerous."

"Why was it there?" I asked. "It wasn't before."

"A mystery I intend to solve, François. Rest assured of that."

Then—with a sudden panic—I remembered why I'd gone to the Hollywood Sign in the first place. I bolted upright. "Wait," I said. "Cassie texted me about a death priest in New York. Do I need to—?"

Rosewood cut me off. "No," he said firmly. "I will deal with that personally."

I paused a moment. There was something about the way he said that last bit that gave me a chill—like beneath the charming accent, Agent Thomas J. Rosewood was a serious, *serious* badass.

"Thanks," I told him.

"Just get some rest, François. I'll be in touch."

Chapter Eight

You Like Me

THE NEXT MORNING, I lay in bed staring at the ceiling after an incredibly fitful night of non-sleep. I had my phone lying next to my ear, but I still hadn't heard any news about Cassie. I thought several times of calling Rosewood, but I didn't want to bother him. He'd call me when he knew something. Still, it felt like I'd been staring at that ceiling all night. I was about to call it quits and get up for some coffee when there was a quiet knock on the apartment door. (Not my room, but the main door to the apartment.) I fumbled out of bed to see who it was. A tiny thrill of hope spiked through me as I thought it might be Cassie. When I opened the door, however, I was greeted with a surprise. Meagan stood there, holding a shoebox and biting her lip. "Hey," she said. Her voice was a lot softer than the last time I saw her.

"Hey," I answered.

She raised the shoebox a fraction. "I brought some of your stuff. Can I come in?"

For a split second, I thought about how strange it was that Meagan was *asking* if she could come in. For a year and a half she hadn't needed an invitation. Yet now, she did. It was one of those weird relationship things. It's like as soon as it ends, this little wall springs up and there's nothing you can do about it.

"Yeah, of course," I said, standing aside.

172

She slipped past me and took a few steps before spinning around. "Can we talk?" she asked.

"Sure."

"Like, privately?"

"We can go to my room?" I suggested.

"Okay."

She didn't move but waited for me to lead the way. Once we got there, I closed the door behind us. She set the shoebox on my dresser and fidgeted with a toy Army Man that was crouched behind a pair of socks. (I'm not sure why he was there. It's not like I still play with toy soldiers when no one's looking. I don't. I swear.)

Meagan put him down and turned to me with a tiny smile. "I see some things never change," she said.

"Who?" I said. "G.I. Jackson? I have no idea how he got there."

She gave me a look. "Right. So how've you been?"

"Um ... busy. You?"

"The same. Mostly school stuff."

She then hesitated and I hesitated and we both just kind of stood there for a second. It wasn't an "awkward" silence exactly, but I wouldn't call it comfortable either. Eventually, Meagan took a sudden step forward. "So last week was kind of ..." She paused mid-sentence and stared at me.

"Crappy," I said after a moment. "I was kind of a jerk. I'm sorry about that."

Her eyes widened and she stepped back. "*What?*"

"When I told you to get out of my apartment," I said. "That was mean. I shouldn't have said it like that."

For some reason, she looked suddenly furious. "François, are you kidding me right now?"

"What?"

"Are you really that clueless?"

I furrowed my brow as she looked at me like I was a space alien. "I suppose it's possible ..." I said hesitantly.

"The reason I was so mad was that you weren't *more* of a jerk! I mean, I *cheated* on you! Like, a lot! And then you were being all calm about it and I felt like the worst person ever!"

"I still shouldn't have kicked you out like that," I said.

"You're still doing it!" she screeched.

"Sorry?"

"*Ugh!*" She balled her fists. "You're not going to make this easy, are you? It would be so much better if you started yelling and throwing things. At least then I could start throwing things back."

I looked around and spotted one of G.I. Jackson's tiny companions on my bed. I picked it up and threw it at her.

"That's not funny," she said flatly. (I caught a tiny smile, though.)

"Look, Meagan, it's alright," I said. "I mean it sucked when I saw you with him and it still sucks when I think about it, but it's over now. Don't worry about it. I'll be fine. And you'll definitely be fine. There's not a guy in this whole school who wouldn't go out with you in a heartbeat."

"*God ...*" She looked at me and sighed. "Anyway. I just wanted to say it's not like I never liked you or anything, okay? I did like you. Or ... I *do* like you. And you *were* my real boyfriend. Not Jake. I mostly just said that to piss you off."

"But you are ... seeing him though, right? That wasn't just a one time thing?"

She groaned, but not at me. "I'm definitely *not* seeing Jake. After I left your apartment I called him. Thirty seconds later, I realized how excruciating it is to actually *talk* to that guy. He and I never did much of it. It was more of a ... *physical* thing."

"Hmm." I nodded solemnly. "That's what I like to call TMI. But thanks for the mental image."

She winced. "Sorry."

"But I get it," I told her. "Besides, it's not the end of the world. We had a lot of fun together, right? You were the first girl I ever danced with who didn't punch me in the face. That has to count for something. Plus, I'll be dining out on stories of your father for the rest of my life. Do you know he called me a 'flapping pussy' when we were in the bathroom at Spago? I mean, it sucked at the time, but now it's actually pretty funny."

Meagan's mouth fell open. "He *said* that?"

"Yep."

She tried—unsuccessfully—to stifle a grin. "Wow. He is kind of an asshole, isn't he?"

"He is. But he obviously cares about you. I've heard stories about dads trying to intimidate their daughters' boyfriends, but he really took it to the next level."

"I guess he did," she said, and then looked up at me. "So ... you don't hate me?"

I stepped closer to give her a small hug. "I don't hate you. I don't hate anybody. Besides," —I pulled back to look at her— "you have a lot of really hot friends. It'd be a shame to waste a resource like that."

"Oh my God, you're mean!" She punched my shoulder.

"I don't mean for me," I said quickly. "Crap, that came out wrong. I just mean my roommates would kill me if I didn't ask for some introductions. Especially Brian. He needs all the help he can get."

Meagan pushed back. "Which one is Brian?"

"The short one."

She scrunched her nose and shook her head. "The tall one is who I'm thinking of. The one with the accent."

"Buckner," I said.

Her eyes suddenly lit up. "*That's* the one. I totally forgot to tell you. You know my roommate, Krista?"

"The one who hates me?"

"Yeah. She got super drunk a few nights ago at this party and told me she was in love with your tall roommate, but I couldn't remember his name. Do you think he'd like her?"

I told her that he definitely would.

And that was that for me and Meagan Goodman. We were going to be friends. It taught me something really important, actually. Sometimes people do crappy things, but that doesn't mean that's who they are. The fact is there's a whole world going on inside everyone's head, and it's big and it's loud and it's complicated, and it's a miracle when you can learn even the slightest thing about it. Meagan might have cheated on me and it definitely wasn't cool. But someday—and this day may never come—I might screw up a tiny bit myself. And when I do, I'll do my best to fix it. Meagan had just done exactly that. She didn't have to come over this morning. She didn't have to speak to me ever again. (Heck, I'd deleted her from my phone.) But she came over anyway. Not to yell or get back together or anything like that. She came over to make things right. Or at least, *better*. That took courage. And because of it, neither of us lost a friend. I'd have to remember that for the future ...

• • •

By the late afternoon, I couldn't take it anymore. I needed to know how Cassie was doing. I'd tried texting her, but I'm pretty sure her phone got smashed when the Drider jumped on her. Thus, my only option was to bother Rosewood. I knew he'd be friendly if I called him, but I still didn't want to bug the guy.

"Oh, nonsense!" he declared after I apologized. "I was about to call you, in fact. I am pleased to announce that Cassandra is doing very well. The doctors released her a few hours ago."

A tidal wave of relief washed over me. Once it passed, however, there was a teeny, tiny bit of betrayal when I realized she hadn't called me yet. I asked Rosewood where she was and he gave a light chuckle before responding.

"Between you and me, François, I dare say Cassandra is a bit embarrassed. Don't tell her I told you, of course, but I fear she's feeling rather shy at the moment. You must understand, our succubus friend is quite a ferocious creature herself, so to get taken by a Drider is something of an insult."

"Oh," I said. "So … should I not mention it or something?"

"Ha! That's up to you. It all depends on whether you're prepared for hand-to-hand combat with a super assassin."

"Mums the word," I said.

"A wise decision. Now as it happens, I'm due to meet with her here in Washington shortly. Would you care to join us?"

"Oh. Is that okay?"

"Of course. What she and I have to discuss concerns you as well. We will be meeting at the Old Ebbitt Grill in a few minutes at seven o'clock. Although—if I might make a suggestion—I would avoid the backdoor in the Hollywood Sign for the time being. There is another one behind Jumbo's Clown Room. It will put you onto Dupont Circle."

After fiddling with Google Maps for a second, I threw on some clean clothes and headed toward Hollywood Boulevard. I maneuvered *Mary Lou* into the alley behind Jumbo's and found a back exit. It had a small lock above the handle where I could use my key. I said, "Washington, D.C.," and pushed the door open.

When I went through, I looked back to see I'd just exited a bookstore. Also, I realized—a tad too late—that the genius plan I had come up with in LA wasn't so genius after all. You see, I didn't *walk* through the backdoor into D.C. I *scootered* through it. That way, I figured, I'd still have some wheels when I got to the other side. It didn't occur to me that it might look weird to people when I arrived. I was spared no shortage of Should-I-Call-The-Police looks from numerous passersby. Plus, the store was sunken below street level, so I had to rev *Mary Lou's* engine and scooter up a small flight of stairs. I felt like a weirdo. Once I was on the road, though, I blended back into traffic.

I pulled up outside the Old Ebbitt Grill and parked the scooter. (One of the perks of *Mary Lou* was the ability to park her anywhere. It was like being a visiting diplomat.) I spotted Rosewood sitting with Cassie in a dark booth in the far corner. They were both hunched and whispering, though they straightened when I approached.

"Good of you to join us," Rosewood said, half-standing from his seat.

Cassie glanced up, but then looked back at the table.

"Hey," I said to her.

"Hey," she mumbled, but didn't look up.

I sat next to Rosewood. It felt weird not saying anything about yesterday—even something small like, "I'm glad you're okay." But if Rosewood didn't think it was a good idea, I trusted his judgment. He knew Cassie a lot better than I did.

"So," I said, clapping my hands. "How's everyone doing?"

Yeah. That was a stupid thing to say. But I had to say something, right?

Rosewood sighed. "Not so well, I'm afraid." His voice hushed again and he leaned forward. "As I was just telling Cassandra, it concerns our missing professor. The BPI has taken a much greater interest in his disappearance. The Vampire Lord, Aeroth, provided them with intelligence—intelligence that they are not willing to share. They have now begun a full spectrum search for Steinberg, and I fear their motives are not in the best interest of this realm."

I knitted my brow. Weren't the BPI the good guys?

"But I thought you wanted them to find him," I said.

Rosewood nodded gravely. "I did. But I fear my recent efforts have uncovered some unfortunate truths." He glanced sideways before continuing. "I believe the BPI to be compromised," he whispered. "I cannot be sure, but their behavior has changed in unsettling ways. There is a darkness to them now that wasn't there before. They have two agents tailing me—which I assure you is quite unprecedented. Several of my colleagues are under surveillance as well. This is a very troubling development. It is *also* why I must rely so heavily upon you. There is only so much I can do while I am being watched. I need you two to do something for me."

Cassie suddenly looked up. "Anything," she said. Her eyes, I noticed, were fierce.

"I need you to return to the Grand Library," Rosewood said. "There is a book there—a very old book that you will need permission to read."

"From the library?" I asked.

"Yes. And it must be *you* to do it, François. The book can only be read by a wizard."

"What is it?"

Rosewood studied the table a moment. "It was written by a very extraordinary man of magic. You know him as Galileo Galilei—one of the fathers of modern science. He was, in fact, the most brilliant alchemist the world has ever known. The book you seek details several of his most prominent inventions. I need you to find a certain passage, *Inter Regna Telescopio.* Here, I've written it down." He slid a small paper across the tabletop. "Your task will be simple. I need you to memorize the full passage. It will be in Latin, of course, but there is no other way. The words will not appear in a photograph and magic is not allowed in the library."

I unfolded the little paper to see a number of Latin words penned in a delicate hand. It made me a little nervous. Memorizing a bunch of Latin didn't sound easy.

"How long is the passage?" I asked.

"A few paragraphs at least." He gave me a pleading look. "You can do this François. Just take it one sentence at a time. Once you're confident that you know every single word by heart, call me and I will take it down. I would do it myself, as you know, but I cannot let this clue fall into the wrong hands. The consequences could be quite dire."

I told him I'd do my best, and a few minutes later, I found myself trailing Cassie out the restaurant's front exit. (Rosewood had used the rear, which had a direct backdoor to the SIA.) She still wasn't looking at me, even as I followed her to where she'd parked. I wasn't surprised at all when I saw her ride. It was possibly the most aggressive looking speed bike I'd ever seen. It was jet black, just like her Mustang, with big angry wheels and a massive engine. Once seated, she finally looked at me. Her face was hard to read. "So you want to follow?" she asked.

If I had to guess, I'd say she looked *annoyed*. I wanted to ask her if I did something wrong. I mean, did I miss something? Why was she being so weird? Instead, I just asked if we were going straight to New York.

"I know a backdoor that will take us to the library," she said

"Okay," I said, and then paused. I cracked a small grin as I glanced down at her motorcycle. "Just, uh, take it easy, okay?"

She frowned.

"I don't think *Mary Lou* can keep up with that thing," I explained.

Cassie followed my eyes to the insane motorbike between her legs and looked up. "Oh," she said. "Yeah."

"Cool."

• • •

The sun was beginning to dip behind the Manhattan skyline when we arrived on the library's front steps. One of the cool things about New York is that it gets dark a little early because the skyscrapers block the sun before the horizon gets a chance.

We headed through the crowded library until we arrived at the ultra-modern magic library. Cassie seemed to know exactly where to go. I followed her down a dozen flights of stairs until we reached a small librarian's booth amidst an entire floor stacked with books reaching to the ceiling. Sitting at the booth wearing a dark suit and glasses was a balding middle-aged man who—even at a distance—looked incredibly creepy. As we approached, he had this awkward, serial killer smile attached to his face like a Lego, and when he spoke, he had a thick, German accent.

"*Guten Tag!*" he said brightly. "Ve don't get many visitors down hyere! Zis must be my lucky day, ja?"

"We're, uh, looking for a book," I told him.

"I should think so! Zis is a library! Hahahaha. Do you know ze title?"

When he laughed he literally said ha and ha and ha. I recoiled slightly, but managed to fish the paper Rosewood had given me from my pocket.

The Nazi interrogator from *Raiders of the Lost Ark* adjusted his glasses and took a look at it. "Hmm." He licked his lips. "Ja, zis is a good one. Hey!" He looked up excitedly. "Are you avare of ze dance beats of Felix Jaehn?" He started bobbing up and down in a little dance. I glanced at Cassie and she gave me a shrug. I turned back to our librarian who had raised his arms, bent at the elbows, and started club dancing behind the booth.

"So …" I said slowly. "It's kind of important. Is the book available?"

He kept swaying his hips with his arms raised. "Life is short, ja? You have to dance, dance, dance! Vhy is zis book so important, heh? You have zis beautiful *fräulein* hyere!" He gave a slow wink to Cassie, who suddenly spoke up. "It's for a bet," she explained. "Our friend Quentin thinks he invented something new. We bet him a hundred bucks he was wrong."

The librarian stopped dancing. "Ooo!" He rubbed his hands together. "An itsy-bitsy wager! Zis is most exciting!"

"Yeah, so we're really in a hurry," I said. "Is there any chance we can—"

"*Nein! Du musst mir alles über diese Wette erzählen!*"

I took an involuntary step backward. Then, in a blink, Creepy Librarian looked bashful.

"Oops! Sometimes I get excited and ze German comes out! You need zis book right away?"

"Yep."

He flashed me a grin. "Your vish is my command, heir ... ew, I do not know your name!"

"François," I said.

"Ah! *Ravi de vous rencontrer, François!*"

"Thanks."

"I am Hans Müller! I vill get ze book right away! You two vait hyere, ja?"

With that, he bounded into the endless stacks and disappeared. I turned to Cassie and gave her a "what the fuck was that?" look. She just smirked and gave another shrug.

A few minutes later, Hans reemerged carrying a dusty, leather satchel with the book inside. He climbed back into the booth and laid the case on the countertop with care. "You must sign hyere," he said, indicating an open logbook accompanied by a little ink jar and a feather. I couldn't help but get a little excited. My inner five-year-old had always wanted to scratch his signature into an old book with brittle pages using ink and a quill. (That's not weird, is it? Surely I can't be the only one ...)

Cassie and I made it back up to the main room where we found an empty table. There were only a few other library-goers quietly reading nearby, and I noticed that all of them looked human. Although, who can tell?

"Have you found it?" Cassie asked after I'd flipped through the pages for a few minutes.

"I think so," I said. "Check this out."

I showed her the passage for *Inter Regna Telescopio.* Her eyes scanned the page until they flicked up to mine. They flashed with what appeared to be poorly restrained amusement. "That, um … sucks," she said after a pause. Her lips remained curved in a small smile.

"Yes," I agreed. "It sucks."

The passage for *Inter Regna Telescopio*—only a "few paragraphs," according to Rosewood—was frighteningly long. *And* it was all in Latin, in case you've forgotten about that part. The writing looked like the Seventeenth Century version of fine print—and it covered an entire encyclopedia-sized page from top to bottom. And I had to *memorize it.* Word for word.

"So, um, maybe I'll just leave you to it?" Cassie suggested.

I frowned at her. "Sure," I said. "I'll just be here. For the rest of my life."

"Cool." She grinned and bounded away from the table in a flash of ponytail and cut-off shorts.

I scowled after her a moment and then down at the book. I could've sworn the full page of dense Latin was laughing at me. I began reading, sounding out the words and using my finger to trace under the lines. It didn't take more than a few seconds before I realized how hopeless this was. Then—in my despair— I got an idea. It was the type of idea that makes you feel like an idiot for not having it sooner. I didn't need to memorize the entire page at once. I could memorize a small chunk of it, run outside so that I could use my phone, and then call Rosewood to give him the passage in pieces. Genius, right? I thought so. The only problem was that I didn't know if I could leave the book unattended while I escaped outside. And there was no way I was going back downstairs to leave it with Hans Müller. Thus, I'd have to wait for Cassie to return so she could watch it. In the meantime, I set to work on memorizing as much as I could.

When she finally got back—three freaking hours later—
she was carrying a flimsy, pink, cardboard box.

"Make any progress?" she asked and flopped down into an
empty chair. She slid the box in my direction and rested her
chin on her palms. "Here," she said. "I got you some donuts. I
ate a couple, though. There's only one left."

I opened the box and found half of a jelly donut resting in
a little puddle. I looked up and told her I was touched.

"Hey, it's not my fault," she said. "This assignment is so
boring and I didn't want to bother you and ... *whatever.* So are
you like halfway done, or three quarters or what?"

I frowned down at my place in the book. "Three and a half
sentences," I said.

Now, I know what you're thinking. You're thinking three
and a half sentences doesn't sound like much, right? You're
wrong. These were long sentences. And in Latin. Let's see how
far *you* get in three hours.

"Is that a lot?" Cassie's nose wrinkled.

"No," I said. "But I've got a plan. I'm going to memorize it
in pieces. Every couple sentences, I'll duck outside and call
them in to Rosewood. I just need you to stay with the book."

She looked miserable. "Ugh ... Are you sure there's no
other way?"

"Positive."

"*Fiiinne.* Go call him. Just hurry, okay?"

I told her I'd be back in a flash—though to be honest, I
was a little annoyed. Apparently even Cassie had her quirks,
and one of them, it seemed, was a serious dislike for hanging
out in the library. It wasn't like *she* had to memorize a bunch of
Latin. Was she still miffed about the spider thing, or what?

When I got outside, I realized it was getting pretty late. It
was almost 10:30, and I still had a million hours to go. I called
Rosewood and gave him my three and a half sentences. He—
unlike Cassie—seemed duly impressed and encouraged me to

keep going. He also promised he'd do whatever he could to figure things out. With any luck, he said, he might find what he was looking for without me needed to memorize the whole passage.

Back inside, I found Cassie standing on her head in the middle of our table.

"Having fun?" I asked.

"A little." She grinned and then vaulted back onto her feet. "So do you want to take a break?"

I looked at the book. The dense Latin looked very uninviting. "Can we?" I said. "I think Rosewood needs this right away ..."

"A few minutes won't matter. Come on."

She took my hand and yanked me toward the shelves. I managed to grab the book before we left. I followed Cassie deep into a labyrinth of shelves until we got to a quiet, secluded corner. She spun around and looked oddly nervous.

"So," she said. "Hi."

"Hey," I said.

I noticed she was shuffling her feet a little.

"So yesterday ..." she started, and then paused. "Well, I've been acting kind of weird today and I'm sorry. I was just embarrassed."

"Are you talking about that spider thing?" I asked.

She shook her head. "Seriously, François, that *really* shouldn't have happened. I mean, I want you to know I'm better than that. Like, way better. I was just ... distracted."

I paused to think a moment. I wanted to make sure I said the right thing here—even if I still didn't fully understand what she was so embarrassed about.

"Cassie, that thing came out of nowhere," I said, trying to gauge her reaction. "How could you avoid something like that? Besides, you're looking at a guy who got his ass kicked by a garden gnome the other day."

"That's different," she said, frowning. "Besides, Howard just has a crush on me. But anyway, I still want to explain. It's like ... I don't know. If you were a musician or something, and this cute guy that you really liked came to hear you play, and then you totally screwed it up, it would suck, right?"

"That actually happened to me once," I said. "I had a piano recital in the fifth grade and Denise Walton was in the—"

I cut myself off. I was babbling.

"So you know then," Cassie said earnestly. "That's what I felt like. I mean, before this, I've taken down some serious monsters you couldn't even imagine. I've saved the world. *Twice.* Plus, I'm supposed to be protecting you. I take that job really, really seriously. And I'm not going to let my guard down like that again, I promise."

I studied her a moment and saw that she was deadly serious. So, in an effort to reduce the tension a bit, I said, "Well look at it this way: The whole thing has boosted my self-esteem. I've gone from gnomes to spider women. I'm on my way to becoming a total badass."

"Shut up," she groaned. "I'm serious. And I feel stupid."

But then—quite suddenly—she stepped back and gave me a funny look. "But yeah ..." she said slowly. "You did kind of charge in there like a hero, huh? I wonder what you were thinking ..."

I stood a little straighter. "Just doing my job, ma'am. It's nothing."

"Nope." She shook her head. "That's not it."

"What's not it?" I asked.

"You like me," she said. It was more of an accusation than a statement. "You *really* like me."

"What?"

"It's okay, you can admit it."

"Cassie, I don't, uh ..."

"You've got googly eyes right now. You're all smitten."

"No I'm not."

"Are too."

"I am not smitten," I insisted. "And I have to memorize this!"

For the first time ever, I was actually glad to have the Latin assignment. I held up the heavy book for emphasis, yet Cassie just looked at me. "Do you?" she asked.

Her face was enigmatic, but I'd known her long enough to realize something was up.

"What do you mean, 'do I'?" I asked cautiously.

She shrugged. "I don't know. Maybe I brought more than just donuts."

"Cassie if you're telling me I just spent the past three hours buried in this stupid Latin book when I didn't have to, I'm never speaking to you again."

"So …" She hesitated. "Do you want me to tell you that you have to keep going then?"

I stared at her a moment with an odd mix of shock, delight and fury. "I don't have to memorize it, do I?" I said. "That's why you've been acting all bored, isn't it?"

She looked like she was doing everything in her power to keep a straight face. "So you wanna see what I brought?" she asked.

"Yes," I said. "I do."

She immediately pulled a small device from her pocket that I could've sworn was a miniature tricorder from *Star Trek*. "I went and got this from Q," she said. "It'll scan the page and email the whole thing to Rosewood. Cool, right?"

"I thought we couldn't use technology in here," I said. "Or magic. And I thought only a wizard could read the text?"

She shrugged. "It takes care of all that. That's why it's such a cool invention. Wanna give it a try?"

"So that's all there is to it? A little device from Q?! You've gotta be kidding me. Cassie, if I could tackle you right now, I would. You know that, right?"

She flashed me a devilish grin. "You know," she said, stepping closer. "I might not mind getting tackled. Let's see what you're made of, wizard boy."

Blushing, I quickly said, "Just gimmie the stupid thing," and snatched it from her fingers. "How does it work?"

She snatched it back. "It's complicated," she said. "Only a trained professional can do it. Watch."

She pointed the tricorder at the open page and clicked a little button. "Done," she announced. "Rosewood should get it any second now. You should go call him."

"Yes," I said, "I'll do that then," and turned toward the exit. I only got half a step before Cassie caught my sleeve and pulled me around.

"Not *that* way." She rolled her eyes. "*This* way."

She tossed the book aside and led me across the back of the library until we reached an exit. When we stepped through, we emerged directly onto the open-air roof of the library. Cassie took my hand and pulled me over to the edge where we had a sweeping view of Bryant Park. A small crowd was milling about the grass as a giant screen got hoisted up for the showing of an outdoor movie. According to the nearby posters, it was going to be *Casablanca.*

"It's like a drive-in," I said.

Cassie half turned. I noticed she was still holding my hand. "Hm? Oh, the movie thing. Yeah. It better not be *Cars 2.*"

"It's not," I said with a chuckle. "I think it's *Casablanca.* Humphrey Bogart. Coolest guy ever. Did you know that line 'play it again, Sam,' is actually a misquote? In the movie, Bogart just says, 'play it!' and it comes across as vaguely racist as he orders the black guy to play piano for him."

Cassie shifted a little closer. "So you're really into movies, huh?" she asked.

I *was* really into movies. I was also really into babbling incoherently because Cassie and I were standing alone together on a dark rooftop holding hands.

"I guess," I said. "It's kind of dorky, isn't it?"

"It's not dorky to be passionate," she said. "Girls like passionate."

"So what are you passionate about?" I asked.

She giggled slyly. "A bunch of things. But as a succubus I need to retain my air of mystery. I guess you'll have to work for it."

And then neither of us said anything for way too long. And by "way too long," I mean about thirty seconds, but it might as well have been an eternity. Because that's the thing about awkward silences: They're awkward, yes, but they're also the ultimate green light to kiss the girl you're standing next to. Heck, awkward silences are the very cornerstone of romance when you really think about it. And all you need to make them *un*-awkward is to cowboy the frack up for a split freaking second and just kiss the girl for Christ's sake.

Or you can totally chicken out and say something like, "So should I call Rosewood to make sure he got the page?" And then you feel her hand loosen a smidge as she says, "Um, yeah. I can do it if you want?" And then the green light turns to yellow ... and then to red.

"Okay," I said.

She let go to bring her phone to her ear. After a moment, she chirped, "Hey boss! Did you get my email?"

A pause.

"I know, right? Yeah, okay. I'll tell him. Okay. Bye!"

She put the phone back in her pocket and looked at me. "Rosewood says hi," she said. "He also said you did a great job. Or actually, he said 'smashing job,' and it was cute."

"Oh," I said. "Thanks."

Cassie looked back out over Bryant Park with me again—although this time there wasn't any handholding. I silently cursed myself.

After a moment, she said, "So I guess this doesn't qualify as a 'height,' huh?"

I looked at her, not understanding.

She nodded and pointed down at the park. "You're afraid of heights," she said. "But you seem fine right now."

Huh. She was right. Normally I would've been totally bugging out standing on the edge of a roof like this. I hadn't even thought about it this time.

"It's not that bad," I said. "I guess I was a little distracted. Speaking of which, you said that earlier you were distracted by something."

"When?" she asked.

"When you were talking about the spider woman thing.'"

"Oh. That."

"So? What was it?"

She blew out a breath. "A boy," she said simply. "He's been driving me crazy and he's kind of clueless."

"Like, 'good crazy?'" I asked.

Her shoulder rubbed against mine. "What do you think?"

I thought a lot of things—one of which was: *Why, François, can you not just turn your stupid head, lean in a little, and kiss this ridiculously awesome girl who clearly wants you to?* (I also thought about the Hubble Space Telescope. It just slipped in there somehow.)

Then there was *another* awkward silence. Can you believe that? Another one. A second chance. And you know what I did with it? Nothing. It then occurred to me that this was one of those cringe-worthy moments I'd remember for the rest of my life. I'd be taking a shower thirty years from now, remember that time on the roof with Cassie and then wince at how incredibly stupid I was.

After a moment, she took my hand again. "Come on," she said. "I have a better idea." She pulled me back to the rooftop exit and took out her key. She muttered something under her breath and opened the lock. I didn't quite understand what I was looking at until I stepped inside. The door led to an indoor pool—totally dark, except for the soft light shimmering up from the water. Cassie followed me through and shut the door behind us. The click echoed across the wide, windowed walls, which looked out over the Manhattan skyline.

"It's closed to guests past ten," she said, walking ahead of me. "It's all ours now."

When she walked, she put one foot directly in front of the other, which did something amazing with her hips. She then casually lifted her shirt over her head and undid her ponytail. Her hair cascaded down her back as she half turned to look over her shoulder with her eyes. "Coming?"

I gulped. She was naked from the waist up, save for a pair of thin straps at her shoulders. "You mean in the water?" I asked.

Now, if you're thinking that was a stupid question, you're correct. It was a very stupid question. But I'm going to warn you that at this juncture you shouldn't expect anything from me approaching eloquence. If I so much as manage to string three words together, you should be incredibly impressed.

"Um, yeah?" Cassie frowned a little. Somehow it was like she was smiling at the same time though.

"Okay," I said, but I still didn't move. It felt like my feet were firmly planted in a bed of concrete. Once it was clear they weren't going to start working any time soon, Cassie gave a little snort. "I guess when you're ready," she said and her hands moved to her waist. I could tell in the darkness she was unbuttoning her shorts. Then they were sliding down her legs and pooled at her feet.

She gave me another look over her shoulder before diving gracefully into the pool. Her head reemerged from the water with her long hair slicked back with allure. After a moment, she said, "Come on, jump in. I won't bite."

I drew a breath and suddenly my feet were working again. I peeled off my shirt and hopped on each foot to pull off my jeans. My shoes proved problematic at the end, so they, my socks and my jeans came off as one. I should also mention—most importantly—that some days I wear tighty whities, while other days I wear boxers. Today—thank God—I wore boxers.

I jumped into the water feet first and got my hair wet. When I came back up, Cassie was noticeably closer.

"So," she said. "Do you like my pool?"

My eyes widened. "Is this like your apartment or something?"

That was another stupid question. The bottom of the pool, which was lighted, had a hotel logo for *Le Parker Meridian* emblazoned across its surface. However, I should remind you of what I just mentioned: Don't expect anything intelligent to come out of my mouth for quite a while.

Cassie, for her part, looked amused and cocked her head. "I could probably tell you anything right now and you'd believe it, huh?"

"Pretty much."

"So if I told you my intentions weren't entirely honorable, would you believe that?"

I nodded.

"Good. Because they're not."

She suddenly pushed away and swam to the other end of the pool. She was—of course—an expert swimmer and glided through the water like a dolphin. I followed, but with a lot of flailing limbs and splashing. When we got to the other side we both had to tread water to stay afloat. She couldn't have been more than three feet away and I noticed the slight curve of her breasts peeking just above the waterline. I stared, but only because looking at her eyes was even more dangerous.

"Can I ask you something?" she said after a moment. She dipped her chin and a tiny spray came from her breath.

"Sure," I said.

"Do you want me?"

I had a slight suspicion that she already knew the answer to that. Yet sometimes it needs to get asked anyway. Especially when the guy is an idiot.

"I do," I said.

Her chin ducked again. "Then why haven't you kissed me?"

"Just nervous, I guess."

She gave me a small smile and rose a little taller in the water. "I told you. You don't have to be scared of me. I'm nice."

"It's not that."

"François, you know this is cruel and unusual, right? I've been trying to kiss you since the night we met."

"You have?"

"I have."

She'd been steadily drifting closer as we spoke. There was something vaguely intimidating about it.

"So remember what I told you on the Ferris wheel?" she asked.

I frowned and told her I didn't remember anything about anything at this particular moment.

She grinned and inched closer. "I can't kiss you unless you give me permission," she said.

"Because you're a succubus," I said.

"It makes life suck sometimes."

"I can't imagine why anyone wouldn't want to kiss you," I said.

She gave me a look.

"What?" I asked.

"Ugh, François! If you don't kiss me in the next two seconds, I'm going to hurt you!"

So I did.

Her lips met mine and tasted vaguely of strawberries and fresh rain. Her head tilted aggressively until we were kissing sideways and I felt her breasts against my chest. I struggled to stay afloat as my right hand slid down her back until my fingers met a tiny clasp. They fumbled at it, but failed. Cassie smiled into our kiss and giggled, "Need some help?"

"No, I've got it," I said.

Her grin widened and she leaned back in.

Unfortunately, I never did "get it." I could only concentrate on one thing at a time. There was no room to solve the blasted Rubik's Cube of the bra clasp while Cassie's tongue wrestled with mine. And I have to admit, up until that point in my life, I'd never understood why people—usually girls—say, "you're a good kisser." I mean, is it really a skill? Well, apparently, yes. Cassie was phenomenal at it. It took everything I had just to keep up with her.

Eventually, we drifted back to the shallow end where Cassie's feet found the bottom before mine. (Which was embarrassing.) Then, still kissing, she pushed forward until my back was against the poolside. Her hands slipped off my shoulders and roamed down my sides. They slid gently into the waistband of my boxers, and with a sudden strength, jerked them down.

I'll be honest—it made me jump a little. Did she really want to go all the way, right here, in the middle of the pool?

She continued sliding them down until she lifted her leg and finished the job with her foot. For some reason—perhaps it was instinct—I stepped out of them. It took a few seconds, but I soon realized that I was officially completely naked in the pool. Cassie still had her underwear on. It wasn't fair.

However, I didn't get any time to balance the scales. Her lips moved from mine down to my neck, then my chest, kissing their way to my stomach before disappearing below the waterline. I felt a small peck on each thigh, and then ... nothing. I looked down and saw Cassie gliding away under the water. Her body was slick as a seal as she lightly kicked her legs. When she resurfaced a few yards away, she had the biggest, evil grin on her face I'd ever seen.

"You are so in trouble," she said, almost singing the words like a taunt.

I was about to ask why, when her hand rose above the water, clutching my dripping shorts.

"Can I have those back?" I asked.

She shook her head and then disappeared below the water. I didn't react until I saw she was heading for the steps. When she reemerged, she was already halfway out—dripping and swaying her hips with each step.

She's not planning on ...?

Oh no. She scooped up our clothes in a single swoop and then glanced between me and the exit. The implication was very clear. I made a mad dash to scramble out of the water and yelped, "Don't even think about it!"

"Don't even think about what?" she asked innocently.

With that, she made a beeline for the exit and burst through. A shaft of light exploded into the room. I ran after her stark naked and dripping. When I got to the door, I stopped. I had nothing to wear. No towel. No underwear. *Nothing.* Not even my socks.

I stuck my head out and peaked around the corner. The hallway was brightly lit, yet mercifully empty. Except, of course, for Cassie who was skipping away in her underwear. It was wet and clung to her backside in a way that would've tempted the devil himself. Then she turned and skipped backwards. The view from the front was even better. She saw me staring and her eyes flashed back in a silent dare.

Normally, I might have hesitated a bit longer, but it wasn't like I had a choice. It was either follow Cassie now, or get discovered by a hotel employee tomorrow morning. (Then, mostly likely, get arrested.)

I left the security of the doorway and did my best to cover myself as I ran. Cassie turned and put her long legs to use, flying down the hallway like a gazelle. She gained another thirty feet before dipping around a corner.

I whisper-shouted for her to stop, as if that might actually work. When I rounded the bend, she was right there. I ran straight into her and my momentum twirled us both against a wall and we were kissing again. It took all of .01 seconds before I forgot all about the "stealing my clothes" thing. My fingertips found the clasp again, but failed for a second time.

I thought: *Damn!*

Then there was a sudden *ding* and the sound of elevator doors opening. Cassie pulled me with her until we were inside. I felt one of her hands leave my waist and frantically stab at the buttons. The doors closed and we slammed against the wall. Our hands were everywhere. I was also coming to realize that Cassie Chu was quite a bit stronger than me. And I'm not talking about "athletic" strong, either. I'm talking about "can lift a school bus over her head," strong. Which—I'll admit—was a little frightening.

The *ding* sounded again, followed by the doors opening. I expected to get yanked outside again—when instead, Cassie immediately let go and jumped back. I heard a sudden gasp.

So, remember how I told you about "cringe-worthy" moments that you'll remember for the rest of your life? Well now, I'd just acquired two in a single night.

On the other side of the open door was a short, elderly lady in her nightgown delicately carrying an ice bucket. Her face was pure shock. I did my best to ameliorate the situation.

"It's, uh, not what it looks like," I said.

My hands had both moved to cover myself as best as possible. Cassie had done the same. "Sorry," she mumbled.

We went down a single floor before the lady got out and scurried down the hall. When the doors closed after her, Cassie and I burst into laughter. I had to prop myself against the wall just to stay upright. When the doors opened again, I managed to ask her where we were going.

"I'll let you work that out for yourself," she said, and took me by the hand.

She pulled me down the hall until we stopped outside a pair of doors. A room key appeared and then we were inside.

I can't really tell you what the hotel suite looked like, other than to say it had a really nice bed. Cassie pushed me onto it and pounced like a jungle cat. I'll spare you the blow-by-blow details (that was *not* a pun, by the way), other than to say it was the most intense night of my life. Cassie—while usually quite friendly—allowed her succubus side to take over. To say that she was a tad "aggressive," might be a bit of an understatement. Still, the sight of her finally undoing that clasp behind her back turned me to putty in her hands. She'd been sitting up tall, straddling my waist when she asked, "Are you ready?"

I *thought* that I was, but then I learned a thing or two about what it's like to be with a girl who could literally pick up an elephant and throw it at you. It was no joke. No joke indeed.

When it was all over—several hours later—I was a wreck. I could've snapped my fingers and fallen asleep in an instant. Yet I found myself fighting to stay awake. Cassie was pressed against my side, her head on my chest and her leg hooked possessively over mine. The feel of the curves of her body was like heaven on Earth.

Sleep, however, is a powerful force. Fighting against it is always a losing battle. Yet before it overtook me, Cassie's voice drifted up to my ear in the dark. She quietly asked if I was still awake.

I told her I was, but that was only half-true. I was right on the precipice of a deep, magnificent slumber. Still, I heard her whisper, "Thanks. By the way."

"Hm?" I asked.

"For saving my life," she said.

Her grip tightened a little, and her cheek readjusted against my chest. My arm moved up to her shoulder.

"Anytime," I told her.

Chapter Nine

The Great Man's Cathedral

MEAGAN GOODMAN WAS THE FIRST GIRL I ever slept with. I'd had a girlfriend in high school, but never made it past first base. Anyway, I noticed that after sleeping with Meagan I seldom felt very refreshed the next morning. Usually, that was because I didn't sleep very much on those nights. The other reason was her insistence on keeping the bed nuclear hot with eighteen different blankets. (I'm exaggerating. It was more like nine or ten.) There were even times when I felt like I had the flu afterwards.

Yet when I woke up next to Cassie that next morning, I felt like a million bucks. Or maybe a billion. I could've taken on the entire world and had energy to spare—so much so that I began to suspect something supernatural at work. Perhaps I was experiencing the magic of being with a succubus. But weren't they supposed to *drain* magic from people? I figured I'd ask her when she woke up—which happened to be only a few seconds after me. Her voice was still raspy from sleep as she lifted her cheek and smiled.

"Hey there, cowboy."

"Hey yourself," I said. "So last night was, uh …"

"Awesome. I know."

"Yes." I nodded. "Very awesome."

"What can I say?" she said. "I've got skills. Speaking of which, what are your thoughts on early morning trysts?"

"I tend to be for them," I said.

She smiled broadly, but didn't move. She just stared at me for a long moment, her eyes searching like she was expecting something.

"What?" I asked.

"You have to kiss me," she answered. "The whole 'asking permission' thing resets with every sunrise. It's annoying."

"Oh," I said.

"So?" The expectant look returned.

After I kissed her, it was on—big time. Her face surged forward and the succubus side took over again. She flipped on top and before I knew it, her hips were rolling against mine. Then her pace quickened until ... okay. I was going to say something about the sound of skin slapping on skin, but it's probably best to leave out those kinds of details. This isn't a porno, after all.

So, fast-forward about an hour—or it could've been more—and Cassie and I were staring up at the ceiling catching our breath.

"You know," she panted. "For someone who is so shy, you're really good at this."

"You did most of the work," I said.

"You did plenty," she chuckled back. "Besides." She rolled onto her side and propped up her chin. "You're quite, um ... *impressive*."

I turned my head, still panting. "Impressive?"

Her eyes flicked to the side and then back with a hint of devilment. "Down below."

Oh.

It's a plain and simple fact that there isn't a single guy on the entire planet who doesn't like to hear that. And it never gets old either. He can hear it over and over and over and over and each time is as good as the first.

"Thanks," I said.

"I should be thanking you. I haven't been able to do something like this in forever."

I rolled onto my side to face her. "Really?"

I was suddenly curious about Cassie's supernatural love life. Had she slept with other guys before? I mean, she must have, but didn't she say something about not wanting to hurt anyone? I still didn't understand how the whole "succubus" thing truly worked.

"Yeah," she sighed. "It's been torture. We succubi kind of enjoy sex. Obviously."

"So how does it work?" I asked.

She gave me a look. "How does what work?"

"I mean when you sleep with someone, isn't it supposed to be really dangerous? Like, for the guy? Because of the succubus thing?"

"For non-magic guys, sure. Probably fatal."

"But what about me?" I asked.

She scooted closer. "You," she said. "Have an endless supply. That's what being a wizard is all about."

"I do?"

"Oh yeah."

I chewed my lip a moment in thought. "So you only sleep with wizards then?"

Her eyes left mine a moment and she actually blushed a little. "Um, no," she said. "You're my first, actually."

"Wait. So you were a …?" It felt awkward to complete that sentence, but Cassie just laughed. "A wizard virgin, yes," she said. "The rest is … complicated. Are you sure you want to know this stuff?"

I was sure that I did *not*. Especially not right now. "You've got a point," I told her. "So what do we do now?"

She shrugged. "Room service?"

"No, I mean you and me and the SIA and all that. What do we do now?"

"I don't know," she said. "Have lots of fun between assignments? Speaking of which, I think we should take full advantage of our current—"

Right then, the hotel room's telephone rang sharply. It was surprisingly loud, with a jackhammer-like quality to it. Cassie rolled over immediately to grab it.

"Boss?" she said with a level of distress that made me sit up. It was like she'd just answered the Bat Phone and automatically knew something was wrong.

"Okay," she said. "We'll be there. Don't worry."

She hung up and jumped out of bed—completely nude, which is something I just have to mention—and found her underwear. Then, searching the rest of the floor, muttered, "Crap. I think I dropped the clothes ..."

"Who was that?" I asked. "Rosewood?"

"Yep. There's an emergency in Florence. We have to go right away." She stood up straight and nodded to herself. "Stay here, okay? I'll get our clothes."

"But—"

"I'll explain on the way," she said as she was already disappearing out the door.

She was back in less than a minute and tossed me my stuff.

"There's a Larva Mage in the *Museo De Galileo* in Florence," she explained as she hopped back into her shorts. "Rosewood needs us to destroy it before it finds what it's looking for. He thinks it has something to do with Steinberg."

Since the other day's incident with the Drider, I'd taken a moment to read Thaddeus Kroeber's *Introduction to Dark Creatures: Where to Find Them and How to Destroy Them.* Thus, I knew a fair deal about Larva Mages. They were essentially powerful magicians—not quite wizard-level though—whose bodies were entirely made of worms. And not only that, but they could supersize their worms into giant larva creatures that were almost as deadly as the Larva Mage himself. (I'm assuming most Larva Mages were male, but I'm not sure. The book didn't say.) Anyway, the thought of fighting a Larva Mage didn't exactly fill me with joy—primarily because of the words, "*larva creatures*"—but if Cassie was going then so was I. I didn't know how much good I'd be with my four spells, yet as a wise man once said, "Four spells is better than no spells." That's an actual quote, too. I'm not kidding.

I started pulling on my jeans and hopped toward the bathroom. I know most stories tend to skip these kinds of details but I'd just woken up after a long night of insane sex. So by the time I finished taking the piss of a lifetime, I reemerged to find Cassie fully dressed. She gave me an earnest look and threw me my shoes. "We have to hurry," she said. "There's a backdoor that will get us close to the museum, but we have to make a stop first."

"Where?"

"We need guns," she said. "I've got a big stash nearby. Or sort of, I guess. It's in Istanbul, but the backdoor is really close."

"Okay. Do I get a gun?"

"No."

About ten minutes later we were in the basement of a kinky-themed nightclub off Istanbul's infamous Taksim Square. (It's like the Turkish Times Square.) The entire room was a dream come true for any eleven-year-old boy, or any U.S. Marine. It was stocked wall-to-wall with every type of awesome weapon you could possibly imagine. There were heavy machine guns, sniper rifles, grenade launchers, shotguns, and not one, but *two* flamethrowers.

Cassie—with a somewhat disquieting level of professional efficiency—began taking one of everything and zipping them into holding discs. She also changed her clothes, which in spite of the situation, I couldn't help but enjoy. When she caught me blatantly staring, she gave me a playful slap. (It still hurt, though.) She'd changed from her shorts and tank top to what I assumed was her battledress—which was somewhere between *Lara Croft* and *The Matrix*. It looked good. Really good.

Something else that looked really good was the modified, special forces-style M4 carbine with a laser scope resting on a pair of hooks to my right. It looked like the centerpiece at a fine art gallery. I went to pick it up—just for fun—but Cassie seemed to read my mind and batted my hand away. "You're a wizard. Stick to magic," she said.

"I only know four spells. And did you know that Larva Mages can conjure giant fire-breathing centipedes that move as fast as a cheetah?"

"They can also make 'larva dogs,' which can bite your head off," Cassie said. "They're really intimidating. And if you have a gun, you'll end up freaking out and shooting yourself in the foot. Or me. Which would suck."

"Come on, I need something," I said. "No dude can walk into this room"—I gestured toward all the gun racks—"and not leave without at least a hand grenade."

Cassie paused, stared at me, and then blew out a breath. "Fine," she relented. "You can have *this*." She opened a small hard case and took out a tiny pistol. She pressed it into my hand and the entire thing was barely bigger than my palm.

It was a two-shot derringer. How do I know what that is? Because I've seen a lot of westerns. You probably know what a two-shot derringer is too. You've seen them a bunch of times. They're those tiny little double-barreled pistols that a gentleman, circa 1872, could keep tucked away in the small pocket of his waistcoat. *Or* he could keep it tucked away up his ass and barely feel a thing.

"Cassie, shit, what am I gonna do with this?" I said.

"The bullets are special," she explained. "Believe me, you're packing some serious firepower there."

I looked at the tiny derringer. "Really?"

"Oh yeah. They pack a bigger punch than their appearance suggests." She winked at me. "Kind of like someone else I know."

"Shut up," I said.

I put the pistol in my pocket and clapped my hands. "So," I said. "Is there a game plan? What do we do when we get there?"

Cassie zipped a bulletproof vest clipped with Ice Grenades into a holding disc. (I knew that they were ice grenades because they had a little snowflake on the side.) "Ice and fire in combination," she said briskly. "I've got a lot of ice weapons from Q, but you're going to need to supply the fire."

"Isn't that a flamethrower over there?" I asked, pointing.

"It is. But I wanted you to feel included."

"That's harsh," I said.

"Not as harsh as a fire-breathing centipede. Besides, I may actually need you on this one. I fought a Larva Mage once before and it was tough. But this time—with the two of us working together—it should be a cinch. Sort of."

A few minutes later we were back in New York riding on my scooter toward the backdoor to Florence. Cassie said it was in Central Park. When we got there—a small public restroom—she didn't waste any time unlocking the door and hopping back on the seat. We rode through it together, and then we were zipping down a narrow and crowded Italian street. We fit right in on the Vespa.

I didn't get a chance to take in much of the city, but I did notice one thing. Florence had that permanently historic look to it, as if all the modern additions like paved streets and traffic lights were just a temporary nuisance to the original buildings of centuries past. It was as if some guy traveled back in time to stick a STOP sign outside the drawbridge of a medieval castle.

It only took a few minutes to get to the *Museo de Galileo* with Cassie shouting directions in my ear. How did she always know where everything was? I could barely get around LA.

The building itself—from the outside at least—looked surprisingly unimpressive. It sat on the corner of a crowded intersection and looked like a brick cube with a few windows up top. Inside, however, was a different story. The lighting and décor was modern with a lot of high-tech display cases and security cameras. I—a man who has a slight weakness for museums—took a second to glance at some of the exhibits. The museum was basically about the birth of science, back when science was a steampunk paradise. Intricate contraptions of polished brass and carved wood lined the walls behind protective barriers, while bell jars housed lighted gases and rested on podiums. I couldn't help but think: *This was from a time when science was magic. They were literally the same thing. When did that change?*

Cassie brought me back to reality with a tap on my shoulder. "Really interesting, huh?" she said.

"Sure is," I said breathlessly.

"When we're done, we'll take a little stroll and look around."

"Yeah, definit—oh. You're joking."

"I am."

I refocused. "So where's the Larva Mage?"

"Not sure. At least the museum is empty, though. I was worried there'd be people here."

"The sign outside said it was closed for renovations."

Cassie shook her head. "That was an illusion spell. I'm almost positive. The Larva Mage probably made it so he could be alone. They're very solitary."

"How do you know?" I asked.

She gave me a sideways look. "His face is made of worms. I doubt he's very sociable."

We moved deeper into the maze of exhibits. It really was a *maze*, too. Each room led into another until I felt totally turned around and had no idea where I was. Ordinarily, that wouldn't be too scary, but in this particular circumstance, I thought it best to remember the fastest way to the exit.

Cassie and I were both moving on tiptoes, ears straining for any sound, when I felt a tiny tap on my shoulder. I thought it was Cassie so I turned to her, but she was staring fixedly at something up ahead. My eyes naturally drifted downward and I flinched. A little curled up larva twisted around on my shoulder and then rolled off. Definitely not a good sign.

I turned to whisper to Cassie, but she held up a fist. It was the same gesture you see Special Forces guys do in the movies.

I felt another tap on my shoulder, and then another and another.

Now, in my defense, Cassie may very well have been doing the "holding up a fist" thing, but unless you're a trained Navy SEAL, there's no way you're not going to jump—and possibly even squeal a little—when a bunch of maggots are falling on your head.

Cassie whipped around, just long enough to roll her eyes at me. When she looked forward again, she muttered, "*shit,*" and then whispered to me, pointing, "One of the centipedes is in the next room. It knows we're here."

I suddenly realized how crazy this whole thing was. (A bit late, right?) Up until now, it didn't seem real. Even after everything I'd seen, the thought of giant, fire-breathing centipedes seemed far-fetched. Yet now, apparently, just such a centipede was about ten feet away on the other side of a thin, plasterboard wall.

"Make a fireball," Cassie whispered, while flipping a grenade launcher out of a holding disc. "When I freeze it, hit it with fire. That's what kills them."

I made a Firebolt and got ready to throw it. It sparked and fizzled around my fingertips, and I knew from painful experience it would explode within a minute if I didn't get rid of it. Cassie shouldered the grenade launcher and aimed toward the door. Then, in a blink, she screamed for me to get down and pushed me to the floor right as a ball of liquid flame shot over my head. I heard a couple low *thumps* followed by the tinkle of crackling glass. When I looked up, I saw that Cassie had hit a gigantic centipede twice and turned it into a gnarled statue of solid ice. And by "solid ice," I literally mean ice, as in frozen water. That's why the Firebolt could melt his ass. I got back to my feet and tossed it at him. Before long, he was a puddle. I stared until Cassie clapped me on the shoulder. "See?" she said. "Easy as pie. But now they know we're here so we have to move."

With that, she yanked me by the sleeve and took us back the way we came. Just above the doorway, the fireball that had missed my head was burning a large hole. The flame looked thick and viscous, dripping down in little clumps like lava. I could feel its heat as we passed underneath.

Cassie led the way through several more rooms until she halted abruptly and held up her fist again. "Three of them," she whispered. "Plus larva dogs. Do you have any protection spells?"

"I have Force Bubble," I said.

"Make it. And don't do anything until I tell you. Even if it looks like I'm about to get eaten. I'll be fine."

"What are you going to do?" I asked, and formed an *Imago*.

Cassie flashed me a girlish grin as she loaded two more grenades into the launcher. She then flipped out a flamethrower from another holding disc. "What I do best," she said, and then launched herself into the next room. Frantically, I did the *Canti* for FB while screeches, explosions, and the roar of shooting flames erupted from the other side of the wall. I'd just formed the bubble when one of the centipedes surged through the door. It came right for me and a burst of flame issued from its mandibles. I held out a palm to shield my face, but the flame missed. The centipede itself shattered against the invisible barrier a split second later. Cassie had tagged him with an ice grenade. When I looked up, I saw her jump back into the other room to finish the rest.

It only took about thirty seconds. She reemerged with both weapons smoking heavily from the barrels. "That was intense," she announced. "But we could use a couple fireballs. The flamethrower ran out of juice."

I stood stunned for a moment until I found my voice. "Happy to help," I said, and popped the Force Bubble. I felt a little embarrassed that I'd been hiding behind it.

After melting the remaining ice statues in the next room, we continued our quest deeper into the museum. The scariest part—for me at least—was going up the stairwell. It was narrow and dark, and I kept thinking that a centipede was going to drop on our heads at any moment. We searched each floor, and by the time we were done, Cassie had killed eight more centipedes and dozens of larva dogs—which weren't actually *dogs,* but giant, fast-moving potato bugs the size of Dobermans. For some reason, they creeped me out even more than the centipedes.

When we got to the top floor, it was clear this was the place. We couldn't see the Larva Mage yet, but his spawn were everywhere. And the weird part was that they didn't attack us. There must have been a hundred centipedes crawling slowly along the walls and ceilings while countless larva dogs roamed the floors.

"*Wow,*" Cassie breathed. We were both standing still as statues. "This is a bit more than I was expecting."

"This isn't what happened last time?" I asked.

"Not even close," she whispered.

"So what do we do?"

She paused a moment. I could tell she was debating whether or not to charge forward with a bunch of guns and just hope for the best. Finally, she frowned and said, "They're all clustered together. If I lob a bunch of grenades I can freeze a dozen at a time." She then paused again and did a little mental math. "Yeah," she said. "I should have enough for that. Probably. You don't know any ice spells, do you?"

"I looked them up once," I said, "but they'll all Level Five. Apparently ice is a lot tougher than fire."

"Well at least you have the fire. Speaking of which, you're gonna need to make a lot of it. I'm all out of flamethrowers."

"I'll do my best," I said.

"Okay. Are you ready?"

For some reason, I had a sudden flashback to when she asked me that same question last night. Same words. Very different context.

"Ready is my middle name," I said before I could stop myself.

Cassie popped the pins on a couple grenades and looked at me.

"Okay, I'll work on that," I said.

"Good. Now on the count of three ..."

She counted to two, and then charged into the room. It was the classic "on three" or "after three" blunder, but within a millisecond it didn't matter anymore. The larva creatures came to sudden life and surged forward. They covered every surface making it look like the building itself was alive. Cassie put well-aimed grenades into the writhing mass while juking around screeching larva dogs like a football player.

I started hurling cantrip Firebolts as fast as I could. I thought I was doing great—making lots of ice puddles—until a large detachment of larva creatures forgot about Cassie and came for me instead. I didn't have any way to freeze them, and as I learned, a Firebolt by itself did precisely nothing. I opened an *Imago* and quickly formed a Force Bubble. The next second, I was completely surrounded. The bugs couldn't break through the barrier, but that didn't stop them from dogpiling on top of me.

Now, in my experience, most insects tend to be at their very grossest from underneath. On top they might have a little carapace or something, but underneath they're all wiggling little feelers and hairy legs and undulating sacks that are truly disgusting. It made me wish that the Force Bubble wasn't so freaking transparent. The view was like something from a nightmare. I was covered in so many giant bugs that all the light was blocked out. I made a Firelight, but upon seeing all the insect bodies, I quickly got rid of it. I also threw a few more Firebolts at some of the exposed underbellies, and while I managed to singe a few legs, most of these guys had six or seven hundred more to spare.

I remained pinned for what felt like an eternity, although it was probably only a matter of seconds. My biggest problem—which had my heart pounding like a drum—was that the Force Bubble would wear out within a few minutes. As soon as it did, I was toast. My only hope was that Cassie was faring better than I was, and that she could throw a couple ice grenades onto my pile of centipedes.

Then I felt a sudden burst of cold, and over the next few seconds, the writhing of countless legs gradually slowed until it came to a complete stop. Now, looking up with a Firelight, I saw that I was buried under a mountain of ice. I started flinging Firebolts two at a time. A few seconds later I was drenched head to toe when the bubble popped. The water was cold—definitely cold—but it was a hell of a lot better than the alternative.

I followed the sounds of fighting to catch up with Cassie in the next room. I was stunned to find every last one of the larva creatures reduced to a puddle. Or actually, there had been so many that the puddles had become an inch-deep flood across the entire floor. Now, Cassie was fighting against the main guy—our Larva Mage. He wore a wizard-like cloak of deep crimson with a large hood that hid his face. His hands were long, spindly and made entirely of worms, maggots and an assortment of crawlers. He held them a foot apart as he formed an *Imago* of his own—only his was dark green. Cassie, meanwhile, had a high tech-looking energy shield in one hand, and a flaming samurai sword in the other. When she saw me, she suddenly screeched for me to get down. My eyes flicked to the Larva Mage just in time to see him whip toward me and cast his spell.

I'm not sure where the rumor started, but a lot people say that right before you die, your life flashes before your eyes. What happens after that, no one knows. But the "flashing before your eyes" thing gets mentioned all the time. I always thought it sounded kind of cool, like a nice way to cap things off. Thus, you can imagine my disappointment when my life *didn't* flash before my eyes. There was just a loud crash, a discombobulated sense of flying, and then waking up some time later feeling dazed and dizzy. As I regained focus, I saw Cassie kneeling over me and gently prodding my shoulder.

"Hey," she said. "Are you okay?"

I pried myself off the floor to sit up. I was drenched from all the puddles. "Am I dead?"

She shook her head. "No, but the other guy sure is. How did you do that?"

I blinked and tried to clear the cobwebs. My whole head was buzzing like a tuning fork. "Do what?" I asked.

"You totally killed the Larva Mage," she said, and I noticed her eyes were wide. "You did some kind of spell."

"I did?"

"Wait, you don't remember it?"

"I just remember he threw a spell at me and then I thought I was dead."

"No, you blocked it with something. This big lightning shield appeared and his spell bounced back at him. He burst into green flames and melted. I don't even know if *Rosewood* could do something like that. How did you learn it?"

I sat up straighter and scratched my head. "I have no idea. But why does my head hurt so much?"

She frowned. "Well, you kind of collapsed afterwards. I figured the spell took a toll or something."

She offered a hand and pulled me to my feet.

"So that's it?" I said. "We're done?"

"I'm not sure. When I found the Mage, he was looking at that old telescope over there,"—she pointed behind her—"but as far as I can tell, there's nothing special about it. Still, it might have something to do with the Steinberg thing. Rosewood thought the Mage was searching for him."

I knew from *Intro to Dark Creatures* that Larva Mages didn't do things on their own. They were always beholden to someone more powerful. So, if that was the case, it begged the question who the Larva Mage was working for, and why was that person looking for Professor Steinberg?

Rosewood was probably right. The professor was definitely up to something, and someone with a lot of power was trying to find him. I mean, you'd *have* to have a lot of power, right? If something like a Larva Mage was your servant? Whoever that dude was, I definitely didn't want to meet him.

I shook my head a final time and the dizziness faded. I looked where Cassie had pointed and saw one of the museum's ancient telescopes lying on the wet floor. I winced when I saw it.

It was probably several hundred years old and made by Galileo himself. At the very least, we needed to put it back in its case.

When I picked it up, I noticed the oddest thing. Even though it was made of wood and had been resting in inch-deep water, it was completely dry. And I'm not talking about waterproofing either. I'm talking about bone dry. There was definitely something supernatural at work. Yet as I turned it over in my hands, I didn't see anything strange.

"What do you think?" Cassie asked, leaning over my shoulder.

I shrugged. "Well, there's *something* weird about it. See how it's not wet?"

She peered closer. "Huh," she said.

"Yeah." Then I had an idea. "Wait," I told her. "There's this spell. I saw it once when I was flipping through my book. It might help."

"What is it?"

I handed her the telescope and fished the Solitar from my pocket. "I forget what it's called. McFadden will know. Let me see if I can learn it."

"Won't that take a really long time?"

"For me? Ten seconds. I'll be back in a flash, sugar."

I was joking when I said that, and I expected Cassie to raise an eyebrow at me, but instead she just beamed. "Okay," she said. "I'll protect the Zippo thing while you're in there. Go be a wizard." She gave me a little peck on the cheek.

I flipped open the cap and sparked the lighter. There was a swirl of melting walls and then I was back on my football field. McFadden was already waiting, standing impatiently next to a chalkboard.

"Any man who isn't a disco dancer in the 1970s who calls his girlfriend 'sugar' should be punched in the face. Nevertheless, the spell you are after is called 'Reveal Magic.' It is a Level Two spell that most of my former students mastered when they were eight years old. Let us see what you can do at age twenty."

"What page is it on?" I asked, sitting at one of my desks and flipping open the book.

"What page, you ask? Well, I suppose it is a bit much to expect you to find it on your own. After all, the index can be quite tricky. The name of each spell is listed alphabetically with a page number next to—"

"Found it," I said.

"Ah. Well done. I dare say you have surpassed my expectations."

"Thanks," I said.

I read over the *Canti* for the spell and it looked doable. There were a few Thetas and Kappas I'd never done before, but they were still a lot easier than the Deltas I had to do for the *Vigilia Temporis*. And speaking of *Vigilia Temporis* ...

"Why are some spells in Latin and others in English?" I asked, still keeping my nose in the book.

There was a brief pause before McFadden boomed, "Well!" He sounded genuinely pleased for once and it made me jump. "François, that may be your first non-imbecilic question! I'm speechless!"

"I try," I said.

"It's so 'not stupid,' in fact that ... well, here." He reached forward and stuck a little gold star on my book. "Well deserved," he said. "And the answer to your question is this: Up until the mid-Renaissance, *all* spells were inscribed in Latin. However, as times began to change, there were movements within the Magic Community to adopt a more egalitarian approach and label certain spells in the native languages of their practitioners. After that, it was merely a matter of happenstance that some words remained in Latin, while others were more changeable. Eventually, this was codified into a proper 'grammar,' if you will, and to this day it remains rigorously enforced by snooty academics such as myself."

"Cool," I said.

"Yes. It is 'cool.' Have you made any progress with the spell yet?"

"I'm trying to memorize it," I said. "It makes it easier to do the *Canti*."

McFadden paused again. "Hm," he said. "Two non-imbecilic remarks in as many minutes. Perhaps this is the beginning of a new era, like when the first chimpanzee used a stick against another. The reason it is easier is that when you remain focused on the *Imago,* you fingers are less likely to stray. I used to teach that very lesson to my former students."

I finally stole my eyes from the page and looked up. "How come you never taught *me* anything like that? I'm a student."

"Oh, François! Dear boy. I may as well ask you why you never taught your family's cocker spaniel to do theoretical physics. I must admit, it simply never occurred to me."

I mumbled that that was mean and went back to memorizing the spell. I thought briefly about ordering McFadden to stand on one leg—which he would have had to obey—but I didn't want to be petty ...

A few minutes later, I felt confident that I had the sequence of *Canti* down pat. Now it was just a matter of doing them. I bid McFadden farewell—to which he made an uncharacteristic retching sound—and I left the Solitar. I found Cassie sitting cross-legged on a dry patch of floor. I emerged right on top of her. It proved to be a mildly awkward moment, if not a pleasantly awkward one, as we both got to our feet.

"So what can I do?" she asked.

I winced and blew out a breath. "Refrain from laughter when I blow up the spell in my face."

She gave a salute. "Never."

(Ah. A question in rhetoric. Never would she laugh, or never would she refrain? Who knew?)

I formed an *Imago* and set to work with the *Canti*. Minute after minute went by as I got it wrong dozens of times. Normally, that would be par for the course. Yet somehow, having a really, really hot girl watching you makes every attempt that's not a hole-in-one a catastrophe.

Still, on my fifty-third try, I got the fucker right as rain.

Oh, and here's another Latin term used in spellcasting: *Ignis.*

The *Ignis* is the little spark of energy that dances around your fingertips after you've successfully formed the spell from the *Imago.* It's then up to you to cast your spell by tossing the *Ignis* at whatever your target is. In this particular case, the Galilean telescope was my target. The second the spell touched the wood, the letters, A, R, and X appeared in a beautiful cursive scroll.

"Arx!" Cassie squealed in delight, beating me to the punch. (Thankfully.) "Remember? That's the word I found in Steinberg's office!"

"Yeah, the one that meant 'fortress,'" I mused. "Why would it be written on a telescope?"

"I don't know. But at least we're on the right track."

I frowned and reexamined the scope. The letters looked worn and faded, as if they'd always been there. The magic—which I "revealed" with the spell—must have turned them invisible. And while that may not seem like a *huge* clue, it kind of was. It meant that the letters were likely carved hundreds of years ago by the great man himself. Thus, the "fortress"—or whatever arx was—was not a new invention. It was an old one. Steinberg wasn't inventing anything. He was discovering something.

I turned the telescope over a couple more times and then put my eye to the lens. (I'll admit, I probably should have thought to do this earlier.) As soon as I did, the walls around me melted in a familiar pattern. The instant they did, I knew exactly what was happening. This telescope wasn't a telescope at all. It was Galileo Galilei's own, personal *Solitar*. Holy. Freaking. Crap.

The inside looked like the main hall of a massive Cathedral—probably out of a sense of irony since the Church kept trying to kill the guy for doing science. However, instead of long pews and a raised pulpit, the entire space had been converted into a workshop. My first thought was: *Iron Man*. This was the Seventeenth Century version of Tony Stark's garage. And if I had thought that the outside museum had a steampunk feel to it, this place took it to a whole new level. Insane-looking contraptions of brass and copper with spindles and gears and pendulums were everywhere. Most of it, I didn't recognize at all. They were undoubtedly magical inventions that never got revealed to the world. The few items I *did* recognize were a cluster of telescopes, as well as something that looked like an ornately carved cuckoo clock.

I stepped between workbenches, marveling at each item. There was no organization to any of it. Everything was strewn about haphazardly like the aftermath of a kids game. I wandered for a good minute or two until I heard a few tiny clinks coming from another room. It sounded like it was coming from near the front of the cathedral where a hallway led to another area— perhaps the back offices for the priests or something. (As you can tell, I don't really know my way around cathedrals. Or any type of church for that matter.) Nevertheless, I quietly followed the sounds until I came upon a small workshop behind the main floor. It appeared to be dedicated to a single invention—one that I recognized from various scenes in movies. I could've been wrong, but it looked exactly like an atomic bomb. But not a new one. It looked the first one ever built—a dark metallic sphere studded with silvery canisters and a million wires sticking out.

Also—crouching next to the invention and tinkering with it—was Professor David Freaking Steinberg. He looked just like the photograph Rosewood had shown us—a carbon copy of Albert Einstein complete with poofy white hair and gigantic eyebrows. I stood in the doorway for a full ten seconds before he noticed I was there. When he did, his eyes lit up in pleasant surprise.

"Why, hello!" he said merrily. "Are you a friend of Carol's?"

It took me a second to remember that Carol was the name of Professor Steinberg's wife. I told him no.

"Oh." The response seemed to puzzle him. "How did you find me then?"

"It's kind of a long story," I said and moved into the room. "My name's François. A lot of people are looking for you."

The puzzlement turned to shock. "*Me?* Why?"

That was a good question. The truth was I still had no idea why anyone was looking for him. Rosewood had thought he was part of a nefarious plot, but didn't have any other details. The BPI, the Larva Mage, and probably a few others were looking for him as well, but once again, I didn't know why.

"I believe they thought you were up to something. You went missing like two weeks ago," I said.

"Two weeks? No. Time is slower in here. Surely it hasn't been that long, has it?"

"I think it has."

His eyebrows furrowed together as he thought a moment. Then he chuckled, embarrassed. "Oh boy. I'm in trouble, aren't I?"

"What do you mean?"

"Carol's going to kill me. You're telling me I've been gone for two weeks and she didn't know where? I'll never sleep in our bed again. And that couch …"

"Professor," I said. "I think you have bigger problems than your wife. My friend and I just killed a Larva Mage that was trying to steal this Solitar. Our friend, who works for the SIA, tasked us with finding you. And the BPI has search parties out looking as we speak. So I have to ask, what are you working on in here? What's the 'arx?'"

"Gracious." He stood a moment, scratching his head in confusion. "A Larva Mage? Here? In the museum?"

I nodded. "When we found him, he was looking at this telescope. Why would he be trying to steal it? What's in here?"

Steinberg kept scratching his head but now turned his gaze on me with a touch of suspicion. "François," he said slowly. "Are you from France?"

"No."

"But you are a wizard, yes?"

"Sort of," I said. "But I only know four spells."

Steinberg frowned a little as his hand moved to his chin. "Well, four spells is better than no spells." (Told you that was a real quote.) "I can't be certain," he said, "but it is very likely that your Larva Mage was sent to steal this." He gestured to the atomic bomb device. "Galileo dubbed it the *Orbis Lux,* or 'World Light.' It was meant to be his greatest invention for the protection of this realm. Yet sadly, he never finished it."

"What happened?"

"He lived in the 1600s. The materials he needed simply weren't available."

I stepped closer and peered at it. "It looks like an atomic bomb. What does it do?"

"Well, its true mechanics are beyond my comprehension. Galileo was an alchemist of unparalleled genius. But what it does is offer a level of protection this realm has never seen."

"So it *is* a weapon?" I asked.

"Only in the wrong hands. You mentioned that you only know four spells. How much do you understand about the Multi-Realm and its various interactions with the Eternal Planes?"

I felt a quick pang of guilt. I'd skipped that particular book in my *Vicipadea*. In my defense, the next book on the list was *A History of Magical Warfare: Key Battles and Lessons Learned*. How was I supposed to know that the "Multi-Realm" book was going to come in handy first?

"Not much," I admitted.

"In that case, I'll give you a crash course. You see, right now you think of Earth as a planet, yes?"

I nodded.

"You believe it exists within a vast universe of countless stars and billions of galaxies—which if you do the math—would suggest there are other life forms out there as well. Is this all correct?"

I nodded again, and Steinberg raised a finger with excitement. "The truth," he said, beaming, "is that the surrounding universe is an illusion—the Fifth Discipline of Magic. You could climb aboard a rocket ship and fly as many billions of light years into space as you wished. All you would find is more space. The reason, quite simply, is that the illusion moves with you no matter where you go."

"So no aliens?" I asked. "That's not cool at all."

"Well I suppose that depends on your definition of 'aliens.' If an alien is merely a person or creature from another world, then my dear boy, there are millions of aliens. I'm sure you've already met a few—including your Larva Mage. You see, Earth is but one realm within the vast Multi-Realm. Each one has its own 'planet' with its own civilizations and peoples and creatures, etcetera. However, realms are only half the equation. There are also the Eternal Planes. The key difference is that realms are for mortal creatures while planes are for immortal ones."

"But what does that have to do with this atomic bomb thing?" I asked. I was getting impatient; worried that Cassie could be in trouble outside. She probably wasn't, but I couldn't shake a tiny feeling like she might be. For all I knew, there could be a second Larva Mage, or perhaps something even worse.

Steinberg raised another finger and skipped over to a nearby chalkboard. "So," he said. "Imagine the Multi-Realm as a giant three-dimensional chessboard with each square representing a separate realm." He grabbed a piece of chalk and drew a hasty Rubik's Cube. "There, you see? Each realm touches several of its neighbors. As such, it is possible to travel between them using an 'arcane gate.' But here's the tricky part. A similar network of interconnected planes overlaps with the Multi-Realm. Therefore, it is also possible to travel between planes. For this, you need a 'portal.' I should tell you that portals are extremely rare and can only be opened by the most powerful beings within the All-Time—which is what we call existence as a whole." He drew a circle next to the Rubik's Cube. "So now," he continued, "we come to the purpose of the *Orbis Lux*. It has the power to either open, or *permanently close*, a portal. This is important because no wizard or warlock or anyone else has ever closed a portal once it has opened."

"I still don't understand," I said.

"Powerful beings from the Eternal Planes offer the biggest threat to the Multi-Realm. Many of the immortals who live there see themselves as superior. As such, many realms have been completely destroyed by evil forces from such planes. Galileo Galilei sought a way to protect Earth from such a fate. Each device, like the one you see here, has the power to close a portal. It can also *open* one, however, if misapplied. And you were right when you described it as an 'atomic bomb thing.' It *is* an atomic bomb, yet with quite a bit of magic in it as well."

"Professor Steinberg," I said slowly, and pointed to the *Orbis*. "Does this thing work?"

"Oh yes! I put the finishing touches on it this morning."

"So are you planning on using it or ...?"

"Me? No. I planned on handing it over to the proper authorities this afternoon. As I mentioned, it could be a terrible weapon in the wrong hands."

I frowned. "You do realize that's probably why a bunch of bad guys are looking for it, right? I think they want to open a portal."

"Yes, of course. But once I hand it over to the authorities it will be perfectly safe. Besides, it is very unlikely that anyone will find me here."

"I think they already have, Professor. We need to get this *Orbis* thing to Agent Rosewood at the SIA. He'll know what to do. If anyone is the 'proper authorities,' it's him. We have to go."

Steinberg hesitated. "Are you sure that's really necessary? I had hoped to do some more experiments ..."

"Professor," I said. "Larva Mages don't work by themselves. They get ordered to do things by someone else—someone a lot worse than they are. Whoever that someone is, he might be coming here right now. Is there any way to disable the bomb?"

"Permanently? No. Not without setting it off. You do, however, need to arm it first, which requires a key. I have it safely stowed away in the Magic Bank. Plus, if worse comes to worst, there is this very clever 'disarm' mechanism as well." He pointed to a comically large red button on the side of the device. "All you need to do is press it and the bomb will go dormant. No problem."

"Okay," I said. That feeling that Cassie might be in trouble was kicking into overdrive. I couldn't tell if it was just paranoia or something else. "The *Orbis* is safe in here after we exit, right? Like, it stays inside the telescope?"

"Oh yes. Precisely."

"Good." I nodded. "So on the count of three, let's go. Are you ready?"

Again, he hesitated. "It's just a shame that ..."

"Professor."

"Okay, okay. On the count of three."

I held up a hand and counted three with my fingers. I thought of exiting the Solitar and the familiar swirl of liquid passed over me and I was back in the museum. Steinberg appeared next to me a second later. I breathed a quick sigh of relief, yet it caught in my throat when I realized Cassie was gone. She was supposed to be holding the telescope. Now it was lying exposed on the floor. I bent to pick it up, but caught sight of her from the corner of my eye. I spun around and there she was—standing still as a statue.

"Cassie?"

I tried to go to her, but I couldn't move. My feet were locked to the floor. She just stared back, unmoving. Her eyes were pleading and a single tear slid down her cheek.

"What's going on?"

She didn't answer, but she didn't need to. He stepped from behind the door the second I asked the question. His eyes twinkled as he wore a broad smile and an impeccable suit.

"I'll have that telescope, François. Now, if you please."

My stomach clenched as Agent Thomas Rosewood stepped forward and held out his hand.

Chapter Ten

Godzilla

"YOU?" I ASKED. I was too stunned to move. I couldn't even lift the telescope. "What have you done to Cassie?"

Rosewood glanced back at her and raised an eyebrow. "Cassandra? Oh, she's fine. I gave her a touch of the old *Rigor Mortis*. Nasty spell. Makes it hard to move."

"If you hurt her—"

"Oh François! I dare say you're in no position to play the hero, now are you?" He tapped my leg with his cane and it made a hollow sound, like knocking on wood. "This particular spell is Level Nine," he explained. "*Arbor Glacialem*—The Frozen Tree. I'm afraid you'll be planted to this spot for quite some time. Perhaps a thousand years or so? Give or take? Now, if you'd be so kind, could you please pass me the telescope? I'd hate to have to resort to violence …"

"Why?" I breathed. "You … I would've brought you the telescope anyway. Why are you doing this?"

"*Why?* Oh. Well, I suppose for the same reason that most people do anything. Because I can. But don't feel badly, François. You and young Cassandra have been very useful in locating our dear professor here." He gave a pleasant nod to Steinberg who stared back in confusion. It didn't seem like he could move his feet either. "Yet as it is with all things," Rosewood continued, "it seems that you and Cassandra have outlived your purpose. I'm afraid our time together has reached its conclusion."

I continued to clench the telescope in my fist, and noticed—oddly—that Rosewood hadn't made any move to take it on his own.

"So everything was a lie," I said. "You've been using us the whole time? And what about Cassie? You told me you *raised* her."

"I did. Quite clever of me, actually. She's been most loyal these past few years. It never hurts to have a trained succubus on your side. Especially one so gifted at killing."

I glanced at Cassie and could see in her eyes that she was struggling with everything she had. Yet somehow, Rosewood's spell had completely frozen her in place. Her entire body was like a piece of iron.

I needed to do something—something to get her free. But how? I could barely move. And none of my four spells would help, not with this. All I could do was stall for time. So I fixed Rosewood with a glare and told him that "because I can" wasn't really an answer. Why *was* he trying to steal the *Orbis?*

"Oh, it's not for me," he explained. "You see, François, we are all servants of one sort or another. Even the most powerful—the kings and the queens—are beholden to the very rabble they call subjects. As for myself, I am but a humble servant as well. And when my master arrives, he will be most pleased with my endeavors."

"And I take it you're using the *Orbis* to get your master here?" I said.

"Quite right, François. Quite right." He then paused and looked at me quizzically. "Oh very well," he sighed. "I suppose there's no harm in telling you the truth. The fact is you are just as responsible for my master's arrival as I am."

"How's that?"

"He's rather taken with you, I'm afraid. I do believe he is planning a most unfortunate future for you and everyone you know. François, *I* was the one who tried to have you killed. I contracted with Aeroth—the miserable sod—who sent those incompetent vampire spawn after you. I also contracted with the skeleton, although in that case, that was a bit of a mistake. After you left my office, I realized you'd be of greater service alive than dead. It just so happened that I couldn't reach the skeleton in time to rescind the order. Nevertheless, our young Cassandra made quick work of him anyway. I was counting on that."

I considered forming a Firebolt with my left hand. It would be out of Rosewood's view and maybe I could do something with it. But what?

"Why would you want to kill me?" I asked. "Up until a couple weeks ago, I didn't know anything about anything. I wasn't even a wizard. And you were the one who lifted the hex!"

"All true. Top marks, François. Truly. That hex was the only thing protecting you—until of course that meddlesome astrologer Greta sent Cassandra to you. With her by your side, you were practically invulnerable. I doubt there's an assassin in the whole realm who'd risk going against her.

"You see, as it happens, you are not just an ordinary wizard—if there is such a thing. You have something much greater than that. But to explain would require *so* much history. I'd rather you just handed over the device and we could get on with things."

Okay. That was the third time he *asked* for it. Now I knew he couldn't take it on his own. Old Galileo must have done something to it—something that barred the likes of Rosewood from stealing it. It had to be *offered* to him, like Cassie with kissing. Still, my only option remained to stall for time. The longer Rosewood talked, the greater the possibility that someone—possibly even myself—might come up with a plan.

"Just give me the Cliff Notes," I said. "I want to know how you could betray Cassie like this. You rescued her. She loved you. And I thought you were the best guy I'd ever met. Then you turned out to be the very worst."

"Oh, you wound me. I'm not as bad as all that. I'm a realist, that's all. My master is coming to this realm—one way or another. And when he does, there will be those to whom he grants mercy, and those to whom he does not. I plan to be in the former camp. Besides, as I told you, it's your fault he's coming here in the first place. It was *your* master who imprisoned him."

"My what?"

"Your master. It hardly matters that you've never met him. After all, how could you have done? He died as soon as he transferred his powers to you. And I see by the confused look on your face that you have no idea what I'm talking about, which of course makes perfect sense. So let me tell you a story. There was a realm not far from this one, perhaps two or three over within the Multi-Realm. It was called Endruvia and was legendary for its extraordinary beauty. It was one of the few realms where peace and happiness flourished for all who lived there. And their magic was the stuff of legend. Absolutely unparalleled. They had some of the best wizards in all existence. Yet when they tried to resist my master, he dispatched them all with barely a thought. There was only one who had the strength to stand against him. His name was Wizenguaard, a warlock of the Thirteenth Order. I'm sad to say, he defeated my master but not before Endruvia was reduced to ashes. He then knew that his time was coming to an end. He traveled here—to Earth—and bestowed his abilities on a newborn infant in Paris. And as his final act, he placed a hex on the child to hide him from other practitioners. That child, of course, was you. Your parents moved to America, and for twenty years you were safe. But the hex wasn't designed to last forever. It was wearing off. After all, what good would it be if you could never do magic? The idea—from what I gather—was to allow you to grow up first. Then you might have a better chance at protecting yourself." He paused. "And now that I think about it, the old warlock must have contacted Greta Garbo as well. *That* was why she sent Cassandra to you when she did. Your own personal bodyguard until your skills increased. Most clever. Most clever indeed."

Now as you might imagine, this was a lot to take in. Foreign realms. Powerful Warlocks. Apparently I'm Luke Skywalker. Etcetera. Yet I have to admit, one of the top thoughts in my brain was: Did he say Greta *Garbo?* As in the 1920s film star? *She* was Cassie's astrologer?

"Just tell me one more thing," I said. "Why didn't you just kill me? Why was I useful to you at all? There was nothing I did that Cassie couldn't have done."

Rosewood shrugged. "I considered it. But there were several excellent reasons to keep you alive. First, if I wanted to kill you, I would've needed to do it myself. No one else would risk going against Cassandra. Then, if I did that, I would've lost my top agent. Second—and I'm most proud of this one—I bugged you."

"Bugged me?"

"The Solitar, François. I told you to keep it on your person at all times—which of course, like the nice little duckling that you are, you did. I've had an eye on you, and by extension Cassandra, at all times. I dare say I felt like a proper spy with that one. You see, I've learned after many years that it helps tremendously to have agents in the field doing one's 'legwork.' It saves so much time, and keeps suspicions of one's actions to a minimum. I wasn't lying, of course, when I told you the BPI was watching me. They are. Though today I managed to 'give them the slip,' as it were. Now it's too late. Even they can't stop me now. Which brings us back to why we are here in the first place. The telescope, François. This is the last time I will ask nicely."

It was time to put my theory to the test—and unless I was mistaken—my theory was the *real* reason Rosewood had kept me alive. He needed someone to *give* him the Solitar rather than take it himself. Cassie wouldn't have been able to discover its secret on her own. Rosewood needed a wizard for that, which made the telescope my only bargaining chip.

"Let Cassie go first," I said. "And Professor Steinberg. When they're safe, I'll hand it over."

Rosewood stared at me a long moment. Then, with a half smile, his eyes twinkled. "Very good, François. Very good indeed. How long have you known?"

"That you can't take the telescope?" I asked. "For as long as you've been talking, asshole."

"Ha! Perhaps old Wizenguaard wasn't such a fool after all! Still, I don't believe you have a proper measure of the situation, my dear boy. I may not be able to take the Solitar from you, but there is nothing stopping me from inflicting a great deal of pain upon your beloved 'Cassie' until you give it me. So. Shall I get to it? Or will you save us all a great deal of time and unpleasantness?"

Damn.

Despite my extensive action movie knowledge, I hadn't considered the "I'll torture your friends until you give it to me" option. I mean, crap. Bruce Willis was probably rolling his eyes at this very moment. Yippee ki-yah, motherf-er ...

"You'd really hurt her?" I asked. "She thinks of you as a father. Does that mean nothing to you?"

I didn't think that'd actually sway him, but I had to delay as long as possible.

"I'm afraid it doesn't. She's a half-breed, François. Filthy. Though I'll admit she has certain physical qualities that are pleasing to the eye. But nothing more. Now." He raised his hands to make an *Imago*. "There is a wonderful little spell called *Brimstone* that I've always wanted to try on a living subject. I dare say you've given me the perfect opportunity ..."

"Here." I put the telescope in his hand without delay.

It was the only thing to do. I doubt I could've lasted five seconds with him torturing Cassie, so why wait? He'd won this round. Simple as that.

Or had he?

Steinberg suddenly spoke up for the first time since we exited the Solitar.

"It won't do you any good," he told Rosewood calmly. "If your intentions are impure, you cannot enter Galileo's Solitar. Plus, the *Orbis Lux* requires a key. You don't have it."

"Is that so?" Rosewood cocked his head. "Well then perhaps you would be so kind as to retrieve it for me." He waved his hand and Steinberg's feet came unglued from the floor. He stepped toward Rosewood. "Why would I do that?" he asked. "You're trying to end the world. Helping you wouldn't make any sense."

"Ha! Well let's just see about—"

Rosewood didn't get a chance to utter another word. Steinberg clicked his heels together and what happened next ... I'm honestly not sure how to describe it. It was sort of like an explosion, but there wasn't any blast and there wasn't any sound. It was just a sudden burst of light and then a million little sparks zipped around the room like angry fireflies. The result? My feet came unglued and I could move again.

But that wasn't the important part. The important part was that Cassie became free as well. And if you were wondering why this chapter was entitled *Godzilla,* now is when you learn the answer.

My girlfriend—yes, that's what I'm going to call her now—charged into Rosewood so hard he flew fifty feet against the far wall and crashed straight through it. She ran after him, re-extending the flaming samurai sword and the energy shield. Her movements were so fast they were practically a blur.

I whipped around to find Steinberg collapsed on the floor. When I kneeled by his side, I noticed he wasn't breathing.

Crap.

Ten thousand years ago, I took CPR as part of P.E. in high school. Like everyone else, I gave it about three percent of my attention. After all, I was never going to need to do *CPR*. No one ever did stuff like that in real life. All I remembered was "Thirty and Two." Thirty chest compressions. Two breaths. So that's what I did. I did it over and over again, but nothing happened. The adrenaline began to pound in my chest. I could've been doing everything totally wrong. I had no idea. All I knew was that I couldn't let this guy die simply because I'd been a crappy student in school.

I redoubled my efforts.

From a floor below, I heard explosions and shouts. Wherever Cassie and Rosewood were, it sounded like an epic battle. Then, in a sudden explosion, they both crashed up through the floor. It was like a landmine had gone off a few yards away. The wood splintered and burst in all directions. Rosewood floated upwards, surrounded by a giant, lightning-infused *Imago*. I figured it was the vastly more advanced version of Force Bubble. Both his hands were zipping with sparks of energy and his eyes glowed red. Cassie jumped to meet him, still defending herself with the shield. All of Rosewood's spells bounced right off it. She lunged with the sword, but his force field was just as impenetrable. It was then that Rosewood disappeared in a blink, and then reappeared right next to me. My arms locked at my sides and he pointed a glowing finger at my head. A spark of energy released and stopped a millimeter from my temple. It hung there, suspended, buzzing like an angry bumblebee.

Cassie froze.

"Put the weapons down," Rosewood ordered her in a changed voice. It sounded deeper and inhuman like he was channeling it from somewhere else.

I felt like an idiot. Cassie probably could've beaten him if it weren't for me. Now, she was slowly kneeling and setting her sword and shield on the floor. Once they were out of her hands, they flew away as if kicked by an invisible foot.

Rosewood's voice suddenly went back to normal. "Jolly good," he gasped, a little winded. "I must say, Cassandra. That was rather a nice workout, what? I've trained you quite well, if I do say so myself."

She spat at him.

"As eloquent as ever!" he said, beaming. "Now, it appears we have a bit of a situation, don't we? I have your boyfriend with a ready spell aimed at his head. I also have the professor here, who will likely die unless I help him. So! I'll make you a deal. A two for one, if you will. I'll revive Steinberg and I'll let your precious imbecile go free. In return, you stay right there, you don't try any funny business, and watch as I leave the way I came in. How does that sound?"

"Don't do it," I told Cassie, but she never broke eyes with Rosewood.

"Do it and leave," she said coldly. "Then I'm coming for you."

"Ha! If ever there was an empty threat! I dare say, Cassandra, I may actually miss you when this is all over."

"Just let him go!" she shouted.

"As you wish. But if I see you move, even slightly, they both die. Is that clear?"

Cassie nodded, fuming.

"Wonderful." Rosewood formed a new *Imago* and began doing a series of lightning fast *Canti* that made me realize just how much of an amateur I truly was. It was like watching a professional violinist after taking lessons for a single day. The skill-level was practically magic in and of itself. Rosewood then cast the spell at Steinberg, whose back arched dramatically as he drew in a massive gulp of air. His eyes flew open as he clutched at his chest, heaving with heavy breaths.

Rosewood grinned and used a cantrip to levitate the professor's body a few feet off the floor.

"I suppose that does it," he said cheerily. He continued to face Cassie as he floated backwards with Steinberg trailing in front. He was heading for an emergency exit only a few yards away. The door opened automatically as he moved. I saw grass on the other side but couldn't recognize any landmarks. Then Rosewood flashed us a final, radiant smile. "In case you were thinking of following," he said. "That would be ill-advised. The ward on this particular door is quite nasty. I designed it myself. Ta!"

And then he was gone. The door closed and the spell hovering next to my temple disappeared. Cassie and I were alone.

• • •

A few minutes later, we were zipping down the streets of Florence on *Mary Lou*. We hadn't wasted any time in going after Rosewood. (Except for a few seconds for Cassie to smash my Solitar with her foot, and then a few more seconds for us to make out. That was it.) We shouted back and fourth as I weaved the Vespa between cars. Cassie had a theory that her former mentor was headed back to LA. She said she'd seen a picture of the downtown skyline on his desk a few weeks earlier. Now, for some reason, she was a hundred percent certain that LA was where he planned to detonate the *Orbis Lux*. The blast wave alone would destroy a good chunk of the city and everyone in it. Then—if that wasn't bad enough—the resulting portal would open a door to the apocalypse. I pictured some sort of evil sorcerer flying through with an army of Fire Demons at his back. So basically, we only had time to guess right once. And since I didn't have any better ideas … Los Angeles it was.

When we arrived at our backdoor, Cassie hopped off with the keys. She'd just reached out to put one in the lock, when her entire body flew backward in a sudden jolt of electricity. She hit the pavement, somersaulted twice, and then landed on her feet. (Possibly the coolest thing I'd ever seen.)

Mary Lou fell on her side as I ran over and asked if she was alright.

"I'm fine," she said, glowering. "He put a stupid ward on the door. I bet they're everywhere in this city. *Fuck!*"

"There's gotta be another way," I said.

"Sure." She chuckled darkly. "An airplane?"

"I don't think that'll make it in time. What about other backdoors? Is there anything outside the city?"

Cassie was already a step ahead of me, digging her phone from her pocket and dialing.

"Q?" she said. "No, shut up. This is an emergency. I'm in Florence and I need the nearest backdoor to LA. But listen. It has to be outside the city."

A pause.

"Yes, Italy! Why would I be in Florence, Ohio?!"

Another pause.

"I don't care if they have good donuts! Just find it! I'm serious!"

I backed off a couple feet to give her some space. It seemed a wise move.

Cassie paced back and forth like a tiger for a minute until she stopped and listened. "Where?" she said. "*Bologna??* That will take hours! No, I'm not yelling!"

She hung up. "Come on," she grumbled. "We're getting gas and then riding a million miles to stupid 'Bologna.' Fucking crap."

I didn't say anything.

A million miles later we arrived in the great Italian city of Bologna, which I'll admit, I'd never heard of before. Seriously. It was a big city too—full of landmarks, culture and centuries of history. But what can I say? I'm an American. When I first heard the name Bologna, my only insight was that it sounded like *baloney*. That's the truth.

Either way, there was no time for sightseeing. We were only in the city for a few minutes until we found our backdoor. Cassie told me to stand back and then tested it with her fingertips. No explosion. We burst through on the Vespa and arrived in LA. It was late afternoon and the traffic was out of control. The entire city was gridlocked, and even on *Mary Lou*, it was hard to maneuver. Cassie explained that Rosewood needed to detonate the *Orbis* on top of a building because it needed the altitude.

"The U.S. Bank Tower is the tallest building on the West Coast," I shouted over my shoulder. We were currently in West Hollywood, which put DTLA about two miles and thirty-eight hours away. Give or take. I could do my best to shave that time with some clever scooter maneuverings, but not by much. Luckily, Cassie had other plans. She told me to take a sharp left down an alley behind a movie theater and then several more turns. We arrived at a dead end.

"Wait here," she said and hopped off. She ran toward the wall and passed straight through it. A few seconds later, a pair of headlights emerged to the tune of a low, grumbling engine. The car was vintage, yet looked brand new. A Dodge Super Bee, if I wasn't mistaken. The door popped open and I got in.

"How many cars do you have?" I asked.

"Lots."

I don't need to tell you that over the next few minutes, Cassie made a handful of traffic violations. If I thought she'd been driving recklessly before, now she was like a vehicular wrecking ball. There was one instance where she angled our trajectory to use a smaller car as a ramp, thereby flying over several other cars—including a tractor-trailer—and then landing right side up. In another maneuver, she took a page straight out of *The Dark Knight,* and started hopping across rooftops. And as far as I could tell, there wasn't anything "magic" going on. She was just *that* good.

It took about ten minutes before we screeched to a halt at the base of the U.S. Bank Tower. I hadn't been able to talk while she was driving, but as I opened the door and stepped out, I reminded Cassie that Rosewood needed a special key to arm the *Orbis.*

She frowned and popped the trunk to select from a wide array of toys. (Guns.) "That's why he took Steinberg with him," she growled. "Rosewood's good enough that he can perform an Invisible Enchantment."

"So?"

"So I don't know if you noticed, but the professor isn't too bright when it comes to security. I'll bet you he put the key in a standard safe at the Magic Bank. All Rosewood has to do is enchant him and he'll go retrieve it. No one will know the difference."

"Oh," I said. "Shit."

"Yes. Shit."

I looked at her. I didn't want to ask my next question, but I had to. There was no way around it. I stepped closer and touched her elbow. "Cass ... about Rosewood ... how are you doing with that?"

She zipped her final weapon into a holding disc and slammed the trunk. "Look," she said. "I'm going to be really, really, *really* pissed off at some point—but not right now. We need to stop him first. Then I'll worry about everyone in my life up till now being a bastard. Okay?"

"Sounds good to me," I said.

"Now kiss me," she ordered.

So I did. (It lasted a bit longer than I would've expected, too.)

Cassie kept her forehead pressed to mine and whispered, "To hell with Rosewood, okay? It's up to you and me to stop him. Deal?"

"Ready when you are," I said.

She pulled back with her first grin since Rosewood betrayed her. "I knew I was right about you. An actual good guy. Now let's do this."

We trotted over to the Bank Tower's grand entrance. It was a giant glass façade that opened into a spacious atrium. When Cassie reached for the door, however, she once again fell victim to an electric shock. Her body flew back a good twenty feet—yet she still managed to do the somersault thing. I didn't bother asking if she was okay since I saw the look on her face. Her eyes were narrowed to thin slits and her lips formed a grim line. A rocket launcher appeared and she hefted it onto her shoulder, biting her lip in concentration. She was about to pull the trigger when I ran in front of it and shouted for her to wait.

"Get out of the way!" she barked, waving impatiently.

"He's on the roof, right?" I said.

"What?"

"Rosewood. He's going to detonate the bomb on the roof."

"So?"

"So I can get us there. Besides, the whole building might be booby-trapped. I can levitate us both to the top."

The rocket launcher disappeared and Cassie stepped closer. She looked down at me with a triumphant smirk. "See?" she said. "I knew having a sidekick would pay off. Let's do it your way."

"We're going to have to talk about the word 'sidekick' at some point, but okay."

I formed a quick *Imago* and did the *Canti* for BL. The *Ignis* zipped around my fingertips until I snapped my fingers and it exploded between Cassie's chest and mine. After that, we were a pair of weightless astronauts. Our ascent was slow, steady and straight up. Cassie and I held hands to make sure we didn't drift apart. And for a few seconds, the whole thing was going quite well. At our current speed, we'd get to the roof within a couple minutes. But then I made the mistake of looking down and saw nothing below my feet. The pavement was falling away. Thirty feet. Forty feet. *Fifty* feet.

Now, it's been well documented that I'm not a big fan of heights. Things like Ferris wheels, roller coasters and tall buildings scare the crap out of me. Yet even with all those things, my feet would still be on solid ground—not hanging by nothing like a cloud, and rising higher and higher with no way to stop.

Panic began to set in.

My forehead—which didn't care that today was a nice afternoon with a cool breeze—started dripping. My heart rate went through the roof.

Cassie noticed my body tensing and gripped my hand a little tighter. "Look straight ahead," she said. "That'll help."

"It's too late." My whole body was shaking and I couldn't breathe. "I already looked down. I'm done for. Just forget about me."

I noticed her roll her eyes. "Look, we'll be there soon. You have to distract yourself."

"With *what?* I'm afraid I left my chess set at home."

"Not chess," she said.

And then we were kissing again.

I'll admit: It distracted me. In fact, it did such a good job that I was startled when we ran out of building and started floating up past the crown-shaped roof. Luckily, Cassie was on it. She quickly fired the grappling hook from her Q watch and tagged a nearby safety railing. It jerked us down until we were standing on the roof's helipad where, sure enough, we found

Agent Rosewood and the *Orbis Lux*. Rosewood looked like he'd been waiting for us. He was sitting pleasantly at a little round table with a flapping tablecloth drinking a cup of tea. The *Orbis,* meanwhile, sat a few yards to his left. It looked totally exposed, and the giant red "disarm" button was calling to me. If I made a mad dash for it ...

"So good of you to join me!" Rosewood shouted, and half stood from his seat. He gestured good-naturedly toward the two empty chairs opposite his own. "I confess I was rather hoping you'd make it! One does not wish to witness such momentous events as these by oneself. 'Tis always better in good company."

My muscles tensed as I thought about charging the red button. Cassie caught me by the wrist. "Don't," she said quietly. "He's ready for us. Nothing is what it seems anymore. Understand?"

I nodded.

"It's not too late to call this off!" she shouted over the wind to Rosewood.

He just smiled and held up the China teapot.

"Come sit," he said. "We have a few minutes before the bomb goes off. Why spend them so angry?"

Cassie and I shared a glance and then sat down. Rosewood poured for both of us. He was quite good at it too, not spilling a single drop despite the heavy wind.

"So," he said, raising his voice as he sat back in his chair. "There's something quite thrilling about the end, isn't there? The finality of it! All our fates are sealed and it's too late to do anything. I dare say, if there was ever a time to 'enjoy the moment,' it would be now, wouldn't you agree?"

"You can still disarm the bomb," I said.

Rosewood cocked an eyebrow. "Can I?" he asked. "I suppose that's a rather philosophical question, isn't it? After all, I've come all this way. I'd judge myself a bit mad if I backed out now. Besides, what would I do afterward? Languish in a magic prison? Get banished to some God-awful plane? No. I do believe my choice has already been taken, François. Sorry."

"You could stand up and fight me," Cassie challenged. "No magic. No weapons. Just you and me."

Rosewood looked puzzled. "And what—may I ask—would I profit from such an adventure?"

"You'd learn what it's like to get your ass kicked, which is what's going to happen in two seconds anyway."

"Ha! Such bravado! Well done! I suppose if you truly wish to 'take a swing,' then I suggest you—"

Cassie took a swing. Hard and fast.

There are some things that when they happen, they don't look natural. For example, when you see a YouTube video of a bulldog riding a surfboard or a cat singing a show tune—they either look staged or in some cases, photoshopped. So when I tell you that Rosewood's hand moved in such a way that didn't look natural, you'll have some idea what I mean. The movement was so quick; it looked like his hand teleported from one place to the other. It caught Cassie's so easily I flinched. Then he squeezed until she screamed.

I jumped to my feet and remembered the two-shot Derringer in my pocket. I yanked it free and pointed it at his chest. His hand continued to crush Cassie's until she dropped to her knees. Tears streamed down her cheeks. Whatever spell he was using, it was powerful.

I looked to Rosewood, who was grinning manically, and I pulled the trigger. The hammer snapped forward, the gunpowder exploded, and then the Englishman turned to me with a curious, knitted brow. The bullet had bounced off his suit lapel like it was nothing.

"I do say," Rosewood said, amused. "Where did that little thing come from? You certainly are full of surprises, aren't you François?"

Another squeal came from Cassie, and I screamed for him to stop hurting her.

"But what if I enjoy hurting her?" he asked. "Perhaps you should try it yourself. It's rather gratifying."

I did the only thing I could think of. I made a quick Firebolt, but Rosewood simply flicked his wrist and the flame extinguished.

"Please, François," he chuckled. "You've done so well. Don't start embarrassing yourself now, I beg you." He gave another wave and the Derringer flew away as well. It landed on the edge of the helipad. Rosewood then cocked his head, still squeezing Cassie's hand, and regarded me curiously.

"I just remembered," he said. "I do believe you are afraid of heights, yes? Cassie confided in me as much a few days ago. Is it true?"

"No."

"Oh, of course it is. You're not a very good liar, you know." He made a fast gesture and my arms were instantly pinned to my sides. He then raised a palm and I floated backwards until my feet left the roof and I was staring straight down at a thousand foot drop.

"I imagine that would be quite scary!" Rosewood called out to me as the wind beat against my ears. I squeezed my eyes shut. "Oh, none of that!" he shouted and my eyes opened on their own. "I tell you, François! I feel extraordinary! Don't you as well? One cannot help but feel an overwhelming sense of 'seize the day' at a moment like this! The world is but minutes from a new future! You will be dead, of course, and so will Cassandra, but I—I shall be the right hand to a new emperor! Is it not marvelous? Simply marvelous?!"

Right then, Cassie managed to hook her leg between his feet and knock him over. His hand released hers and she scrambled to get away. Rosewood floated back to his feet without using his arms. His eyes were glowing red again. "I will enjoy this!" He smiled and advanced on Cassie with long strides. I couldn't move a muscle to help. She backed away, but not fast enough. His hand came crashing down on her wrist and yanked her to her feet. I was surprised to see Cassie do nothing in return. It was like all her strength had left her. Rosewood's free hand collided with her stomach so hard I could hear it. She doubled over, gasping for breath. Without warning, he kicked her in the ribs, sending her rolling toward the roof's edge. He caught her before she went over, only to lift her by the neck until she was dangling above him.

"You see, François!" he boomed over his shoulder. "There is no *creature* that can match a wizard! I *own* this building, do you see? It is under my control. None of this half-breed's pathetic skills will work here. Here she is nothing! He threw her toward the *Orbis* and she crashed into the tea table. She didn't get up. Her body lay crumpled and unconscious in a twisted heap.

My heart practically exploded. "Rosewood, stop!" I screamed, but there was nothing I could do. No spell. No ace up my sleeve. I was pinned and dangling over my worst fear. I wasn't a superhero. I wasn't a spy. I was just a random guy out of his depth. I was—as Rosewood had put it—*nothing*. And that's what being helpless is all about. It forces you to confront just how much "nothing" you truly are.

Rosewood picked Cassie up by the throat, her body hanging limp. He punched her across the jaw once, twice ... I lost count. I couldn't breathe. Her lips were smeared with blood and her cheeks swollen. Rosewood beamed with pure delight, exposing rows of newly sharp teeth. Cassie, I noticed, raised her head a little. The blood made it hard to tell, but I could've sworn her lips curved upward a little.

And that's when I saw it.

There was something in her hand. It glinted in the fading sunlight. Metal. And on the side ... a little snowflake.

Rosewood glanced down. Cassie's weak grin widened as he leapt back in shock, dropping her. I could almost hear him wondering where the grenade had come from. I suppose he'd have to ask Q about that. It exploded before he had a chance to jump away. It was all over in a heartbeat. Rosewood and Cassie were now solid statues of ice.

It was almost like she'd planned it from the start. She'd known the whole time about the grenade tucked away in a micro-disc. She'd just been waiting for the right moment—a moment that I needed to finish.

With Rosewood turned to ice, his spell keeping me aloft disappeared. I hung suspended for a half-second before plummeting straight down. My hands caught the roof's edge. I kicked wildly against the side of the building as I scrambled to pull myself up. The sheer size of the drop pulled at my feet like a vacuum. I clawed my way back an inch at a time, thinking I was going to pass out from sheer terror at any second. When I finally finished, I stood on the helipad, doubled over and panting from the adrenaline. I was so rattled I couldn't even think. All that mattered was the blood pounding in my temples and the desperate need for air.

Yet somehow, I saw it anyway. It lay at my feet like destiny itself and glinted in the pink-grey light—a two-shot Derringer with one shot left. I picked it up, I walked a few paces, and I aimed. I set the sight square on Rosewood's chest. His statue was beginning to glow, like it was trying to break the spell. I cocked the hammer and met his icy eyes.

At the beginning of this story, I told you that I was *not* from France. I told you that I didn't speak French. I told you I was embarrassed of my name and grew up with dorky parents. I told you I was average. I told you I was nothing.

Then I met a girl and learned that I was wrong. I am François Lemieux. I speak French, of course I do, damn it! What do you think my parents spoke all those years? I *am*

French. I am a wizard too. But most of all, I am in love. *So au revoir, Monsieur Rosewood! Vous êtes une merde! This is for Cassie Chu!*

And I pressed the trigger.

A lot of things could've happened after that. The bullet could've missed. It could've ricocheted off the side. It could've dinked against the ice and done nothing. But it didn't do those things. It hit Rosewood center mass like a freight train. His statue exploded into a thousand icy shards leaving his head to drop straight down, shattering on the cement like your aunt's favorite vase.

I won't lie. It was immensely satisfying.

But there was still the *Orbis*. Only a couple minutes remained on its timer. I ran for the big red button. I punched it with my fist, only to discover what it feels like to get zapped with fifty thousand volts and fly backwards. I landed hard on my butt and groaned. As I got back to my feet, I was hit by a renewed sense of panic. I was screwed. We all were. Rosewood had placed a powerful defensive ward around the bomb. There was no way to disarm it. And with only one minute, fifty-two seconds left, the opening of the portal was inevitable. I didn't know the first thing about wards. I didn't know how to create them, and I definitely didn't know how to erase them. If only there was someone who ...

Oh.

Galileo's telescope. It lay right next to the broken tea table. I ran for it and put my eye to the lens.

McFadden—bless the son of a bitch—was waiting for me inside the cathedral.

"There is little time," he said sharply. "If you wish to cancel a ward, you must first learn *which* ward you are canceling. Understand?"

"How do I know which ward it is?"

"Damn it, François! Use that thing between your ears and think! You must go back in time, do you see?"

"*Vigilia Temporis?*" I asked.

"Yes! But quickly!"

I formed the *Imago* and began doing the *Canti*. It took me four tries to get it right. I left the Solitar and cast it. The swirly cloud appeared and the window at its center showed Rosewood forming a spell. I zoomed in to watch his fingers. Quickly, I went back inside the telescope.

"I've got it," I announced, still holding the cloud in front of me.

"That is step one," McFadden said. "Step two is to learn which ward he is making based on the *Canti*. You need to watch closely."

"Why?"

"The only way to cancel a ward is to cast the same ward on top of it. There are hundreds of variants, so you cannot simply 'guess.' You must learn the exact one. Now get to it. Time runs slower in this place, but it does not stop. You have minutes at most."

I re-watched Rosewood perform the *Canti* for the ward. Then I watched him again and again. The guy was *fast*. His fingers flew over the *Imago* in a blur.

So imagine this: Some madman has his finger on the button to destroy the world—maybe he's an eccentric president with the launch codes—and he tells you, "Here. Take a look at this YouTube video of a concert pianist playing Mozart's Fifth Concerto. Now, you have precisely 'a few minutes' to learn to play it yourself. If you don't, or if you fail to do it in time, I'm going to press the button. Go."

There was no way I could learn a spell that complicated just by watching another guy's hands. It was impossible. No one, least of all me, could do something like that. There was no point in even trying.

"There is no choice, François." McFadden's voice came from above as I kept my head down. "It is a difficult task, I grant you, but the most important ones always are. You cannot give up. A great many people are depending on you. Do your best. Keep your chin up. Try your hardest. If you can do that, son—you can do anything."

Screw it.

I raised my hands and formed another *Imago.* The image of Rosewood's hands played beside me as I studied each tiny movement of his fingers. At first, I felt another wave of frustration, as I couldn't make out a single note.

Then I spotted one.

His right index finger pressed inward and I *knew* it was an Omega. Then I watched the other fingers, one by one. A Delta here. An Epsilon there. I was piecing it together. I tried over and over to mimic each movement. Some of them I could do, others I couldn't. Still, I tried. I could feel the clock winding down. Minutes had passed. The timer on the bomb was likely down to seconds. I needed to master this spell, and I needed to do it now.

"François, listen to me," McFadden said softly. "You have learned many spells these past weeks, yet I fear you have not considered *magic.*"

I looked up.

He poked my chest with the head of his cane and held it there. "Magic, my dear boy, is more than just a word. It is more than just a spell. Do you not see? It is that which makes us *believe.* Believe in the impossible. Believe that there is something more than just what is. *That* is what this moment requires, François. You must believe for the very first time since you encountered the uncanny that *magic* ... is real."

This was my last chance. I closed my eyes and did the *Canti* blind. One note after another—each one leading to the next. I heard music. It moved right through me and played across my fingertips. Wherever my thoughts were coming from, it wasn't my mind. There was something else—something from somewhere far away. When I opened my eyes ... the spell was formed.

Outside the Solitar, the *Orbis* was down to three seconds. I cast the ward. I prayed. And I pressed the big, red button.

A second later ... I didn't die.

The next breath I took felt like my first in five years. It was glorious. I'd done it. I didn't know how, but I had. I'd formed an impossible spell in an impossible amount of time. The clock had stopped with one second left. The world had just gotten a second chance. Then, as if on cue, the cavalry arrived. A large BPI helicopter appeared overhead and touched down.

I ran to Cassie's statue and stopped her from blowing over. When I saw her start to tilt, I nearly had a heart attack. A swarm of dark-suited agents emerged from the chopper and went straight for the *Orbis*. Another man followed them, but came running for me instead. It was Professor Steinberg, freshly rescued from wherever Rosewood had left him. His hair was wild. His eyebrows were massive.

"You did it!" he exclaimed over the whir of the rotors.

"How do we help her?" I shouted back, motioning to Cassie. "She blew up an ice grenade!"

Steinberg stopped dead in his tracks when he saw her. His eyebrows furrowed so severely it made my hands shake. He was giving me the look that a man gives when something terrible has happened and nothing can be done.

"Professor!" I shouted. "Please!"

He studied Cassie a long moment. "Wait," he said sharply. "I am detecting a strange hue here." He then looked at me. "Is your friend entirely human?"

"She's half succubus," I said.

Steinberg's shoulders suddenly dropped. He let out such a sigh of relief it overpowered the beating of the helicopter. "Oh, thank goodness," he breathed. He then flashed me a wide, bashful grin. "In that case, the solution is quite simple."

"What is it?" I asked.

"All you must do is kiss her."

"That's it?!"

"There is a good deal of magic in a kiss, you know. A lesson we all learn eventually. Now help your friend before she melts."

I stood in front of her, leaned up a little, and put my lips to hers. They were solid and cold for only a second. Then, as I opened my eyes, they were alive and warm, and Cassie Chu was back.

And *then* … we kept kissing.

She rushed forward, pushing me back until we were both on the ground. We rolled until she landed on top and started tearing my shirt off.

I'll admit the situation was getting a little embarrassing. But Cassie—obviously—didn't care. I caught a few looks from passing BPI agents as they hauled off the *Orbis*. I tried to stutter an excuse about my girlfriend being a "succubus and what can a guy do?" but Cassie kept bringing my attention back to her. Then her hand slid down to my waist and … *Jesus Christ, was she unbuttoning my pants?*

"Cassie, uh, are you …?" I tried to ask around her kiss, but she literally growled into my mouth. Her hand then moved to her own pants and started working them down. I guess that was my answer. It wasn't something I'd normally do, but I didn't really have a choice. Cassie and I were going all the way.

Chapter Eleven

Bond, James Bond

I TOLD YOU EARLIER ABOUT NOTICING cringe-worthy moments as they're happening. We all have them. I'm sure you've had a few yourself. Maybe you asked a girl to a dance once and then noticed that a flap of underwear was sticking out of your zipper? (No? Okay, that's mine.) The point is those moments have a tendency to stick with you forever. The trick is to realize that they're not so bad. Often times—if not always—the most embarrassing moments of a guy's life make for his very best stories.

After Cassie and I finished on the rooftop of the U.S. Bank Tower—in full view of a dozen BPI agents who I *hope* were automatons and not real people—we spent the next few days never leaving a series of hotel suites, rooftops and foreign palaces. It wasn't all just rolling in the sheets, though. We occasionally ordered room service, and I showed her several of my favorite movies.

She thought they all sucked.

Which was fine because that led to some fun arguments, which led to some fun other things.

There were also several more embarrassing moments, including the one where the President of the United States caught us in the Lincoln Bedroom, and we spent the next few minutes running naked through the White House getting chased by Secret Service agents. (We got away, but only after running across the street to another building.)

Our epic tryst finally ended, however, when Cassie got a cryptic call from the SIA. It told her to report to the London headquarters "with all possible speed." It also told her to come alone.

It was now the next day, and I still hadn't heard from her. I texted her several times, but they bounced back with a message saying, "Unable To Deliver."

I was starting to seriously worry. The only other person I could call in the Magic Community was Q, and he told me—in no uncertain terms—that she was probably fine and that I shouldn't be a pussy.

So, all I could do was wait. And since waiting is best done in the company of others, I joined my roommates for a video game tournament of *Duty Bound*. (What else could I do? It took my mind off things.)

"Eat that!"

I blinked in time to see my character get hit by a bunker buster. Brian whooped in delight, as for once, he was thoroughly winning.

I sighed and tossed my controller to Buckner, who caught it with a wide grin.

"I'm surprised the young man can stay upright," he said. "He's been at it for three straight days with that girl. I mean, damn!"

"I never said that," I said.

"Shoot hotrod, it was written all over your face. You didn't need to say nothin'. Speakin' of which, how come you're lookin' all worried? Did she move on to greener pastures already, or what?"

I shrugged. "I texted her, but she hasn't texted back."

"You call her?" Buckner asked

"No, just text."

"Well ain't you a Don Juan for the ages. Call the girl, you dumbass. Tell her you love her."

"You want me to tell her I love her?"

"Chicks dig it when you say that, man. They go all crazy."

I chuckled and checked my phone again. Still nothing.

"I say the whole thing is bullshit," Brian announced, still angling his controller like it would help his character move faster. "You two are the only ones who have seen this mystery girl."

"Man's got a point," Buckner agreed. "You need to bring her around. We gotta meet her. And maybe steal her away if possible ... She's way too hot for you anyway."

"If she texts me back," I said. "And I wouldn't recommend stealing her. You'll hurt yourself."

I hadn't told any of them she was a succubus, so they didn't know what I meant by that. Thus, Buckner just laughed. "Will you look at that?" he said. "Our boy's finally grown some cojones. Atta boy, Frenchie. You keep that girl close."

I was about to roll my eyes when I heard a beautiful sound—the soft *ping* of a text.

I literally dropped my phone and then scrambled to pick it up and ... *yes!* A text from Cassie. It looked like this:

007Girl69: You! Come outside!

Before I could react, a hand snatched the phone from my grip.

"Is that her?" Buckner exclaimed and looked at the screen. "Holy shit, it is, ain't it? 007Girl? And 69? I like her already!"

I jumped to my feet. "Dude, I gotta go."

"Fuckin' eh right you do." He tossed the phone back. "Go get 'em, hoss!"

I was halfway out the door as I heard Brian saying, "I'm still calling bullshit. Why didn't she come up?"

I grinned as I flew down the stairs and burst out the front door. I'll admit I felt a little childish for being so excited to see her, but I couldn't help it. Plus, I was relieved she was alright. After the whole Rosewood thing, I didn't trust the SIA at all.

When I got to the curb, I skidded to a halt. Cassie wasn't there. Instead, there was an eerily familiar silver Rolls Royce with a uniformed chauffeur standing outside. He bowed mechanically and opened the passenger door.

"Hello sir," he said with an equally mechanical voice. I noticed a well-concealed hinge near his jaw. "You are requested in London. Please come with me."

"Where's Cassie?" I asked.

"Agent Chu is awaiting your arrival, sir. I have instructions to bring you to her location."

"I'm not getting in that car."

The automaton blinked in confusion and I heard the whir of gears inside his head. Then, after a pause, he said, "Sir, please come with me."

I got out my phone to call Cassie's new number, but no one answered.

"Sir?" the automaton asked. "Are you attempting to reach Agent Chu?"

"She's not answering," I said. I then squinted at him and formed a Firebolt. "If you work for Rosewood," I started to say, but stopped when his head fell back unnaturally and a 3D hologram shone out of his gaping mouth. It showed Cassie sitting at a desk, and for a split-second, she looked surprised when she glanced up from some papers. "Hey!" she said, brightening. "You met Jeeves!"

I stepped back and frowned. "Who?"

"My new automaton. Every agent gets one. Plus the Rolls. But I like my old car better. Anyway, what are you doing outside? He's supposed to bring you here."

"I didn't want to get in," I said. "It was freaky."

She wrinkled her nose. "You mean, Jeeves? He's cool. Come on, we have important things to discuss. I got a promotion, you know. I'm big time now. Full secret agent status."

"So that's why you sent your driver to come fetch me, huh?"

I was trying to sound offended but I couldn't stop grinning. Just seeing Cassie's face had that affect on me. (Usually.)

Her eyes glanced down and she gave a sheepish grin. "I was showing off. You're not impressed?"

I looked at the brand new Rolls and then at Jeeves. "No, I'm impressed," I said. "So I guess I'll see you in a few minutes?"

She nodded curtly. "That would be correct, my hot new boyfriend. Bye!"

Her hologram disappeared and Jeeves's head snapped back into place. "Hello sir," he said again. "You are requested in London. Please come with me."

• • •

The trip to London took about an hour. The coolest part of the journey, and partly why it took so long, was that we drove across L.A. to get to the famous Griffith Park Tunnel. It's fame hails from its role as the entrance to Toontown in the movie *Who Framed Roger Rabbit.* (Arguably an astounding work of cinematic genius.) When we passed into the tunnel, we instantly popped out the other side of a different tunnel in London. From there, it was only a short drive to a small pub on the corner of Chiswick Street and Mistyshire Lane. (I just made those up. I didn't actually see the street names.) The Rolls stopped at the curb and Jeeves hopped outside to open my door. "It is this way, sir." He motioned toward the pub.

"In there?" I asked.

"Yes, sir."

I followed him inside. The place was dark, musty and deserted. I wasn't surprised, though. London was eight hours ahead of LA. It was four a.m. local time. Jeeves led the way before coming to an abrupt halt and pointing to a supply closet.

"This is the entrance, sir. Use the passcode 'Cherry Trolley Manchester,' to arrive at your destination. Have a safe trip." He bowed again and then marched away.

I looked at the door. I knew it was just a standard issue backdoor, but I couldn't help but feel a little nervous. The SIA had a long way to go before I trusted it again. In fact, it was kind of stupid that I had ever trusted it at all. What did I know about any of this stuff? I was a college student in a den of magical spies. If ever there was a sitting duck ...

I spoke the passcode aloud before turning the key. The door opened to a drab room with a gated elevator on the far wall. Beside it stood a familiar old man in a starched conductor's uniform.

The scary guard, I thought.

I closed the door behind me and the old man morphed into his true self—an eight-foot tall, flaming-headed angel thing with a giant sword.

I gave him a nod. "George,' I said.

We stared at each other until the elevator gave a loud clatter and its doors opened. The screech of rusty metal on metal was like fingernails on a chalkboard. I half-expected to see Cassie, but instead it was a middle-aged white guy who I'd never seen before. His suit was grey and businesslike. His face—the same. He didn't exit the elevator but just stared at me a moment. Somehow, I knew he wasn't another Brit like Rosewood. There was something about his clothing, his no-nonsense posture, and his salt and pepper hair that suggested he was an American, and most likely, a former Marine.

"François Lemieux," he said with a slight squint. (I was right. American. Marine. No-nonsense.) He stepped forward and extended a hand. His other gripped a heavy file folder. "I'm Agent Brewer. Let's have a chat, shall we?"

"Where's Cassie?" I asked.

"Agent Chu will join us in a moment. I wanted you and I to meet first. Let's go."

I hesitated, but stepped inside the elevator anyway. The guy had the tone of a cop, which somehow compelled me to follow his instructions. The doors clattered shut behind me and he didn't say a word as we dropped at least a hundred floors before they reopened.

"It's this way," he said, and walked ahead.

I was mildly disappointed to see that we were in a bland hallway lined with closed doors. I'd hoped the headquarters of the Supernatural Intelligence Agency would be a little cooler than *this*. This was like the basement of the Internal Revenue Service.

Agent Brewer showed me into a windowless room with no furniture except a simple table and three chairs. I'd seen plenty of rooms just like it on TV. This was the room where the homicide detectives questioned their suspects. There was even a big mirror on the back wall that wasn't fooling anyone. I stared at my reflection a second—mildly panicking—and asked Brewer where we were.

"This is the interrogation level," he explained as he sat in one of the chairs. He pointed to the other. "Have a seat."

"Am I in trouble?"

"Depends," he said, and opened the file.

I sat opposite him and waited. My plan was to look as cool and casual as possible. I looked straight ahead as Brewer scanned a few pages in silence. There was something strangely familiar about him. Perhaps I *had* seen him before. I just couldn't place where. He glanced up as I was staring. "Wizenguaard, huh?" he said. "Why'd he pick you?"

He was referring to the foreign warlock guy who had apparently bestowed his abilities on me when I was a baby.

"No idea," I said.

"No? Well look, here's the deal. I need to make sure you're on the level before we proceed any further. Tell me about the night you met Agent Chu. Give me the play by play. All of it."

I took a deep breath and told him everything I remembered about the party, the vampettes, the car chase, and Cassie taking me back to my apartment. Brewer took copious notes. When I was done, he said, "Alright. Now tell me about the next day. Tell me about meeting Agent Rosewood."

So I did. After that, a pattern developed. Brewer asked for the details of each day for the past few weeks and I told him everything I knew. When I got to certain days, like when Cassie and I visited the indoor pool at *Le Parker Meridian*, I used some creative language to avoid lying. If Brewer could tell the difference, he didn't let it show. His face—which at this point looked so familiar it was driving me crazy—was like a piece of granite.

By the time we were done, at least three hours had passed. He made a final note with his pen before closing the file with a heavy thud. His face was unreadable.

"That's quite a story," he said. "I'll be double-checking the facts, rest assured of that. But so far, everything squares with Agent Chu's debrief. Well done."

"So what now?" I asked.

"Agent Chu has requested that you continue on as a special consultant to the SIA, serving as her personal assistant. I'm inclined to grant her request, but on a provisional basis only."

I frowned. "She called me her personal assistant?"

Brewer gave me a look—his first visible emotion since we'd met. "I believe Agent Chu was looking for the most diplomatic title possible. And quite frankly, in your future role, it fits."

At that moment, there were two big thoughts in my head competing against each other like a game of tug-of-war. The first thought was that I still didn't trust the SIA. Rosewood had been an SIA agent, and look what happened there. How could I know if Agent Brewer wasn't just as bad? I didn't know the first thing about the guy. And *why*, dang it, did he look so freaking familiar?!

The second thought was that—here in this little, dingy room—I was essentially being offered a job by a super secret magical intelligence agency for a life filled with mystery, adventure and intrigue. How in the world could I possibly betray the dreams of my eleven-year-old self by turning it down? Plus, I'd be working with Cassie Chu—a dream of my thirteen and onward-year-old self.

"I'm in," I said.

The door suddenly swung open and Cassie strode in purposefully. She wore a sharp-looking suit that was professional, yes, but also sexy as hell. She even wore glasses, which I doubted were necessary, but completed the "hot businesswoman" look quite well. Her face was completely neutral. Just like Agent Brewer's.

"This is your contract, Mr. Lemieux," she said in a cold, even tone and placed a massive stack of papers in front of me. "Sign at the bottom, please."

I squinted at it. First, I was a little weirded out by Cassie's demeanor. It was like she'd morphed into a corporate lawyer overnight. And second—why *do* lawyers give you the entire contract, anyway? The thing was at least five hundred pages long. You could've given me a desk, a reading lamp, and an endless supply of Oreo Cookies and it would've taken me six weeks to read the entire thing. So what was I supposed to do here and now—"look it over?" I signed it.

I caught a tiny flash in Cassie's eye, but it was immediately extinguished.

"Good," Agent Brewer said crisply. "Now we can speak freely. The contract you just signed has confidentiality agreements of a—shall we say—'magical nature,' that will prevent you from sharing sensitive information. I'd now like to discuss some of the revelations Rosewood explained to you after stealing the *Orbis Lux*."

"Yes," I said. "I am the Chosen One."

Cassie snorted but quickly returned to lawyer face.

Brewer grimaced at me. "You may think this is funny, son, but I assure you it isn't. As of this moment, you are now what we like to refer to as a 'Being of Interest.'"

"BOI," Cassie agreed solemnly.

"That's right," Brewer said. "We'll be keeping an eye on you. But before you get a big head about that, remember where you are. This is the SIA and it sure isn't our first rodeo. So you went and got yourself some special wizard powers from some special wizard from some special realm. I'll tell ya, that kind of thing is par for the course around here. That being said, your skills may be of value someday. Not right now, but someday. And I like to plan ahead."

"When do I reach double oh status?" I asked.

"God damn it. Do you know how much paperwork went into that contract you just signed? Don't make me regret it."

"Sorry," I said.

"Now look here, son." He leaned forward and pointed an accusatory finger. "I don't trust beings like you. I've been around the block too many times. It's all these damned wizard feuds and sorcery shenanigans from other realms that gets *this* realm into a whole pile of trouble. And my job is to keep this realm trouble-free, you understand?"

I saluted. "Yes, sir."

The salute was actually totally genuine. I'm not even kidding. I just did it.

"Good," Brewer said. "Now I checked with Archives, and they do indeed have records confirming what Rosewood told you. There was a realm a few spheres over from ours called Endruvia, and it was destroyed by a sorcerer who goes by 'Delvious.' Shortly after his victory, however, a warlock named

Wizenguaard from yet another realm, this one called Arpathia—which is a hell of a long way away—arrived on the scene and banished Delvious to the Infernal Plane. At this point the details are a bit hazy, but apparently the battle weakened Wizenguaard and he saw fit to pass his abilities onto another. Why he chose this particular realm, and why he chose you is a mystery that I intend to solve sooner rather than later. In the meantime, I suggest you do whatever Agent Chu tells you to do, and maybe you'll live long enough to learn the answer for yourself."

I told him I'd do my best. Yet right as I did ... I noticed something unmistakable. There was a certain crease in Agent Brewer's forehead. I couldn't believe it. I knew *exactly* where I'd seen him before. "You!" I nearly shouted and stabbed a finger back at him. "It's you, isn't it?"

To my utter shock, he cracked a tiny grin. "Only took you a few hours, kid. That's gotta be some kind of record."

"You're the creepy German librarian!"

"That's right."

I turned to Cassie who remained stone-faced like she'd known all along. My head whipped back to Brewer. "Holy shit! Are you, *you* right now, or is this a disguise or ...?"

"It's called tradecraft, son. You better study up. And if I'm doing my job right, you'll never know which is which."

• • •

After a few more minutes of stern warnings from Agent Brewer/Hans Müller, he finally left Cassie and me alone together in the little interrogation room. I was genuinely dumbfounded when she did *not* drop the corporate lawyer routine.

"Do you have any additional questions, Mr. Lemieux?" she asked with her hands neatly folded on the desk.

I scratched my head. "How come you're acting so—"

"Good," she said abruptly. "If there's nothing more, come with me."

She got up and headed out, expecting me to follow. I practically had to jog to keep up with her. We reached the elevator in silence, and once we were inside, she turned to me and put a finger to her lips. She then inserted a key into the elevator's archaic control panel and pressed the top button. When we arrived at what I assumed was the top floor, it opened onto another endless hallway lined with doors.

"This way," Cassie said, resuming the lawyer voice and raising her chin a little. "Follow me, please."

"Cassie, I don't—"

"Agent Chu."

I rolled my eyes. I knew in my bones that this was some kind of prank—especially knowing Cassie—but I had no choice but to go along with it.

"Okay," I said. "Agent Chu. Where are we going?"

She stopped at one of the doors with an abrupt about-face. "I am your training officer, Mr. Lemieux. I have designed your first lesson and I need you to come with me. Is that a problem?"

I shook my head.

"Good. It's this way." She opened the door, and with a not-so-gentle hand, shoved me through. I stumbled into a small space that looked like a little submarine-shaped gondola. Its walls were made of glass, offering a wide, panoramic view. I stood up taller and my heart beat faster. We were high up— *really* high up. And the view, on all sides, was of the vast metropolis of London. The door clicked shut and I turned to see Cassie grinning wickedly.

"Mr. Lemieux," she said.

"Agent Chu."

She stepped forward. "I thought we'd cure that fear of Ferris wheels once and for all. This is one of the tallest in the world."

My heart beat even faster, but for an entirely new reason. "So I guess this means I can call you Cassie again?"

She shook her head. "I prefer Best Girlfriend Ever. Just … not in front of other agents. They kind of frown on inter-office romance around here. And then I'd have to quit because I'm not giving you up for anything."

I put my arms around her waist and kissed her. After a moment—before I knew she'd start losing control—I pulled back. "Cass," I said. I wasn't sure if this was the right time or not, but there was something I needed to say. It was probably going to be a huge mood-killer, but I couldn't help it. Because as much as I *wanted* Cassie, I liked her even more.

Her eyes opened questioningly.

"We haven't really *talked* much since that night with Rosewood," I said slowly. "Up on the roof, I mean. I'm not saying we have to right now, but I'm here whenever you're ready, okay?"

She studied my eyes a moment longer. Then something new appeared in hers—a faint glow. "I know," she whispered. "And I will."

"I just wanted you to know."

She smiled and then playfully grabbed the scruff of my collar with both hands. "Listen," she said. "You're my boyfriend. But you really *are* my personal assistant, too. That wasn't a joke. When I tell you to do something, I expect you to do it."

"I get it," I said with a solemn nod. "It's life and death out there."

"Just so long as we understand each other." Her hand moved to her neckline and began unbuttoning her blouse. "So first, I'm going to need you to remove your pants ASAP. If you don't, there will be consequences."

From that day on, I was never scared of heights again.

Werewolves, yes. Unicycles, sort of. But heights? No.

They now reminded me of the best three hours of my life. And then another three at my apartment.

My name is François Lemieux. And as it turns out—though I suppose it's up to you—I don't think I'm too shabby at this whole "writing" thing, after all. Perhaps I'll keep doing it as a hobby.

When I'm not being a wizard, that is.

And don't forget, dear reader, if there's one thing you should take away from my story it's this: I went twenty years thinking I was Mr. Average—a complete nobody. But you never know what tomorrow may bring. Perhaps a black Mustang and a girl with a ponytail.

Keep looking.

THE END

Thank you for reading "True Magic."
If you liked it, please take a second to leave a review.
We authors thrive on reviews. Big time.

Also, be sure to check out my other titles including,
"Downfall: Book One of the Deadlander Series," as well as
"Where the Dragons Go," a heartfelt young adult contemporary
novel written under the penname C.W. Sims.

Thanks again for reading. You rock.

About the Author

After growing up in the quiet suburbs of Silicon Valley, Colin Sims decided journalism might be a good way to see the world. Thus, after college, he moved to Cairo, Egypt where he studied Arabic and worked as a freelance reporter for three years. Once he returned to the U.S., he worked in television news but couldn't shake a growing desire to try his hand at fiction. So, in a fit of lunacy one day in 2011, Colin quit his job, bought a motorcycle, and spent the next few months riding across the country and writing his first manuscript. He has been dedicating himself to the craft ever since ...

You can find Colin on Facebook:
www.facebook.com/colinsimsauthor

Twitter: @colinsimswriter

Or reach him by email at: colinwsims@gmail.com